考官親自出馬與你分享，
教你練出最靈活、最讓考官喜愛的高分英文口語！
真的不是權威不出書！

學習有捷徑
夢想最接近

使用說明

　　雅思考試是全球數一數二重要的英語考試，也是給讓許多華人考生痛苦到不行的考試。沒關係！只要正確使用本書，你也能夠達到以下四個目標：

一、把你從 5 分以下的泥潭中解救出來，送上 7 分甚至更高分的平坦大道。

二、並非僅僅獲得雅思高分，而是能真正為國外大學的學習以及日後的工作做好準備。

三、激發你的想像力和創造力。在口語考試中，考官非常重視你的答案是否有創意，因為太過平淡無奇的答案他們早就聽膩了，不會留下好印象。

四、養成高效率的練習習慣與思考模式，因為在口語考試中需與真人考官對話，非常重視快速的臨場反應，若習慣於緩慢而穩定的思考，在有限的時間內肯定無法表現出自己最好的一面。

　　這本書的目標不是讓你死背「正確答案」或「優美的句子」，考完就忘，而是要真正提高你的語言能力。只要語言能力夠高，那什麼都不用背了，不是嗎？無論遇到什麼話題，你都能自信地融入與考官的談話之中了。

　　本書根據考官親身經驗，為考生們量身打造的結構與使用方式如下：

▶第 1 章 考官偷偷告訴你

★從雅思考官的角度向你全面介紹雅思口語考試的流程、評分標準。

★說明準備考試時容易遇到的問題，讓你在準備考試時不會做白工，也可以將有限的精力花費在最有用的訓練上！

★從經驗豐富的雅思考官角度介紹，絕對最權威！

★偷偷跟你洩露考生常有、考官最討厭的錯誤觀點！

⊃ 來看個例子！

學習七大秘技，解決你的問題

❶ 創造力和獨創性是西方教育體系最為重視的特質，而雅思考試也體現出了這一點。你越具有創造力和獨創性，你的表現就會越好。

❷ 想進步，就必須經常練習。在語言學習的過程中，沒有什麼能取代反覆練習。

❸ 想進步，你還得變得積極主動。想想你會感興趣的話題，查查字典，提些問題，變得主動起來。不要等著老師把想法填鴨式地灌輸進你的腦袋。

④ 在雅思考試中，就像在任何一場對話中一樣，任何一個問題都沒有「正確答案」。只有比其他回答更流利、或詞彙更豐富、或文法更準確的回答，但沒有正確答案。像如果我問：「你喜歡花嗎？」這個問題就沒有正確答案。

⑤ 死記硬背是一條死胡同。很多學生都會背誦文章和詞彙表，然後告訴自己「我都學會了！」但我們這本書要告訴你，一定要放棄這種做法：如果你在考試時背誦以前的文章，你的得分永遠不會超過 5 分！

⑥ 想在雅思考試中有不俗的表現，詞彙和想法很重要。但請記住，詞彙學習不僅僅是背單字而已。如果你只是背單字，不管背誦的單字多麼有趣，你運用詞彙的能力都不會有任何進步。你應該做的是養成用詞彙連續說上兩三分鐘的習慣。

⑦ 多閱讀、多思考、多查閱和記錄詞彙、頻繁練習語言的流暢度，這才是你提高口語水準的最佳方法。

▶第2～4章 考官教你征服雅思考試！

★三章分別涵蓋雅思口語考試的三個部分！

★由最瞭解雅思考試的考官丹尼爾的角度、和最瞭解華人考生的陳思清老師的角度，分別針對三個部分進行講解，教你最關鍵的闖關秘技。

★分別點評了真實的考生範例，讓你知道如何回答才能得到考官的青睞，避免哪些錯誤才能不讓考官給你打低分！

➔ 來看個例子！

考官獨家披露 12 種常考的問題類型！具體如下：

❶ Where you live: place

❷ Where you live: house or apartment

❸ What you do: I'm a student

❹ What you do: I work

❺ Gifts

❻ Happiness

❼ News

❽ Noise

❾ Swimming

❿ Children

⓫ Time management

⓬ Weather

▶第5章 用考官的評分標準要求自己！

★帶你從考官的眼中看世界，詳細描述了考官評分的四大標準。

★告訴你如何按照這些標準去練習，最終才能達到考官的高分要求。

★清楚告訴你什麼樣的表達是高分表達、什麼樣的表達是陳腔濫調。

★告訴你用什麼樣的詞彙才會拿到 7 分！

★告訴你哪幾個發音是華人考生最難發對的！

❷ 來看個例子！

設想考生在描述一個他認識的人，而這個人一直喜歡吃大量的速食。

5 分考生會這樣描述：He is too big, too fat. 他塊頭很大，很胖。

6 分考生會這樣描述：He is fat and overweight. 他很胖，超重了。

7 分考生會這樣描述：He is seriously overweight, I mean, way beyond plump!
他嚴重超重。我是說，他可不僅僅是偏胖。

8 分考生會這樣描述：He has ballooned out to an incredible size. He's so fat now he
can scarcely walk. 他像吹氣球似地胖了起來，塊頭大得嚇人，
胖得幾乎都走不了路。

▶第6章 高分考生面面觀

★怎樣的考生才會拿高分？本章全面總結了高分考生必備的五大要素，讓你知道考官
眼中的理想考生是什麼樣子！

★當然，也有具體小撇步，幫助你成為這樣的理想考生！

❷ 來看個例子！

高分考生一定要……　　　　　　　　　　　　　　高分考生一定不會……
‧享受使用英語的樂趣　‧積極地應對考試　　　　‧背誦所謂的「正確答案」
‧說話時練習用手勢　　‧要有重音、語調和感情

▶第 7 章 考場外的準備

★告訴你從考前一週到考試當日應該如何「臨時抱佛腳」。

★從多個角度展現了中外文化的不同，讓你未出國門就能瞭解未來學習和生活的環境。

⊃ 來看個例子！

考前一週：
確保補充蛋白質和足夠的睡眠

考前一天：
準備好考試報名表、身分證或護照、手錶、筆與橡皮擦

▶特別收錄

★為你揭秘了考官一天的監考生活，帶你走進考官的內心世界。

★對全書介紹過的口語練習妙招進行了進一步闡述和總結。

　　現在你對全書的結構和框架有了大致的瞭解，就可以制訂出學習計畫囉！別忘了，全書只瀏覽一遍是不夠的，一定要一天練習一點，擴大單字量、提高語言流暢度。相信你最終一定能成為雅思口語達人！

Preface 作者序

Dear Readers,

Think of this book not just as a way to achieve your dream IELTS score, but as the first step in a learning journey that will also carry you to success in your university studies and your future career.

Remember, memorization is for losers! To score higher than 6 in the IELTS speaking test, candidates have to be willing to engage with the examiner—creatively, energetically, and fluently. Think of the test as an intelligent conversation in which you say what you think about the topics that come up and back up your opinions with information gleaned from the media and a wide vocabulary. You need good grammar, clear pronunciation, good rhythm, fluency and a wide vocabulary to get a 7 in the IELTS test.

Regular work on your vocabulary and fluency is essential. That is why this book exists—use it consistently over a period of six months, and we guarantee you will lift your IELTS score.

Your country needs international talents, creative and outspoken managers, teachers, journalists and researchers. The authors believe that, by taking a proactive approach to the IELTS test, candidates can develop key skills that will serve them all their lives.

This learning package shows you how.

Yours sincerely,
Daniel Cotterall, Chen Siqing

親愛的讀者：

當你拿起這本書，不要僅僅將它當成能幫你雅思口語考高分的幫手，還要把它當成能助你向學習的旅程邁出第一步的朋友，引領著你走向大學學業和職業生涯的成功。

請你一定要記住，單純靠背誦來準備口語考試是失敗者的學習方式！要想突破口語 6 分，考生必須樂於與考官互動，要有創意、有活力並流利地與考官對話。不要把雅思口語考試當成一場考試，而是把它當成在跟一個知識豐富的人聊天。你可以針對一些話題表達自己的觀點，並利用從媒體獲得的資訊和豐富的詞彙來論證自己的觀點。

為了達到雅思口語 7 分的目標，你需要有扎實的語法基礎、清晰的發音、流暢且有節奏的語言和豐富的詞彙儲備。經常針對詞彙和語言流暢度進行練習是必不可少的。這也是本書的目的所在！利用它連續練習六個月，我們保證你的口語分數一定能顯著提升。

您的國家需要國際型的人才，需要有創造力和說話坦誠的管理人才、老師、記者和研究人員。筆者相信，通過以積極主動的態度備考雅思，考生們一定能培養起讓自己受益終身的重要技能。而我們的書就能告訴你如何去達成這一切。

你們的朋友，

丹尼爾‧科特拉爾（Daniel Cotterall）、陳思清

Contents 目錄

第1章 考官偷偷告訴你

第2章 考官教你征服雅思口語考試第一部分

第3章 考官教你征服雅思口語考試第二部分

第4章 考官教你征服雅思口語考試第三部分

第5章 雅思考官評估考生的「四大標準」！
讓你一一突破考官心防，輕鬆滿分！

第6章　高分考生面面觀

第7章　考場外的準備

特別收錄

開始前，先來認識一下雅思！
What's IELTS?

▶ 雅思是什麼？

雅思的基本介紹

　　IELTS（International English Language Testing System）國際英語測驗為一種全球認可的英語測驗標準。以台灣而言，每月定期都有舉辦考試，在北、中、南各地均有試場及超過 80 個報名地點。

考雅思有什麼用途？

★大多數英語系國家，如：澳洲、英國、紐西蘭、加拿大及德國等高等學府都偏好雅思為英語能力認證的標準。

★美國現今已有超過 3,000 所大學院校承認 IELTS 成績，含美國十大知名院校在內的高等學府，都接受 IELTS 成績作為申請入學者須提供的英語能力證明。

★不只是學術機構接受 IELTS 成績，凡是申請至英國、澳洲、紐西蘭及加拿大移民者，或是英國及澳洲各政府部門實習生及參加專業公會人士，如國防部及公共醫療會議等，又或是申請在美國從事特定職業，如：醫師、護理師等，都得在申請時一併提供 IELTS 成績以證明其英文能力。

★全球目前已有超過 9,000 所的各式機構或組織採用雅思成績。

★ IELTS 考試內容全面，涵蓋聽、說、讀、寫四個項目，評估考生在英語環境中學習、工作、生活所具備的語文能力，是目前國際公認最符合生活情境及實用性最高的英語能力檢定。

欲查詢美國接受雅思成績的單位，請至：http://www.ielts.org/ielts_in_the_usa.aspx

欲查詢全球接受雅思成績的單位，請至：http://bandscore.ielts.org/

為什麼要選擇雅思？

方便：每月提供 3 至 4 次考試，成績單於測試後 13 天發出，線上即可報名，考生號碼均會以 e-mail 與簡訊寄發，無須列印准考證等，人到現場即可。

全面：不同於其他一些英語能力證明只涵蓋聽與讀，雅思也測驗「寫」與「說」的能力。成績單詳細列出每個考試部分（聽力、閱讀、寫作及口語）的成績及總成績。

國際化：全球超過 130 多個國家都有舉行 IELTS 考試，成績適用英語系國家及大多數國家。

可靠：由 IDP-IELTS 澳洲、英國文化協會及 Cambridge English Language Assessment 共同規劃執行 IELTS 考試。

現代化：IELTS 注重測試考生使用英語的能力多於文法及辭彙知識。

嚴謹：定期更新試題及嚴謹之批改程序，政府部門及專業團體都認可此測試。

▶雅思考什麼？

IELTS 考試分為 Academic（學術組）及 General Training （一般組）。

　　學術組的閱讀及寫作部份，是用來評估考生在修讀學位或研究所課程時，是否適合以英語作為學習或培訓的媒介；一般組的閱讀及寫作部份，則適合前往英語系國家就讀中學、工作、或參與非學位培訓計畫的考生。

　　測試內容涵蓋 Listening（聽力）、Reading（閱讀）、Writing（寫作）與 Speaking（口語）四個項目。Reading 與 Writing 會因組別不同而給予不同題目。

　　考試的時間與內容參考下表：

	時間、篇數	內容
聽力	30 分鐘／四大主題／共 40 題	◆第一、二個主題以生活語言為主，第三、四個主題偏重學術性語言。 ◆有配對、是非、填充、選擇、簡答、標籤題等不同的答題方式隨機出現。 ◆給予額外 10 分鐘讓考生將答案填寫於答案卡上。

閱讀	60 分鐘／ 3 部分／ 共 40 題	◆分 Academic 組與 General Training 組，都為 60 分鐘的測驗時間。 ◆A 組有 3 篇文章，每篇約 1000 字，題型含配對、選擇、填充等，主要測驗考生閱讀長篇文章時快速抓到重點的能力；而 GT 組則約 5 篇文章，含短篇如廣告、公告、簡介等。 ◆答題方式亦包含配對、是非、填充、選擇、簡答、標籤題等。
寫作	60 分鐘／ 兩篇	◆分 Academic 組與 General Training 組。 ◆A 組的 Task 1 為圖表練習，以描述及比較各類圖表為主，考生需於 20 分內寫完 150 字的描述。Task 2 則為申論題，範圍廣且有深度，考生需按題目分析及表達個人意見或做優缺點比較等。 ◆GT 組的 Task 1 則與 A 組有別，通常為書信的撰寫如：邀請函，抱怨信，道歉信等，至少 150 字。而 Task 2 就與 A 組類似，為申論題。
口說	11-14 分鐘／ 三部分	◆由口試官跟考生進行一對一、面對面口試。 ◆內容分為三大部份： 一、自我介紹與一般話題交談 二、依據提示卡做個人表述 三、較深入的闡述

▶雅思考試當天的流程

時間	流程
8:10	雖然考試九點才開始，但一定要在 8:30 前到場報到。建議可 8:10 就抵達考場，工作人員會宣布考生注意事項。
8:15	將個人物品放置於置物間。
8:20	簽名報到、指紋掃描、現場拍照。

8:45	開放入場。入場前會先檢查文具用品與護照。場內只可攜帶文具用品、護照與水，且水杯上不可有文字，如有需先撕去。橡皮擦的套子上經常會有文字，也需要先拿掉。
9:00	測驗開始，順序為聽力測驗（40 分鐘）、閱讀測驗（60 分鐘）、寫作測驗（60 分鐘）。
12:20 後～ 5:30 左右	考試當天，每個人的口試時間將會公布在考場，考場桌上的考生號碼標籤上也會註明，請在公布的時間前半個小時回到考場報到，準備口語考試（約 11 ～ 14 分鐘長）。

▶考前的小提醒

★凡報名雅思者均會在 e-mail 中收到「Road to IELTS」的帳號，可免費登入 Road to IELTS 雅思練習網站。其中不但有模擬試題線上練習，更有應試準備的相關訓練，且涵蓋題型廣泛，都是在正式考試中可能會遇到的。Road to IELTS 中的題目均有分級，可依考生需求選擇從哪一種開始。

★ 8:30 後到場視同遲到，不可入場，所以一定要看好考場的地圖。若考場為任何一家美語補習班，要注意記好地址，不要跑錯家，因為同一家美語補習班可能會有好幾家分支在附近。

★考試當天需攜帶有效護照正本，否則不可入場應試。

★只可攜帶一枝鉛筆或自動筆與一個橡擦入場應試，其他文具則不可攜帶。不可使用原子筆作答。

★筆試進行中並無休息時間，想上洗手間之考生請避開播放 CD、考試規則講解時、各科考試結束前十分鐘及收、發考卷的時間；並請舉手等待，由監考人員陪同離場。

★考場一般會有時鐘或者以投影機在考場前方顯示時間，所以不必擔心沒有帶手錶。電子錶不可攜入考場。

★成績單將於考試後 13 天寄發，也可線上查詢，並會以簡訊通知分數。

＊資料來源：台灣 IELTS 雅思官方考試中心網站

"第1章"

考官偷偷告訴你

第一節 考官帶你解讀雅思考試
Key Success Factors for Each Part of the Test

　　雅思口語考試分為以下幾個部分與步驟，現在就讓我們以考官的角度來告訴你，每一個部分該怎麼考才能得高分吧！

步驟	內容	這樣考才能得高分！
簡單介紹 Introduction	考官自我介紹，詢問考生的姓名、來自哪裡，檢查考生的號碼。	✓ 發音清晰 ✓ 態度積極 ✓ 肢體語言靈活
詢問基本情況 Questions about Yourself	考官問考生一些簡單問題，例如住在哪裡、念哪個系、做什麼工作等。這些問題可以讓你放鬆並克服緊張情緒。	✓ 良好的詞彙運用能力 ✓ 簡潔清晰的回答 ✓ 稍微展現出一些個人特色
第一部分 Part 1	針對各種話題提一些簡短的問題，話題可以包括花、寵物、電視、跳舞等任何方面。不要只是簡單地回答「是」或「不是」，也不要用事先背誦好的答案回答。口試應該像聊天一樣。如果你單憑記憶背誦，考官會打斷你，然後問你另外一個問題！	✓ 理解問題的能力 ✓ 提供非抄襲的原創回答的能力 ✓ 轉換思路、繼續回答下一個問題的能力，因為考官可能會打斷你的長篇大論
第二部分 Part 2	給考生一張話題卡和一分鐘的準備時間。考生必須針對這個話題進行兩分鐘的發言，中途不能出現長時間的停頓。 如果考生很快就無話可說，考官會說「你能針對……再說一說嗎？」之類的話。	✓ 能夠迅速寫下一些想法，這有助於你構建發言思路，填滿兩分鐘的時間 ✓ 流利地說兩分鐘話的能力 ✓ 語言具有連貫性，即能夠圍繞中心話題發表讓人易於理解的觀點 ✓ 單字量大 ✓ 運用多種時態 ✓ 既能使用簡單句，也能使用複合句 ✓ 語音清晰，語調優美，重音準確

步驟	內容	這樣考才能得高分！
第三部分 Part 3	這一部分是與第二部分內容有點關連的討論。口試進行到這一部分，考生已經提供了一些個人資訊，也已談論了個人的喜好和習慣。而在這一部分中，考生要更全面地談論一些觀點。雙方的討論會變得更複雜，考官可能也會提到考生之前說過的觀點。在這種情況下，考生就要為自己的觀點辯護，或更加詳細地論述之前已表達過的觀點。	✓ 知識面廣，對於世界時事有一定的認識 ✓ 單字量大 ✓ 能夠自信地表達自己的觀點 ✓ 能夠融入與考官的對話之中、捕捉到考官表達的要點
結尾 End	考官在結束時可能會說「謝謝，口語考試結束了」之類的話。這時候你就可以收起你的身分證和口試卡。考試結束了！	✓ 面帶微笑地離開 ✓ 不要問考官你的分數，這會讓考官不悅

第二節 雅思考官評估考生的「四大標準」有哪些？
Four Criteria the Examiners Use to Score Candidates

　　雅思考官用來評估考生的四大標準有：語言的流暢度與連貫性、文法知識的廣度和準確度、詞彙以及發音。那麼在這四個方面，考官具體會聽什麼？考生要有哪些具體表現才能符合這些標準呢？

▶標準一：考官會聽什麼 What the Examiner is Listening for

語言的流暢度與連貫性 Fluency & Coherence

❶ 語言是否流暢。考生能否連續地說，還是需要放慢語速才能繼續說下去？是否需要重複說過的話才能保證不停頓？能否自然地使用停頓與過渡的詞語（如 oh、I mean 等）？

❷ 語言是否連貫。考生說的話是否言之有理？是否回答了問題？能夠一直緊密圍繞著話題講嗎？

我們在本書中編排了一些可改善語言流暢度和連貫性的練習。由於語言是一個有機的整體，豐富的單字量能使你的語言變得更通順。你腦海中的詞彙越多，你就越能自然流暢地表達自己的觀點，也就能避免發言時卡住和放慢語速（這些都是會造成考生得分侷限在 5 分以下的問題）。

▶標準二：考官會聽什麼 What the Examiner Is Listening for

文法知識的廣度及準確度 Grammatical Range & Accuracy

❶ 文法廣度。考生是否能運用簡單句和複合句？是否會使用各種時態？

❷ 文法準確度。考生用的文法準確嗎？是否用對了形容詞比較級和名詞複數形式？是否能做到主詞、動詞一致？動詞的形式是否正確？代名詞和介系詞的使用是否正確？

考生需要向考官展示出自己能正確運用文法的能力，比如能正確使用介系詞和動詞時態。但只是做到準確還不夠，考生還要掌握各種文法結構。考官會看考生有沒有正確使用過渡詞語、是否能使用複合句。介系詞用對了嗎？會使用比較級嗎？能運用幾種動詞時態？會使用條件句嗎？

▶標準三：考官會聽什麼 What the Examiner Is Listening for

詞彙 Vocabulary

考生的單字量有多大？所用詞彙是否多數屬於基本詞彙，只是偶爾夾雜一兩個不常用的詞彙？詞彙的使用是否正確？是否能夠始終用豐富的詞彙表達各種意思？

背單字的確會有用，但掌握詞彙的捷徑永遠是閱讀。如果你真想得到 7 分，你就應該開始閱讀英語書籍。

▶標準四：考官會聽什麼 What the Examiner Is Listening for

發音 Pronunciation

❶ 發音。考生是否能夠掌握好英語的發音，比如 development 或 vital 中 v 的發音？發音是否容易讓人理解？

❷ 節奏。考生是否能夠掌握英語的說話節奏？停頓的地方正確嗎？語言的語調和重音是否自然？

大部分華人考生都可以讓考官理解他們的意思，但卻掌握不好說英語的節奏。現在上網、看電視都很容易找到英文聽力的資源，所以這個問題可以通過不斷模仿和練習來克服。

第三節 華人學生口試最容易犯下的「七個致命錯誤」
Seven Misconceptions About the Test

考生們對於雅思口語考試普遍有一些誤解，下面我們來討論一些常見的錯誤準備方式！

▶ 1. 錯誤觀點：考官的問題有正確答案。

考生觀點：考官問我有沒有去過海邊、河邊玩，但我不知道正確答案應該回答什麼。

考官點評：在對考試的所有誤解中，這種觀點是最普遍的，也是最有害的。數學題有正確答案和錯誤答案，在對話中，你也可能會犯文法錯誤或發錯音，但就內容而言，是沒有對錯的！有些回答可能會有點長，或有點詼諧，或有點創意……。如果你事先背答案，考官一定聽得出來。死記硬背的考生通常在第三部分會露出馬腳，因為他們把全部精力都放在努力回憶答案上了，而不能積極思考和融入對話。

▶ 2. 錯誤觀點：要多用很難的字來回答問題，才會高分。

考生觀點：如果多用一些很生僻的單字來回答，就能得高分。

考官點評：這一觀點的問題是，如果你突然用到一個很生僻罕見的詞，或一個非常複雜的句子，它們與你的回答相符嗎？還是顯得很突兀？那個單字或句子運用得合適嗎？如果不合適，就會出現連貫性的問題。如果你運用的大部分詞彙都屬於很基本的詞彙，卻突然說出 "Yes, I like flowers because of their gossamer-like fragility"（是的，我喜歡花是因為它們如薄紗般脆弱）之類的話，考官肯定會驚訝地豎起眉毛。而且如果那是你能說出的唯一一個高級詞彙，考官就會判斷出你的整體詞彙運用水準並不高，會為你打出相應的分數。

▶ 3. 錯誤觀點：外表有魅力就能得高分。

考生觀點：穿得性感，得分就會比較高。

考官點評：這種策略肯定會適得其反。男性考官和女性考官都不會欣然接受這種企圖明顯的操縱。事實上，穿著性感的考生得到的分數反而可能會更低，因為考官討厭這種試圖操縱結果的企圖。同樣，如果考生在考試開始時說「我只想說，你今天真是太漂亮、太帥了」之類的話，這純粹是在浪費口舌，只會給自己惹麻煩。應試態度要積極、禮貌、友好，但不要試圖操縱考官。

▶ 4. 錯誤觀點：這只是個語言考試而已。

考生觀點：雅思口語考試只是考英文能力，不會考什麼其他的能力。

考官點評：考生這麼想是情有可原的，因為英國大使館文化教育處也是這麼公開宣傳的。但事實上，雅思考試不僅僅是語言測試！這也是本書想要闡明的一點！考試其實也考你的應對能力，並希望你對英語國家的文化有一定的瞭解。所有的語言都以文化環境為「根」，所以語言交流的本質也就是文化的交流。要想在雅思考試中拿高分，考生就必須「遨遊」在英語國家的文化中。

▶ 5. 錯誤觀點：講得越快越好。

考生觀點：說得越快，就表示語言越流暢。

考官點評：雖然偏慢的語速會導致考生在語言流暢度方面得分偏低，但反過來就不一定成立。考官不僅會聽考生語言是否流暢，也要聽是否連貫。所以即使考生的語速很快，但如果不斷重複，而且還出現很多邏輯錯誤，同樣也得不了高分。

▶ 6. 錯誤觀點：要講得跟老外一樣才會高分。

考生觀點：考試時，我要刻意講得像老外一樣。

考官點評：考生沒有必要像老外一樣講話。你本來就不是老外，你的文化背景、教育背景、母語的語音系統等都跟外國人不一樣，考官也知道，所以就算你講話不像老外，也完全不會影響考官對你的感覺。

▶ 7. 錯誤觀點：要多用優美的句子。

考生觀點：句子越優美，應該就會越高分。

考官點評：讓我們想像一下，如果有位考生在描述她和男朋友去南京旅遊時說：

So, in the end, he went by train and I took a plane and, when I got to the airport in Nanjing, I texted him and he met me at a subway station and then we walked to the hotel. One day we visited Sun Zhongshan Park and walked right up to the temple at the top where there is a statue of Sun Zhongshan and then, that evening, we went to a bar to listen to some music and, I remember, when we came out, the moon like a silver disc suspended in the starry sky seemed to bathe our destinies with a silvery glow. And the next day it was the end of our holiday, so we went back to Beijing.

在這段話中，標色部分就是一句「優美的句子」。但雖然這句夠優美，考生在此之前和之後說的話都完全不優美，所以這句格格不入。聽到這麼格格不入的句子，考官會立刻判斷考生是硬背的而打低分。

第四節 學習七大秘技，解決你的問題
Seven Key Ideas

① 創造力和獨創性是西方教育體系最為重視的特質，而雅思考試也體現出了這一點。你越具有創造力和獨創性，你的表現就會越好。

② 想進步，就必須經常練習。在語言學習的過程中，沒有什麼能取代反覆練習。

③ 想進步，你還得變得積極主動。想想你會感興趣的話題，查查字典，提些問題，變得主動起來。不要等著老師把想法填鴨式地灌輸進你的腦袋。

④ 在雅思考試中，就像在任何一場對話中一樣，任何一個問題都沒有「正確答案」。只有比其他回答更流利、或詞彙更豐富、或文法更準確的回答，但沒有正確答案。像如果我問：「你喜歡花嗎？」這個問題就沒有正確答案。

⑤ 死記硬背是一條死胡同。很多學生都會背誦文章和詞彙表，然後告訴自己「我都學會了！」但我們這本書要告訴你，一定要放棄這種做法：如果你在考試時背誦以前的文章，你的得分永遠不會超過 5 分！

⑥ 想在雅思考試中有不俗的表現，詞彙和想法很重要。但請記住，詞彙學習不僅僅是背單字而已。如果你只是背單字，不管背誦的單字多麼有趣，你運用詞彙的能力都不會有任何進步。你應該做的是養成用詞彙連續說上兩三分鐘的習慣。

⑦ 多閱讀、多思考、多查閱和記錄詞彙、頻繁練習語言的流暢度，這才是你提高口語水準的最佳方法。

考官語錄

The more creative and original you are, the better you will perform.

考官語錄

If you rely on memorized passages in the test, you will probably only get a 5!

考官語錄

Remember that vocabulary is more than word lists.

"第2章"

考官教你征服雅思口語
考試第一部分

第一節 第一部分闖關秘技
Keys for Success in Part One

第一部分沒有第二部分和第三部分那麼重要，只是一個熱身，要給考官留下良好的第一印象。

如果你想給別人留下良好的第一印象，你會怎麼做？微笑，運用豐富的肢體語言，仔細傾聽，再微笑……考試一開始，考官會問幾個簡單的問題，比如考生住在哪裡，或有關考生工作或唸書的一些事情。然後，考官會提出兩個問題，且兩個問題的話題不一樣。可能的話題有：童年、旅行、時間管理、新聞、游泳、大海、假期、跳舞、鳥類、噪音、電視或做家事等。你不可能預測考官會問什麼，因為考官經常變換話題。但不管是什麼話題，問題一般都比較直接，例如：

- Do you like flowers?
- Do you think you watch too much television?
- What was your favourite school?

考官語錄

Candidates who have prepared for the test have a pretty good idea what kind of topics will come up—topics like childhood, travel, time management, the news, swimming or the sea, holidays, dancing, birds, noise, television, or doing housework.

第一部分成功的關鍵是反應迅速、回答主動、發音清晰。

考官語錄

The keys for success in Part 1 are quick reactions, spontaneity and clear pronunciation.

考生的回答必須清晰、生動。如果你能用一兩個有趣的單字或不太常用的時態，那就更好了。當考官和考生開始交流時，背誦是一大禁忌。記住，雅思口語考試是為了讓你展現你個人的表達能力，所以不要背誦和複述別人的答案，也不要像鸚鵡一樣重複上課學到的內容。答案要跟別人不一樣。

千萬不要低估了考官！考官的工作就是傾聽考生說話，然後打分數。在他們的考官生涯中，已經考過成千上百的考生，所以他們非常清楚你到底是在自由表達還是在背誦提前準備好的內容。

第二節 60 個通關問題
60 Questions

這個練習的目的是使你在第一部分的表述更自然，語言更流暢。練習的目標是在五分鐘內回答 60 個問題。

▶ 遊戲規則 How to Play

Track 001

可以跟你的同學或朋友一起玩這個遊戲。如果只有兩個人，一個人可以回答 30 個 或 60 個問題，看你們怎麼玩而定。如果有六個人，那就是每人回答 10 個問題。如果有個同學當考官的話，那麼每人就是 12 個問題。玩法是大家圍坐成一圈，第一輪要集中精力簡短迅速地回答問題，目的是提高反應速度。第二輪，再次回答問題，這次要說出原因，像在進行第一部分的考試一樣。

1. Which is better: emails or text messages?

2. Were you obedient or rebellious as a child?

3. Describe computer games in just two words.　必考 感情！

4. Are you hard to get to know or easy to get to know?

5. Do you think children should do household chores?

6. Do you go online every day?
網路 正 ㄒㄨˇ or

7. Do you like flowers?

8. Which is better: swimming in the sea, in a pool or in the river? 丂、鴨子

9. What floor do you live on?

10. Do you look better in dark clothes or light clothes?

11. Are you physically strong or mentally strong?

12. Is unhappiness always a bad thing?

13. How often do you watch TV?

14. Do you reckon daily life is too noisy?

15. When you think of your mother, what's the first image that comes to mind?

16. Have you had driving lessons?

17. Do you prefer calling your friends or texting them?

18. What makes you happy?

19. Which is better: news on TV or on the Internet?

20. Do people spend enough time outdoors these days?

21. Who's the sexiest film star in the world?

22. Which is better: Valentine's Day or Qixi（七夕）?

23. Can you swim?

24. What will you do next weekend?

25. What was your favourite game when you were a kid?

26. Who do you phone most often?

27. What kind of clothes do you like?

28. Do you like physical exercise?

29. How many emails do you write every week?

30. What's the longest car journey you ever went on?

31. What's your favourite TV series?

32. What's the noisiest place you know?

33. Have you ever been hiking?

34. What's the best thing about mobile phones?

35. What do you remember about your primary school?

36. Are you an organized person?

37. Three adjectives to describe one of your grandparents.

38. Who would you most like to go on holiday with?

39. How often do you work out in the gym?

40. How many languages can you speak?

41. How old were you when you first used the Internet?

42. What's your favourite weather?

43. What's your favourite colour?

44. When was the last time you gave someone a gift?

45. What's the coldest weather you ever experienced?

46. Which are better: Western universities or Chinese universities?

47. Is your apartment spacious?

48. Where would you like to go for a holiday?

49. What's your favourite animal?

50. Do chrysanthemums have any special meaning in China?

51. What language would you like to learn?

52. Is fashion important?

53. How do you feel when you get a handwritten letter?

54. Did you learn to dance when you were a kid?

55. Three adjectives to describe your father or mother.

56. What is the most important holiday in China?

57. What is the best job in the world?

58. Three adjectives to describe the perfect girlfriend/boyfriend.

59. What would life be like without the Internet?

60. If you were an animal, which one would it be?

第三節 12種常考問題：考官為你點評真實案例！
Case Studies

在本節中，我們會一一列出第一部分常考的 12 種問題類型，並結合考生真實案例進行分析。在前六個話題裡，每個問題都給出了兩種版本的回答。看一看考官對每個回答的點評，你就會發現，得分更高的回答不一定更長，但文法更準確，詞彙更豐富，聽起來更自然。

12 種常考的問題類型具體如下：

1. **Where you live: place**

2. **Where you live: house or apartment**

3. **What you do: I'm a student**

4. **What you do: I work**

5. **Gifts**

6. **Happiness**

7. **News**

8. **Noise**

9. **Swimming**

10. **Children**

11. **Time management**

12. **Weather**

考官語錄

Good replies are not necessarily longer, but they are more grammatically accurate.
They contain a better range of vocabulary, and they sound more natural.

其中最後四個話題的回答都是 7 分級別的，也就是說如果這些題目回答得好，就比較容易拿到高一點的分數。

▶ 1. 你住在哪裡：地點
Where You Live: Place

以下問題考官都有可能會問到。看看考生回答和考官點評吧！

考官： Let's talk about where you live. Are you living in a small town or a big city at the moment?

我們來談談你住的地方吧。你目前住在小城鎮還是大城市？

考生 A： I ~~living~~ a small town in the Hebei province. It's near Baoding, ~~do you know that~~?

考官點評 第一個動詞的時態就用錯了，正確結構應該是 I am living。但這個小城鎮是該考生長期居住的地方，所以改為一般現在式，用 I live。Hebei 前不用 the。問考官是否知道這個地方是不明智的，他們沒有時間來回答你。

考生 B： I live in a small town in Hebei province. It's near Baoding.

考官點評 回答得很好，清晰且乾脆。第一部分中考官並不想聽到大段的回答。

↗ 現在完成進行式

考官： How long have you been living in this town?

你在這個鎮上住多久了？

考生 A： I ~~am living~~ this town for twenty years—since ~~I born~~.

考官點評 回答得不好。這些都是在開場白時間的簡單問題，考生應該已經準備過了，沒有理由犯這種錯誤。注意，考官提問時用的是現在完成進行式，考生也應該用同樣的時態回答：I have been living in this town for...。另外，還需注意，後半句應該改為 since I was born。

現

考生 B：Well, I was born there but now I have entered Nankai University in Tianjin so I live in Tianjin. But I go back to my hometown quite a lot. It's not very far from Tianjin, about two hours by train.

考官點評　回答明確。考生用的現在完成式 I have entered 有加分效果，而且考官肯定也注意到了談話中用到「about two hours by train」，用得既恰當又自然。

考官：**Is your town an interesting place to live?**
你居住的城鎮有趣嗎？

考生 A：I think it is very interesting because it has many ~~cultures~~ and many modern facilities and ~~transports~~, so it is very convenient ~~to~~ me.
　　　　　　　　　　　　　　　　　　　　　　　for

考官點評

- 名詞 culture 和 transport 很少用到複數形式。這句話最好表達為：It has a lot of culture, good transport and many modern facilities.
- convenient for me 才對，而不是 to me。
- 這個回答的主要問題是聽來不自然，應該是提前準備好的，像是從補習班學到的。

考生 B：Actually, I can't stand my hometown. There's no nightlife there and nothing to do, not like Beijing. Honestly, I feel much more at home in the big city.

考官點評　回答得很好，聽起來是考生自己的觀點。考生在詞彙方面的得分來自：can't stand、nightlife 和 feel at home。

考官總評：考試前背誦口語範文或模板有用嗎？

　　一些考生一上來就背一段對於家鄉的描述，冗長且俗套。這並不好。考官很容易就會看出這是背好的，所以通常都會打斷考生。建議考生仔細想想自己到底是喜歡還是討厭家鄉，並把這種喜惡表達出來。考生應該用自己的語言陳述，因為自己的語言才是真情實感，聽起來才真實。

▶ 2. 你住在什麼樣的房子裡
Where You Live: House or Apartment

考官：Let's talk about where you live. What do you like about your house or apartment?

我們來談談你的住處。你喜歡它的什麼地方？

> **考生 A：** My ~~department~~ is very nice because it is on the third floor. We have two rooms, one for my parents, and one for me.

考官點評

- 基礎詞彙用錯了，department 應該是 apartment。
- 考生描述了公寓，但並沒有回答考官的問題：「你喜歡它的什麼地方？」所以缺乏連貫性。

> **考生 B：** Actually, I am living in a dormitory in the university with three other guys. But my parents ~~are having~~ a flat in our hometown, in Wuhan.
>
> *have a flat*

考官點評

- 首先在文法方面，存在一個動詞時態的問題。I am living in a dormitory 是正確的，因為 -ing 形式表示暫時的狀態。但用 -ing 形式形容武漢的永久住所是不合適的，所以應該用一般現在式，改為 my parents have a flat...。
- 其次，這位考生也沒有正面回答考官的問題。

考官：What is your favourite room in your apartment?

你最喜歡你公寓裡的哪個房間？

> **考生 A：** In my parents' flat, it's the living room, because we have a piano and ~~much~~ books and a fan under the roof so ~~it is staying~~ cool in summer. At university, our ~~dormitory only~~ one room, so that's my favourite!

考官點評

- 考生說的內容還可以。fan 和 piano 都是很好的詞彙。

- 從文法上講,應該是 many books 而不是 much books。而且在英語中,「風扇在天花板上」的正確表達應該是 on the ceiling,而不是 under the roof。it is staying 用錯了時態,應改為 it stays。

- 最後一句少了動詞,應該是 our dormitory only has one room 或 our dormitory is only one room。

考官:What would you like to change about your apartment?
你想怎麼改變你的公寓?

> **考生 A**:Yeah, I want to change my dormitory. When I ~~am graduated~~ I can look for my own apartment and invite my friends and ~~have it more private~~.

考官點評

- 該考生理解錯了考官的問題。考官問的不是「你想換公寓嗎」,而是「你想怎麼改變你的公寓或改變公寓的什麼地方」,比如改變牆的顏色或換傢俱,甚至是改變公寓的大小。考生因為理解錯誤而失分。

- 從文法上看,考生應該說 when I graduate,而不是 when I am graduated;應該說 have more privacy,而不是 have it more private。

> **考生 B**:What would I like to change about it? Mmm, the size, maybe. I mean, it's too small. The location is good, but we really need more space.

考官點評 考生重複了一下問題。你在思考怎麼回答時是可以這麼做的,但不能每個問題都重複。除了這一點,其餘的回答聽起來都很自然。雖然沒有令人印象深刻的詞彙,但用詞恰當。

考官總評：考試時我應該怎麼說才能讓考官感興趣？

如果你沒有意識到這不僅僅是簡單的對話，你的雅思口語成績就拿不到高分。你說的話可能會讓考官很有興趣，也有可能讓他昏昏欲睡。表達生動意味著要有更多的細節或例子，因此你的陳述要有個人色彩。如：「我的房間很小，害我不能做伏地挺身」就比單說「我的房間很小」來得有趣又有個人色彩。

▶ 3. 你是做什麼的：我是個學生
What You Do: I'm a Student

考官：Let's talk about what you do. Do you work or are you a student?
我們來談談你的身份吧。你是上班族還是學生？

> **考生 A**：I'm a student. I study at Xi'an Jiaotong University. Our campus is very beautiful with many trees and parks where we can hang out and relax ~~ourselves~~.

考官點評 這個回答基本上還可以。介紹校園的句子和問題本身並無太大關係，但這麼回答還說得過去，只是聽起來像是背的。另外，沒有 relax oneself 的用法，直接用 relax 即可。

> **考生 B**：I'm a student. I study at Jiaotong University in Xi'an and my major is Chinese philosophy.

考官點評 回答很簡潔，但很清楚，切中要點。

考官：What do you find most interesting about your studies?
你覺得學習中最有趣的地方是什麼？

> **考生 A**：I think the ~~calculate~~ that we do are interesting. We must handle many figures because maths is very important for the finance, you know. I think this major is very hot and ~~it help~~ me to have a bright future!

考官點評

- 回答恰當，但並沒有展現出考生有過人的語言能力，內容也談不上新穎。「前途光明（bright future）」之類的說法屬於陳詞濫調。

- 從文法方面看，calculate 應是 calculations；it help 應是 it can help 或 it will help；finance 前不必加 the。

> **考生 B：** Well, I love my major. A lot of my friends are studying finance or accounting or whatever, but I have always loved Chinese and I think that this field is interesting and that I can probably teach Chinese overseas in the future!

考官點評 回答好極了，沒有文法錯誤。文法結構多樣，用了三種不同的動詞時態：一般現在式（I love...）、現在進行式（my friends are studying...）和現在完成式（I have always loved...）以及含情態動詞的句子（I can probably teach...），還用到了複合句。用詞恰當，話語標記 or whatever 的使用使回答顯得更流暢。

考官： **Which is more important to you—the teachers or the other students on your course?**

老師和班上的同學相比，誰對你來說更重要？

> **考生 A：** I think the teachers ~~is~~ the most important for us because they can teach us many things and give us many ~~informations~~ and ~~advices~~. They have ~~many experience~~ so we should listen to them.

考官點評 給考官留下深刻印象的是不可數名詞的錯誤使用。information 和 advice 均為不可數名詞，所以沒有複數形式。teachers 後面還出現了主詞動詞不一致的錯誤，所以正確的句子應是：I think the teachers are more important for us because they can teach us many things and give us a lot of information and advice. 同樣，experience 也是不可數名詞，應該用 a lot of experience。

> **考生 B：** Both, really. The teachers can give us a lot of knowledge and advice. But my classmates help me a lot, not just with class assignments and presentations, but also with their encouragement and support, so they are really important to me.

考官點評 回答得非常流利。第一句很自然流暢。不可數名詞 advice 和 knowledge 的用法正確，還用到了可以加分的詞：assignments 和 encouragement，文法準確。

考官總評：我怎麼給考官留下好印象？

當考官問你問題時，你一定要注視著對方。儘量避免使用像 this can broaden my horizons 或 this major will give me a bright future 這樣的陳腔濫調。如果你能用一些使說話顯得自然的詞，如 actually 或 not really 等，就會給考官留下更好的印象。

▶ 4. 你是做什麼的：我是上班族
What You Do: I Work

考官： Let's talk about what you do. Do you work or are you a student?

我們來談談你的身分吧。你是上班族還是學生？

> **考生 A：** I working a factory in Hunan.

考官點評 這個開頭很不好，有文法錯誤。動詞時態用錯了，用一般現在式就可以：I work in a factory in Hunan，也可以用現在進行式：I am working...，但 a factory 前少了一個介系詞 in。文法方面的嚴重錯誤使得考生可能只得 4 分。

> **考生 B：** I work. I've been working for three years now. I work for a software company as a marketing assistant.

考官點評 表達清晰、流利、準確。回答這種問題是考生用現在完成進行式（I've been working）的最好時機。這個時態的使用會使文法方面加分。後面提到市場助理的職位時也説得很好。

考官：**Do you find this job interesting?**
你覺得這份工作有趣嗎？

> **考生 A：**Yes, it's pretty good. I like it.

考官點評 回答得可以，但有侷限性。文法沒有錯誤，但回答過於簡短。這會讓考官產生疑問：這位考生有能力説得多一些嗎？所以考生應該多説一點，否則考官會問：「為什麼？」

> **考生 B：**Yes, it's pretty good. I get to meet a lot of clients and I have to make presentations and do research. I like it. But I also have to work a lot of overtime which is not always very convenient! My boyfriend often complains about that!

考官點評 這段回答沒有動詞時態的變化，均為一般現在式。但語言自然，而且用到了一些很好的詞彙：research、presentations、overtime 和 complains。

考官：**Why?**
為什麼？

> **考生 A：**Because it is very interesting to me. I like it.

考官點評 考生只是重複了上一個問題裡的關鍵字，這表示他不會展開思路，這會讓考官認為該考生的語言能力有限。

考官：**Do you want to continue doing this type of work in the future?**
你將來還想繼續從事這類工作嗎？

> **考生 A：**I think so because this job can give me a bright future.

考官點評 回答簡單，且有點老套。像前面提到的，give me a bright future 這類表達屬於陳腔濫調，在雅思考試中最好避免。

> **考生 B：**Well, I would like to continue doing marketing or PR work but not necessarily in relation to computers. I have a friend who works in PR for a car company... PR is an area I would like to try if the right opportunity comes along.

考官點評 考官會注意到 to continue doing something 的說法。在流暢度方面，回答很自然，用詞不錯，如 necessarily 和片語 comes along。如果考生能正確發出 necessarily 的音，考官也會注意到。

考官總評：第一部分我可以簡短作答嗎？

雖然第一部分的問題很簡單，但回答不能太簡單。我們知道第一部分相當於熱身階段，但考生也要認真對待。如果你能快速理解問題，給出生動、準確的回答，第二部分和第三部分肯定會表現得更沉著、自信。

▶ 5. 禮物
Gifts

考官：Let's talk about giving and receiving gifts. When was the last time you gave someone a gift?
我們來談談送禮物和收禮物吧。你上一次送禮物是什麼時候？

> **考生 A：**Actually, it was on Valentine's Day. My girlfriend gave me a watch. I was very ~~moving~~ because I know it is a lot of money ~~to~~ her. Next year, I ~~going~~ buy the same watch for her and ~~writing~~ on it, "Forever love". I think she will be very happy, she will love me forever.

考官點評 回答很生動，但明顯離題。考官問上一次送禮物給別人是什麼時候，但考生卻回答自己上一次收禮物的時間。還有許多文法錯誤：應用 moved，而非

moving；a lot of money for her，不是 to her。明年是將來的時間，所以應該是 I am going to buy、I will buy 或 I want to buy。同樣，writing 應改為 I'll write on it 或 I will write on it。

考生 B： The last time I gave someone a gift? Mmm, actually, it was only about a week ago. I gave my mother some flowers for Mother's Day. Just a simple bouquet.

考官點評　對話比較自然。考生用了 Mmm 和 actually，讓對話更流暢。而且單字 bouquet 的使用會為其在詞彙方面加分。

考官：Do you find it easy to choose gifts for friends or family？
你覺得為朋友或家人挑選禮物容易嗎？

考生 A： No, it is very difficult to me. I never know what my family members really want. It is ~~so trouble~~ to me. I am very ~~confusing~~. If it is for my family, then my girlfriend helps me. She knows ~~every people want~~.

考官點評　文法錯誤太多了。考生應該説 difficult for me 和 it is a lot of trouble for me，而更好一點的説法是 it is a real headache for me。I am very confusing 的用法錯誤，應該説 I get confused 或 I am at a loss as to what to buy。最後一句應為 She knows what each person wants。過多的文法錯誤意味著該考生在文法方面只能得 4 分。

考生 B： Not really. I don't always know what my family members want, so I have to trust my instinct. For my dad, no problems, because he's happy with socks or a book. My mum is more complicated; she likes surprises. She likes scarves and jewellery but ~~it's~~ so expensive. She likes cosmetics too. I know what her favourite brands are, but if I give her moisturizing cream, there's no surprise!

考官點評　回答得很流利、很自然。介系詞使用正確，難詞的發音也正確，如 jewellery、cosmetics。沒有背誦答案的跡象，聽起來像是考生自己的想法。一些詞彙用得不錯，如 trust my instinct、complicated、cosmetics 和 night cream。有一處小文法錯誤：it's 應為 they're。

考官：**Do you think it is important to buy expensive gifts?**
你覺得買貴重禮物很重要嗎？

考生 A：Sometimes. In China, ~~our face~~ is very important so sometimes we must think about the ~~money~~ of the gift. It depends ~~who is the person~~.

考官點評　還不錯。考生應該說 face 而不是 our face，因為 face 在這裡是抽象概念，表示「面子」。money 應換成 cost。最後一句的語序應為 who the person is。

考生 B：No, I don't think so. I think what's important is the feeling you have when you give something to your friend, when you try to make someone happy. My cousin gave me a painting she did by herself. It's very lovely; it's very meaningful for me.

考官點評　答得很好。聽起來也像是考生自己的想法和感受。誠實比背答案好。

考官總評：要怎麼得高分？

首先要仔細聽考官的問題，不要離題。回答要生動，要用自己的話表達自己的觀點。在雅思口語考試中，沒有正確答案。

▶ 6. 快樂
Happiness

考官：**Let's move on to talk about happiness. What makes you happy?**
我們來談談「快樂」這個問題吧。什麼能讓你感到快樂？

考生 A：Lots of things. Dumplings! Having free time at the weekend. My boyfriend—well, sometimes anyway, not all the time. Mmm, what else? Eating tanghulu in winter. It's a kind of Beijing delicacy that you can get at street markets. Walking in the park with my mum and my dad... Reading books. Sitting in a café with my friends gossiping, haha. So many things!

考官點評　一般來説，在第一部分，考官不會讓考生説很長。但讓人印象深刻的是這位考生有這麼多話要説。她的表達很流利，情緒很高興，且對這個問題有很多想法。她的詞彙量也大：dumplings、delicacy（美味佳餚）、street markets（路邊攤）、gossiping（聊八卦）。英國人很少見過糖葫蘆，所以這裡直接用中文也沒有關係。在文法方面，考官注意到考生可以自如地使用 -ing 形式：having free time、eating tanghulu、walking in the park、reading books。如果該考生的發音語調都很好，且重音正確的話，那麼她的總分會提高。

考生 B： I like to play basketball with my friends. I have a lot of friends. We all play basketball. I like Kobe Bryant. He is really great.

考官點評　這個回答聽起來有點俗套。文法正確但水準有限：只用了一般現在式和很簡單的句子。這可能會讓考官想，該考生會複雜的文法嗎？

考官：Do you think money is necessary for happiness?
你覺得有錢是快樂的必備條件嗎？

考生 A： No, I don't think it. Money cannot buy the happiness. Happiness is your family, your friends. That is the happiness. Money is the advantage of the work but you family is the more important for you.

考官點評　這個回答還不夠好，有幾處文法錯誤，意思表達得不清晰。考生應該説 I don't think so 或 Money cannot buy happiness。關於 the 和 a 的用法，可參見本書第五章中專講文法的第三節。我們在談論抽象概念（如快樂）時不用 the。考生想説的可能是：No, I don't think so. Money can't buy happiness. I think the real source of happiness is family and friends. Money is something we earn from working, and it is true that we need it and it brings us many benefits, but I think family is much more important than money.

考生 B： I guess so. I mean, if you don't have the money, what can you do? If you want to travel, you need money. Or even just for your studies and to get some nice clothes so you can go to the job interview, you always need money.

考官點評 回答得很有自信。文法和詞彙都還可以。唯一的文法錯誤是 the 用錯了：這裡應為 money，因為我們是在談抽象概念的錢，而不是指具體的錢。同樣的道理，應該是 a job interview，因為考生並沒有特指哪場面試。另外，請注意 clothes/kləʊðz/ 的發音，因為很多考生會讀錯。

考官： Do you think that unhappiness is always a bad thing?
你覺得不快樂總是一件不好的事嗎？

考生 A： Yes, of course. If you are unhappy, you are sad, and that is not good for you or your friends. You need to ~~look the~~ bright side.

考官點評 回答太簡單，應該再深入一點，比如可以談談樂觀和悲觀。文法方面漏了一個介系詞，應該説 you need to look on the bright side。

考生 B： No, because sometimes when we are unhappy, that makes us think and it also makes us turn to our friends and they can help us to find a way to deal with it. I remember, when I broke up with my girlfriend, I was really sad and unhappy but it made me think about a lot of things and my friends were great. They really supported me. We went to dinner together and drank some beers. It helped me feel better.

考官點評 回答得很從容，也很連貫。文法準確，但文法結構單一。詞彙比較豐富，片語 broke up 和 feel better 用得很好。

考官總評：第一部分的回答最關鍵的是什麼？

生動細節和個人情感容易讓別人產生共鳴，不要説俗套的話。記住，每個人都有獨特的內容可以説，用自己的語言去表達自己的感受吧！如果平常多練習的話，每個人在考試時都可以做到與眾不同。

▶ 7. 新聞
News

考官：**Let's talk about the news. Do you prefer to read newspapers or watch TV to keep up with the news?**

我們來談談新聞。你比較喜歡透過看報紙還是看電視來瞭解新聞？

考生：Actually, neither. I ~~following~~ the news on Internet and on Weibo. I mean, when something like a train accident ~~occur~~, you can get photos and info straightaway on Weibo. But I also look some news websites, Chinese websites mainly, but also foreign ones like yahoo.com and basketball sites.

考官點評　英語中並沒有 I following 的用法，應該改用一般現在式 I follow，以表達經常性的習慣動作。主詞 a train accident 是單數形式，所以動詞應是 occurs。此外，考生應該說 look at some news websites，少了介系詞 at。整體來看，回答的內容不錯，但文法方面會丟分。

考官：**Why?**

為什麼？

考生：Well, I like to have different ~~informations~~ and reading yahoo.com, or sports websites from the US, is really good for my English.

考官點評　information 是不可數名詞，不能在後面加 s。這是華人考生會犯的一個普遍錯誤。如果沒有這個錯誤，這段回答雖然簡短，但還是很不錯的。

考官：**How important is it to you to be able to keep up with the news?**

瞭解時事新聞對你來說有多重要？

考生：It's important. I mean, people need to know what's ~~happen~~ in the world. I'm only 20 now, but in a few years I will have a job and a wife and a child and I need to make good decisions so I need good information.

考官點評 動詞 happen 要用現在進行式：what's happening。I will have a job 用了一般未來式，用法正確。這一回答也很連貫、機智，但 happen 的時態用法錯誤屬於基本錯誤，影響了整體分數。

考官總評：一開口時態就出錯，怎麼辦？

很多考生有豐富的文法知識，但一到考試就變得很粗心。有什麼對策？自己一個人的時候要進行說話訓練，並且要經常訓練，這是糾正基本文法錯誤的重要手段。考生可以經常用英語進行自我對話，也就是說給自己聽，這樣腦子中所想的和嘴上所說的之間的聯繫會逐漸加強，會越來越統一。

> ▶ **8. 噪音**
> **Noise**

考官：How do you feel if you have to work in a noisy place?
如果必須在喧鬧的環境中工作，你會有什麼感受？

考生：I don't like it; it makes me nervous and uncomfortable. Sometimes I get crazy because I cannot ~~concentrate my~~ work. Often we go to the library on campus because it is ~~quite~~ there.

考官點評 回答還算過得去，前後連貫，但動詞 concentrate 的用法有錯誤，應該是 concentrate on my work。另外，用 go crazy 會比 get crazy 好一點。再來就是單字 quite 和 quiet 完全不同，不應該混淆。

考官：Are there any sounds that you particularly like or dislike?
你有特別喜歡或不喜歡的聲音嗎？

考生：I like the sound of birds singing, and the sound of kids laughing. Actually, there are a lot of sounds I like. Even the sound of the bus arriving in the morning. I mean it is an engine noise so it's not that pleasant but for me it's a reassuring sound because it means I won't be late to class!

考官點評 該考生對於詞彙和文法都把握得很好。-ing 形式使用得準確、到位。考生在 engine 前正確使用了 an。engine 和 reassuring 都是出色的詞彙。開頭提到了鳥叫和孩子的笑聲，有點落入俗套，但考生很快用汽車的聲音這個新穎的說法來彌補。

考官：Do you think daily life is becoming more noisy?
你覺得日常生活變得比以前喧鬧了嗎？

> **考生：** Definitely. I mean, there are more and more people living in this city and an incredible number of cars, so life is really noisy. People bang on their horns and shout. I guess the only way to escape from the city noise is to wear headphones and immerse yourself in your own music.

考官點評 該考生使用了一些高級詞彙（incredible、bang on、horns、I guess、headphones、immerse yourself），分數有可能會達到 7 分或 7 分以上。儘管考生自始至終只用了一般現在式這一種時態，但有兩個文法正確的複雜句子。回答連貫從容，各方面都把握得不錯。

考官總評：第一部分在詞彙和文法方面有哪些需要注意的地方？

考官會注意到你使用的詞彙和文法，即使在第一部分也是如此。你不必故意使用很長的單字或很複雜的文法，只要準確、多變就可以。在日常生活中經常進行細緻的觀察，對回答這類問題非常有用。

＊以下 9 ～ 12 題的回答都能達到 7 分。

▶ 9. 游泳
Swimming

考官：**Let's move on to talk about swimming. Did you learn to swim when you were a child?**

我們來談談游泳吧。你小時候學過游泳嗎？

考生：Yes, I did, when I was about eight. I remember, my mum took me to the swimming pool every week. I think the class was on Wednesday, and the instructor was really nice. He encouraged me a lot. At first I could only swim like, like a dog and then I learnt to do the, you know, the...the... a different style. If I have free time, I always swim. It helps me to ~~relax myself~~.

考官點評　回答比較流利，在這一部分，考官可能會給 6 分。回憶以 I remember 開始，與前面連貫得很自然。文法沒有錯誤，特別是正確使用了一般過去式（did、took、was、encouraged、learned），可惜犯了一個錯誤：relax myself（在中文中，可以說「自我放鬆」，但在英語中 relax 後面不加 oneself）。詞彙還不夠豐富，考生知道 instructor 這個單字，但不知道 crawl 或 freestyle（自由式）怎麼說。

以下是含 relax 的正確句子：

• I like to relax.
　我喜歡放鬆。

• It helps them to relax.
　這讓他們很放鬆。

• Students need to relax a bit after a long week of study.
　學生在漫長的一週讀書後需要放鬆一下。

• I spent the whole weekend relaxing.
　我整個週末都在休息。

考官：**Do you think it's important for children to learn to swim?**
　　　你認為學會游泳對小孩重要嗎？

考生：Yes, I do. I think there's something a bit scary about water, at least at the beginning, so it's good for kids to get over that fear and discover that they can swim. It helps them build their confidence... and it's a great sport for people who want to build their bodies, and stay slim. You know, that is important for us, especially for girls.

考官點評　　回答得很流利，發音也很清晰。考生開始感覺放鬆後，回答得自然就更好了。這表示分數會超過 6 分。文法把握得很好，沒有錯誤，還使用了一些很好的用詞，如 scary、get over that fear、build their confidence、build their bodies 和 stay slim。不過得 8 分的考生可能會用 overcome that fear。

考官：**Would you prefer to swim in a pool or in the sea?**
　　　你更喜歡在游泳池還是海裡游泳？

考生：A lot of people prefer to swim, prefer swimming in pools because they think it's ~~more safe~~ but I like the sea. You know, when I was a teenager, I used to go to Qingdao with my parents. My dad would always encourage me to go out further from the shore so I slowly got braver. If he hadn't pushed me, I guess I would have always stayed in the shallow water. But I love the sea. It's a great feeling being in the water.

考官點評　　回答流利，思路清晰。考生在使用動詞 prefer 時有點拿不定主意，出現了 prefer to swim 和 prefer swimming 兩種說法，兩者都正確。文法把握得很好，使用的文法結構讓人印象深刻，特別是條件句 my dad would always encourage me 和 if he hadn't pushed me, I guess I would have always stayed in the shallow water 的使用。如果沒有漏洞的話，考官會給 7 分。但考生犯了一個小錯誤：more safe（單音節形容詞的比較級在詞尾加 -er，不需要用 more 來修飾，如 fatter、smaller、cleaner、safer 等），但這並不影響她整體出色的文法表現。雖然這只是考試的第一部分，但這位考生為最終 7 分的成績奠定了基礎。

考官總評：怎麼讓我的回答更有趣、更吸引考官？

考試時最好能舉一些例子。例子能讓你的回答顯得有趣，還可以用上豐富的詞彙。想一想記憶中的事情，把你經歷過的事說出來吧！

▶ 10. 兒童
Children

考官：Let's move on to talk about children. What kind of a child were you?

我們來談談小孩吧。你小時候是個什麼樣的小孩？

考生：I was a pretty happy-go-lucky, easygoing kind of kid, I suppose. I was lucky because there were a lot of kids in the hutong where I grew up and we all used to play together after school. We got up to a bit of trouble, like all kids... I remember we once lit a fire with some old papers and couldn't put it out.

考官點評 語言流利連貫，可以得 7 分或 8 分。happy-go-lucky 一詞用得很好，很突出。在詞彙和文法方面，考生使用了動詞 light 的過去式 lit，用法正確，且讓人印象深刻。片語 to put out a fire 和 to get up to trouble 用法正確。考生用了中文拼音「hutong」，這完全可以接受，因為在英語中沒有對應的單字。

考官：What kind of activities did you enjoy doing when you were a child?

你小時候喜歡什麼樣的活動？

考生：Well, I loved playing all sorts of games. We had one called zhuomicang; I think you say hide-and-seek in English. That was a lot of fun. And I liked sports at school; I played football and basketball. And we had hobbies too—one of my friends collected insects, for example, we used to spend hours looking at all those insects in their bottles... I mean jars.

考官點評　回答得很精彩。在詞彙方面，insects、jars 和 hide-and-seek 的使用比較突出。除此之外，其他詞彙也很標準。儘管考生在停頓之後才說出單字 jars，但他最終還是說出來了，所以有可能得 7 分，但得 8 分還有點難度。文法把握得很好。動詞時態單一，幾乎都是一般過去式，但如果在考試的其他幾個部分使用多種時態，那也是可以的。動名詞 playing all sorts of games 的用法正確。

考官：How often do you spend time with children now?
你現在會花多少時間與孩子在一起？

考生：Quite often, actually. Ummm, my parents are divorced and my dad remarried so I have a young brother. He's only seven. I hang out with him quite a bit. He's crazy about computer games which I don't think is very good but he also has a bike so we often go riding in the lanes around their house.

考官點評　語言流利自然，使用了讓話題更順暢的 actually。用詞恰當，remarried 以 lanes 都比較突出。在文法方面，幾乎所有的動詞時態都是一般現在式，但這裡是可以接受的。另外，還使用了動名詞（go riding）。

考官：Do you think children's lives are changing nowadays?
你認為如今兒童的生活在改變嗎？

考生：Yeah, a lot. Like my little brother, he's totally into computer games and if we let him, he would do that all day. He likes riding bikes but he is not really interested in sport. In my opinion he spends too much time inside hunched over a screen. I never did that when I was a kid. I guess he really is a product of the computer generation.

考官點評　語言依然流利自然。考生提到了之前說過的小弟弟，且使用了 Yeah, in my opinion 和 I guess。在句子 He's totally into computer games 中，新潮的片語 to be into 用法正確。還用了一些讓人印象深刻的特別說法，如 hunched over a screen 和 product of the computer generation。在文法方面，考生這次把握得也很好，用了條件句 if we let him, he would do that all day。考官肯定會注意到這些的。

考官總評：平時我該怎麼提高我的口語能力？

　　閱讀對於口語能力的提升至關重要！而這裡說的閱讀不是指一般意義上簡單的瀏覽。如果只是看內容，對口語是不會有太多幫助的，要一邊看一邊重點關注詞彙和句型。經過一定時間的累積之後，可以對一定篇幅的文章進行口頭複述或大意的概括。類似這樣的訓練可以有效改進語言表現力，因為這個過程不僅僅有資訊、素材的累積，同時在複述的過程中還可以將閱讀的內容轉化成自己的語言，表達能力自然會得到提升。

▶ 11. 時間管理
Time Management

考官：Let's move on to talk about how you manage your time. Are you good at organizing your time?

我們來談談你是怎麼管理你的時間的。你擅長安排時間嗎？

> **考生：**Actually, I think I am, especially if I compare myself with some of my classmates who do everything at the last minute. I have a sort of instinct for planning. I think I get it from my dad. My parents never have to tell me to do my homework or anything. I plan it out myself.

考官點評　考生的回答有點偏離話題，拿自己和同學進行了比較。但這在談話中很正常，並沒有影響連貫性。流利連貫的回答中還用到了簡單句和複合句。文法簡單，但把握得好。

考官：What would you do if you had more free time?

如果有更多的空閒時間，你會做什麼？

> **考生：**If I had more free time, I would watch more movies, go out more, have more fun. I think young people in China spend too much time studying. You know most of my classmates are in their twenties, and we all have to study like crazy, including the IELTS test. I think we should be enjoying ourselves more. It's so tough in China, so competitive...You know, some of us, we are going

to reach thirty and have a job and a career and a family and maybe a kid, and maybe we'll turn round and say, where has my youth gone? So much pressure, and then so much responsibility, haha. It's terrible!

考官點評　有了這段回答，考生得 7 分的可能性就很大。文法正確，而且結構多樣，使用了條件句（If I had more free time, I would watch more movies...）、動名詞（spend too much time studying 和 should be enjoying）、兩種類型的未來時態（we are going to reach thirty 和 maybe we'll turn round...）和一個現在完成式（where has my youth gone）。精彩的片語有 study like crazy 和 turn round and say。形容詞 competitive 也不錯，如果考生能把這個音發正確的話，得分會更高。整體來說，回答流利連貫，觀點堅定清晰。

考官總評：考官如果不同意我的觀點，會不會對我的分數不利？

　　要以積極的態度面對考試。對話題要有自己的想法，並且自信地表達出來。考官是否同意你的觀點，其實並不重要，重要的是你如何把自己的觀點好好地表達出來。

▶ 12. 天氣
Weather

考官：Let' talk about the weather now. What is your favourite kind of weather?

我們現在來談談天氣吧。你最喜歡什麼樣的天氣？

考生：Wow, that' not easy. I know what I don't like which is really hot weather like we have in Beijing in July and August but, apart from that, I like everything. I like spring and autumn but I also like winter. I like being out in the cold with a scarf and gloves and warm clothes and then getting home and drinking a lovely hot cup of soup.

考官點評 語言流利連貫。考生開始講了自己不喜歡的天氣，但後面就開始圍繞著問題談論，回答得很好。最後一句非常精彩：考生舉例並描述了冬天寒冷的畫面，這讓考生有充分的機會來展示詞彙，如 scarf、gloves、hot cup of soup。片語 apart from that 用得很好，也可作為連接詞。動詞 like 的重複使用並沒有顯得考生詞彙不豐富，反而顯得很自然。文法把握得很好，時態主要是一般現在式，動名詞用得很好，如 being out、getting home 和 drinking。

考官：Is there any kind of weather that you don't like?
有沒有什麼樣的天氣是你不喜歡的？

> **考生：**Yes, like I said, I hate the summer in Beijing. It's so hot. I don't like sleeping with the ~~air condition~~. And sometimes the pollution is really thick and just stays in the air. It's bad for your health. A couple of summers ago, my parents ~~have let~~ me go to Harbin in July and that was fantastic. The weather was ~~more gentle~~. There is a place there called Taiyang Dao and it's really great to hang out there in summer. The temperature is perfect and there are so many things you can do.

考官點評 回答連貫，但有好幾處錯誤，可能會使考生拿不到 7 分。用得比較好的詞彙有 hate、pollution 和 perfect，但 air condition 是錯的，正確的說法是 air conditioner，不過更好一點的說法是：I don't like sleeping with the air conditioning on。stays in the air 中的動詞 stays 不算錯，但要想得 7 分或 8 分，最好用 hangs。

另外，如果用 mild 來描述天氣會比 gentle 更道地。文法基礎扎實，但 more gentle 這一錯誤讓人驚訝（應為 gentler），這是 7 分的考生不應犯的錯誤。有一個動詞時態有錯誤，應該是：my parents let me go to Harbin，因為發生在過去的時間。注意動詞 let 的動詞原形、過去式和過去分詞都是 let。現在考官可能認為該考生只能得 6 分，但後來的優秀表現很有可能會改變考官的看法。

考官：**Do you think the weather is changing in China?**

你認為中國的天氣在發生變化嗎？

考生：Sure, the weather is always changing. We have four seasons...Oh, you mean climate change? Yeah, definitely. I think the summers are ~~more wet~~ now in the north of China and the winters are not so cold. I guess it must be because of climate change...I saw a documentary on TV that said the glaciers in the west of China are gradually disappearing. They showed photos taken about 100 years ago and compared them with now. You could really see the difference. It's terrible. You know, some people say that Shanghai would be wiped out if the sea level rises!

考官點評　回答說服力強、語言連貫。在文法方面，考生又犯了一個形容詞比較級的錯誤，more wet 應是 wetter。除此以外，其他文法知識都把握得很好，文法結構多變。考生使用了情態動詞：you could really see... 和多種動詞時態，如一般現在式（I think...）、現在進行式（the weather is always changing... 和 gradually disappearing...）和一般過去式（I saw...）。條件句 would be wiped out... 和過去分詞 taken 的使用也正確。

在詞彙方面，考生談到了電視紀錄片，這樣就有機會用上很多很棒的詞來介紹。考生在流暢度、詞彙和發音方面的得分都為 7 分，但文法得分在 6 到 7 分之間。考官在第二部分和第三部分會認真聆聽，因為需要進一步的根據確定最後的分數。不可否認，這個考生的表現很好。生動的細節描述、真實的個人情感和少量的文法錯誤，結合在一起肯定能讓考官仔細聆聽並做筆記（儘管他或她會儘量避免讓考生看到）。這位考生在第一部分的熱身做得很好，並為第二部分和第三部分做好了準備。

第四節 黃金法則
Dos and Don'ts

▶一定要⋯⋯ Do...

▸ 展現出你的興趣和活力，發言時聲音要洪亮，肢體語言要豐富。

Project interest and energy, and put energy into your voice and into your body language.

▸ 仔細聽，不要把搞錯問題的意思。然後直截了當地回答！

Listen carefully, and don't misunderstand the question. And then get to the point!

▸ 考試過程中要直視考官的眼睛。

Maintain good eye contact with the examiner.

▸ 盡可能用自己的話來表達。

Be as original as you can.

▸ 儘量使用一些條件句或不太常用的動詞時態，如現在完成式。

Grab opportunities to use some of the less common verb tenses like the present perfect or the conditionals.

▸ 發音要清晰。

Make sure your pronunciation is clear.

▶千萬別⋯⋯ But don't...

▸ 不要機械背誦記憶過的答案，因為聽起來會很無趣。

Don't trot out memorized replies because they sound dull and boring.

▸ 不要問考官問題，因為他們沒有時間來回答。

Don't ask the examiner questions, because they don't have time to reply.

NOTE

"第3章"

考官教你征服雅思口語
考試第二部分

第一節 讓考官告訴你：原創回答得高分
Use Your Own Words and Ideas

　　讓我們這些當考官的納悶的是，很多雅思考生並沒有採用正確的方法為考試和出國留學做準備。他們總是死記硬背很多回答，而且會認為考官的問題有「正確答案」。但雅思考試不是數學考試，不會問你 1 加 1 等於多少這類的問題。當然，學生還是有可能犯文法錯誤、發錯音或誤用連接詞，但考官與考生的對話中並不存在正確答案。

　　舉例來說，如果我問你：「你覺得某某電影怎麼樣？」這個問題是沒有正確答案的，因為電影就是有人會喜歡、有人會不喜歡。你喜歡也好，不喜歡也罷，都是你的個人觀點，重要的是你的回答方式。你的回答可能比較簡短，沒有展現出真正的語言能力，例如「這電影不錯」或「太棒了」。但你也可以展現出很獨到的觀點，並用豐富的詞彙來說明，例如「我覺得這電影很糟糕。雖然特效相當震撼，但故事情節落入俗套……」。前者和後者都不是「錯的」答案，但哪個會得高分應該很明顯了吧！考生喜不喜歡這部電影不重要，重要的是他們的觀點表達得好不好。

　　再舉個例子來說，如果有個考生被問到：「你認為人們在鄉村還是在城市生活比較好？」考生回答：「我認為有兩種人生活在鄉村，一種是一直住在那裡的窮人，一種是選擇了那種生活方式的富人。」這聽起來是個不錯的回答，觀點很獨到，但這時身為考官的我們馬上會發現：這個月已經從其他考生口中聽過三四次一模一樣的答案了，可見這個考生的答案一定是背的！所以，這個聽起來像是「對的答案」的答案反而沒辦法幫考生拿高分，還會讓他被扣分，而且老實說，我們當考官的聽到考生都講一樣的句子，其實不會太高興，甚至會有點惱火，因為我們會有種被騙的感覺。你當然不希望考官對你惱火吧？

　　考官是西方人，我們西方人從小成長的環境有重視批判性思維的傳統。我們欣賞願意融入談話的考生，而不喜歡只會重複背誦語句的考生。對我們來說，這樣等於是在作弊。

　　當然，我們不是叫你們不可以背單字、背片語。背這些當然可以，但背一整段就不行了。而且也別忘了，考雅思的考生大部分是打算要出國唸書的，而西方的大學比起「正確答案」，更重視批判思考的能力，所以如果你永遠只靠著背誦知識，就算雅思過關了，到國外的大學也不會過關的喔！

最後，再總括一次。在雅思這樣的考試中，沒有「正確答案」，只會有多種多樣的回答，有些有趣，有些無聊，有些機智，有些出人意料，有些則是老生常談。如果學生們用自己的語言說出自己真正的想法，而不是背其他人的答案，就會給考官留下更好的印象，也能為進入外國大學唸書做好準備。如果用背誦的句子回答問題，就無法與考官進行有效的交流，而且很難突破 5 分，會困在所謂的「5 分泥潭」中！如果只是背誦固定答案的話，永遠也得不了 7 分。

第二節 第二部分闖關秘技
Keys for Success in Part Two

雅思口語的評分標準之一是「語言的流暢度和連貫性」。而這一標準在第二部分的考試中顯得尤其重要，因為你要針對考官給出的一個話題連續發言兩分鐘！因此，在第五章的第一節《標準一：語言的流暢度和連貫性》中，我們會以「電影」這一話題為例，重點講解如何在第二部分展現出流暢和連貫的語言。

在本章中，我們除了通過分析真實案例，向你展現第二部分得高分的重要因素以外，還會教你從容應對第二部分的方法。想要流暢地表達，前提是你要有自己的想法。其次，你要具備豐富的詞彙，這樣才能避免考試時因在頭腦中費力尋找合適詞彙而出現停頓、卡住。

為什麼在本章中，我們不單純列出以前考過的雅思話題呢？因為這樣無益於你拓展詞彙和改善語言的流暢度。我們有以下三點理由：

❶ 考試的話題經常更新，以前考過的題很快就會作廢。

❷ 考生多半會抱著消極和僥倖的心理去練習這些話題，而不是把它們當成能提高自己語言水準的工具。

❸ 我們編排這些話題的目的並非是對考生進行「填鴨」教學，而是向你們展示如何拓展詞彙、如何使自己的語言更流暢。而一旦語言能力有所提高，你就可以自如地應對有可能呈現在你面前的任何一個話題了。

請記住，在第二部分中，詞彙 + 觀點 + 流暢 = 成功！

第三節 知識要廣：考官為你點評真實案例！
A Good Case Study

　　優秀考生能夠運用豐富的詞彙，在第二部分無論遇到什麼話題都能流利地表達自己的觀點。而且，他們會每天看時事或聽新聞，瞭解世界上正在發生的事情。這表示當他們拿到第二部分的話題卡時，腦海中立刻會浮現出很多想法。只要經常進行流暢度訓練，就能將許多高級詞彙運用到句子中，並能夠使用各種不同的動詞時態和條件句。

　　在第二部分開始前，考官會先說明題目要求，例如：「And now here's your topic. I'd like you to talk about a news story that interested you.」

　　以福島核洩漏事件為例，考生在話題卡上寫下了下面這些單字：

nuclear disaster

safety

radiation –vegetables –traces

contamination

wind

ocean

tsunami

media

考生回答	考官點評
A news story[1] that really impressed me in 2011 was about the nuclear disaster in Japan, in Fukushima. Um, I remember[2] very clearly that night, when the news came out, I was at a bar in Shuangjing, and we started getting	1) 注意 news 和 story 要連讀。 2) 表示要結合個人的經歷來談論，增加了生動性及可信度。

news. People were receiving[3] news on their phones. Some people were trying... onto the net. They were going online, and I know my first reaction was to call my mum and to ask her to close the windows in the house and also I remember[4] texting my best friend who has a young brother and, you know[5], sort of saying to her, "Hey, you need to check out what's happening online. Maybe there's a nuclear disaster happening in Japan." And in fact here in China we were lucky. I mean the wind blew a lot of the, um, the radiation[6] into the ocean rather than[7] towards us here, but even in China they found there had been[8] some traces of radiation in vegetables. But I mean it was an absolutely terrible disaster and the Japanese people were... Actually my dad has been to Sendai. It's so heavily[9] populated... The whole of Japan, it's not a very big country in terms of landmass, but it's got a big population, and people were overwhelmed[10]. That tsunami, terrible... The farmers that lived in that area, I mean they couldn't leave their land because otherwise who would feed their animals and so they just had to kind of sit there and hope for the best. So it was a terrible disaster, and of course it has made people all around the world much more cautious about nuclear power... Um, I saw on CCTV 9 that people in Europe[11] are worried about nuclear power at the moment too, and they want to get rid of their nuclear reactors.

3) 進行時態是華人學生時常忘記使用的時態。

4) 一句話中進行不同時態的轉換，可以起到放慢語速的作用。

5) you know 用來填充短暫空白。

6) 不關注新聞就很難學到 radiation（放射）這樣的詞彙。

7) rather than 表示轉折，這種說法對華人學生來說比較新穎。

8) there be 句型和完成時態的結合，表示一種客觀事物已存在一段時間。

9) 表示程度嚴重的時候，heavily 是比較合適的選擇。

10) overwhelm 表示受到了程度比較大的打擊，同時具有強調結果很嚴重的意味。

11) 說明該考生興趣面很廣，因為他不僅知道福島的情況，也知道其他國家對此事的反應。

譯文

2011 年，給我留下了深刻印象的新聞是發生在日本福島的核洩漏事件。

我清晰地記得在事件發生的當晚，我正在雙井附近的一家酒吧裡。我們開始看相關的新聞。有人通過手機接收資訊，有人上網追蹤事件的進展。我記得我的第一反應是打給我媽媽，要她關上房間的窗戶。我還記得我發簡訊給我的好朋友，她有一個弟弟。我告訴她快上網看新聞，說日本也許發生了核洩漏事件。當然我們在中國還是比較幸運的。我指的是，強風把大量的放射物吹到了海洋裡，而不是我們這裡。但在中國依然發現蔬菜有受過輻射的痕跡。這真是一場慘重的災難，日本人太……其實我父親去過仙台，那裡的人口非常稠密。整個日本從陸地面積來看，不是一個很大的國家，但人口密度很大。人們都被擊垮了。這場海嘯真是太嚴重了……住在那裡的農民們不能離開他們的家園，否則就沒有人照顧他們的家畜，所以他們只能留在那裡祈禱，往最好的方面想。這真是一場可怕的災難，使得全世界的人們對開發核能變得更加小心謹慎。我在中央九台看到，當時歐洲人也很擔心核能問題，想廢除核反應爐。

考官們的總評

考生是如何應對這一話題的呢？他談到了自己對該事故的反應、災難對中國潛在的影響、災難對日本人的影響以及可能對歐洲產生的影響。要做到這些，考生平時就要積累大量的資訊。考生是在福島核事故發生後參加雅思口語考試的，所以對這個事件並不陌生，仍記得風將放射物吹入了海洋，並在中國的蔬菜中檢測出了核輻射物（traces of radiation 讓人印象深刻）。顯然考生也瞭解日本農民處理災後影響的困境，以及災難對他們生活的影響。日本不是一個大國，仙台市靠近福島，這都是常識，所以考生知道這一點。考生還意識到，考試中可能會問到歐洲核安全的問題，所以也進行了準備。

考生對自己所表達的內容加入個人的情感，這樣的語言更容易讓聽者產生共鳴。細節的描述可以有效說明陳述者對話題的瞭解，也增添了諸多鮮活的因素。

第四節 內容要生動：考官為你點評真實案例！
A Good Case Study

考官提出的要求是：「And now here's your topic. I'd like you to talk about a book that you have read and that you would like to read again.」話題卡上的描述是：「You should say what the book was about, what you know about the writer, what you liked or disliked about the book and why you would like to read it again.」

考生在卡片上記下了下面幾個單字：

Gossip Girl

Serena, Dan

luxury

Well, the book I would like to talk about is a book called *Gossip Girl*. Maybe you know it's also a TV series, but I read the book. I read the book in English. I think that was good for me because it helped me develop my vocabulary. Because there was quite a lot of words I didn't know, I had to look them in my dictionary. Anyway, it's a book about some young people living in New York and the life they have. It is a kind of luxury life really. You know, it's very different from the life we have in China. And also it talks about their families and especially their romances,

考官點評

• 文法知識的廣度：只用了一般現在式、一般過去式和幾個情態動詞。

• 文法準確度：非常準確，只有 look them 應改為 look them up。

their relationships, and some of them have secrets from the past. You know, the characters like Serena and Blair, they're much more open than people in China. I guess in some ways I felt sort of envy for the girls because they have so much freedom to do what they want. But in other ways I didn't like their life very much, their decisions. I guess I am more traditional. I don't remember who the writer was. It's a woman. I guess I just remember the characters, especially Serena and Dan. He is a kind of good person but he gets involved in things and it's complicated. I'm not sure that I would read it again because I can always watch the TV version. Maybe I would try to read another book, because that can help me to know more words and knowledge, and also to know more about foreign culture.

- 用詞：用了一些很好的詞彙，如 luxury life、romances、relationship、secrets、envy 和 freedom。形容詞和副詞用得不多，介系詞和代名詞能夠做到準確使用。

- 錯誤率：低

考官們的總評

　　該考生在第二部分表現得很好。她閱讀過英文原著，文法正確，語言流利，用到了一些比較高級的詞彙。但她沒有過多談論這本書。總體來看，她的分數可能為 7 分。

第五節 跟考官練各種口語話題
Practicing Different Topics

一、考官學中文，有六步練習法！
Six Steps to Practicing Chinese Speaking

我是個土生土長的紐西蘭人，對我來說中文很困難，相信我的中文很可能比你們的英文差多了。所以我自己擬了一套練習中文口語的方式，大家也可以試試看用這個方式練練看英文口語！

假設我抽到的是「你去過海邊嗎？請描述你去海邊的一次經驗」這個題目，我會以這六步進行回答：

第一步：寫下單字。

雅思口語考試中，會給你 1 分鐘的時間作筆記，寫下要用的單字，然後再讓你作答。於是，我在紙上寫下一些我需要的詞彙，其中有一些我只知道英文，不曉得怎麼用中文說。

海	海菜
青島	oyster
海灘	魚、蝦
sand	游泳衣服
濤	游泳
lie on the sand, sunbathe	

第二步：口語練習

接下來，就開始作答，用錄音機把所說的內容錄下來。雅思考試中，共要說一到兩分鐘。我說的內容如下：

去年我去了青島，跟我的女兒和我的朋友。我們在青島兩個禮拜，是一個非常美麗的地方。有一個很大的海灘，我們喜歡在青島每年放假，因為我們都喜歡游泳。我的女兒一點害怕大濤，所以在青島對她是很安全，她很高興。別的東西在青島是一個非常有意思的事，是他們的海菜，海菜非常好。我們都喜歡吃魚，吃蝦，這樣的海菜我們都喜歡吃，所以很高興在青島。每天我們很早起床，然後吃早飯，然後去海灘玩兒。我們都有美麗的游泳的衣服，在北京買了，所以在海灘很高興。有很多人，但是我看了一個東西，是在青島中國人一點害怕去很遠……因為我的游泳很屬害，所以我可以游泳很遠。沒有別人，我是一個人在這裡，是非常有意思。

第三步：回饋及改善

接下來，我把錄音音檔寄給我的中文老師，老師給了以下的建議：

* 有很多文法錯誤，尤其是在語序方面。例如，我們中文不說「我去了青島跟我的女兒和我的朋友」，而是「我跟我的女兒和朋友去了青島」。

* 表達不夠準確，不應該說「我可以游泳很遠」，而是「我可以游得很遠」。

* 單字不夠準確，不是「中國人一點害怕」，而是「中國人有點害怕」。

* 發音不是很準確，但是是可以理解的。最明顯的發音錯誤是「去年」的「去」，應該發四聲。

* 用字錯誤：不是「大濤」而是「大浪」或「大的海浪」。

* 用字錯誤：我們很喜歡吃「海鮮」，而不是「海菜」。

* 用字錯誤：中文不說「游泳的衣服」，而是「泳裝」、「泳衣」、「泳褲」。

第四步：拓展單字量

在得到回饋後，我就自己畫了一張單字擴展圖，並在裡面添加了新的單字，還加上新的內容，如下圖所示。

第五步：再練習一次

我利用新寫下的單字再練習了一次這個話題，並努力避免「很高興」、「有意思」、「在青島」等詞彙出現太多次。同時，我也努力糾正「去年」的發音。在這次練習中，我用了更多的單字，語言更流暢，語序也更正確了。

第六步：第三次練習

最後又練習了第三次。這次我不再低頭看筆記，並努力説得更快、更流利。之後，把錄音的音檔存入電腦，接下來就可以進行下一個話題的練習囉！大家也可以試試看用這些方式來練習口語。

二、選擇練習的話題
Finding Topics to Practice on

　　就連網路上找到的考古題都練習完了嗎？還可以再自己想一些其他的話題來說！雅思口語要你回答的話題沒有固定，隨時有可能增加，所以也別以為練完考古題就沒事了。再加上要出國的你，在國外會說到的話題本來就有千百種，多練習絕對只有好處沒有壞處的喔！

　　那自己選擇別的話題來練習，可以如何選擇呢？在日常生活中其實就可以找到。每當在生活中遇到有趣的事情，就可以打開手冊記錄下來。例如：

- 在臉書上看到的話題，如災害、犯罪、政策、名人八卦等等。

- 娛樂事件，如你喜歡的歌手開演唱會、體育新聞等。

- 國際新聞。

- 與藝術相關的話題，如電影、音樂、美術等。

- 虛構的事件，例如假如你現在有 1000 萬元，你會怎麼花？

　　舉例來說，假如你剛參加了音樂會，就可以把這個音樂會當作一個能拿來練習的話題。你可以先記錄下和這個話題相關的單字（中英文皆可），再利用它們造句。也可以透過網路或字典找到自己需要的單字，並替中文單字找到對應的英文。

名詞：	theatre, stadium, stage, aisle, barrier, atmosphere, people, rhythm, melody, beat, guitar, drums, keyboard...
形容詞：	fascinating- I find the music fascinating. amazing- They had this amazing light and laser show. crowded- the stadium was so crowded. scary-We were pressed right up against the barriers. It was quite scary for a while. cool-The guy playing the keyboard was really cool and handsome. My friend couldn't stop looking at him.

副詞：　　totally- Everyone was just totally into it, the music, the atmosphere, everything.

incredibly- I found the music incredibly moving.

動詞：　　dance- People were dancing in the aisles, going crazy.

clap, applaud- Everybody clapped and applauded and people started to call out for an encore.

feel- I feel elated. Honestly, it was one of the most incredible nights of my life.

第六節 有效練習各種話題
Practicing Different Topics Efficiently

一、六步練習法
Six Steps

　　前面已經說過找出話題的方法，那該如何練習這些話題呢？首先要腦力激盪，思考與話題有關的單字，然後錄下你的陳述。在瞭解到自己的不足後，用更快的語速將同樣的話題再說一遍，接下來就可以進入下一個話題。以下是具體的步驟：

第一步：記錄單字

寫下回答話題所需要的單字，注意以下幾點：

- 寫出你能想到的所有單字和片語，如果對單字比較熟，盡量直接寫英文，如果真的不知道怎麼說再寫中文。

- 在字典上或網路查不知道怎麼說的單字，找出英文說法。

- 把這些單字與片語都記下來。

第二部：口語練習

準備好錄音設備，邊看記下來的單字邊進行陳述，並錄下來，盡量説三到四分鐘，用手機或計時器計時。

第三步：回饋、檢查

仔細聽錄下來的音檔，看你是不是有很多地方卡住？是不是有的單字發音不對？是不是有的單字想不起來？重複的地方多嗎？有沒有文法錯誤？是不是還有一些中文找不到對應的英文單字？最好可以找老師或英文好的朋友一起檢查。

第四步：拓展單字

使用接下來即將介紹的詞彙擴展圖，擴展與該話題相關的單字及説法。

第五步：再練習一次

再練習一次這個話題，這次的目標是減少卡住的地方，説得更流暢、快速，調整發音和節奏，並努力運用更豐富的單字。

第六步：第三次練習

第三次練習同樣的話題，這次不要看手冊上的單字，看看自己是不是能夠連續説兩分鐘。盡量多説一些內容，多用一些單字。

完成以上步驟後，就可以進入下一個話題了！充分運用這個練習法，就等於養成了優秀的學習習慣，口語也一定會越來越流利。

二、詞彙拓展圖的多種應用
Vocabulary Expansion

來看看右頁的詞彙拓展圖吧！該怎麼用呢？下面列出了多種應用方法，及不同的劃分方式，你可以從中選擇最適合你的一種。

1. 按照詞性劃分

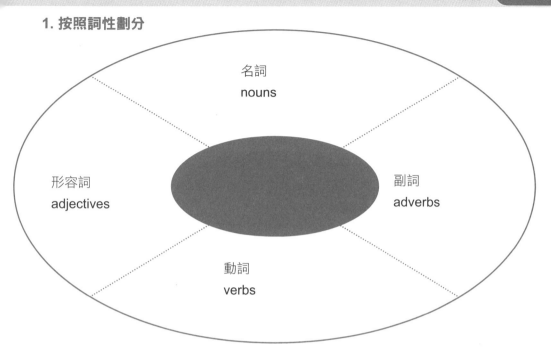

2. 按照論述方面劃分

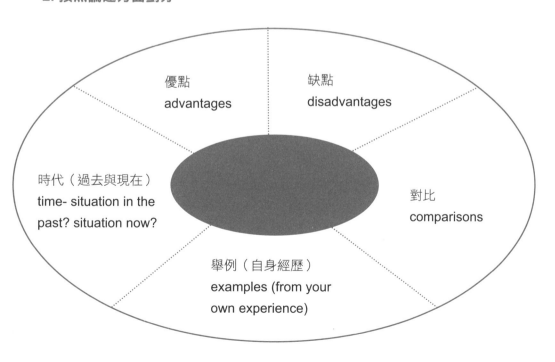

3. 按照「人物、地點、時間、方式、原因」等要素劃分

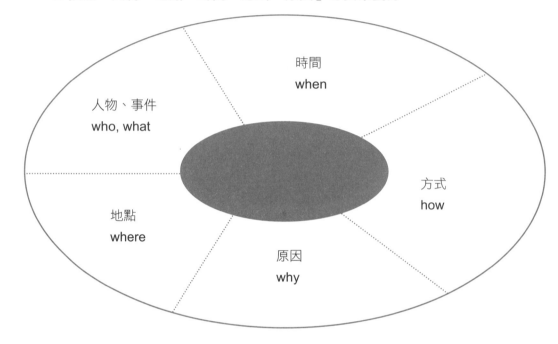

4. 按照陳述順序劃分

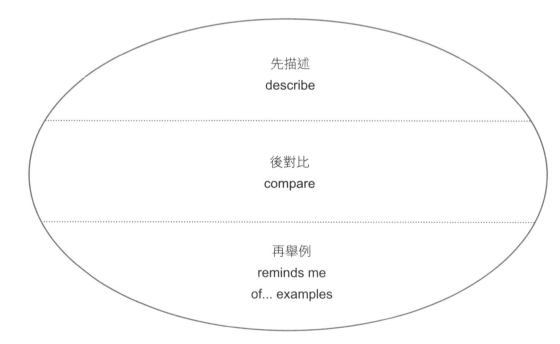

5. 按照描述要素劃分

" 第4章 "

考官教你征服雅思口語
考試第三部分

第一節 讓考官告訴你：成敗在此一刻
Make or Break

雅思口語考試的最後一部分是「討論」，大概持續五分鐘左右。討論的內容與第二部分的話題有關。考官會問考生 4 ～ 10 個問題來展開討論。第三部分的考試非常關鍵，考生無法預測這部分會提出的問題，因此單憑死背回答是沒有用的！如果考官認為你回答的內容是背的，他們就會在第三部分揭開你的「真面目」。事實上，第三部分才是真正的對話，如果你突然到了英國、美國等等英語系國家，要和當地人溝通，差不多就會是這樣子。所以第三部分可以說是成敗的關鍵喔！

有些學生常會誤以為只要第一、第二部分背了足夠的答案，表現得夠好，第三個部分就只要說個幾句便可以過關。但這個觀念完全是錯的！對於考官來說，第三部分才是最重要的。考官會利用這個部分擺脫已設定好的問題，用提問測試考生真實的水準。考生可以在考前先為第一部分和第二部分提前準備、背好答案，但第三部分是開放式的討論，絕不可能靠著背答案來解決。

那麼考生怎樣做才能在這部分取得好成績呢？第三個部分的目的就是「討論」，而「討論」包含了爭辯、思考、評論、尋求解決方法、辯論等等方面的含義。這表示考官和考生應拋開各自的身份，假裝自己並非在考試，而是認真在談論一個話題。考生必須能夠提出一個論點、說出自己的觀點，也應該能夠說出不同的解決方案並進行評論。也就是說，考生不但英文要好，而且知識要夠，腦子裡要有想法。

那麼在第三部分的討論中，考生可以加入自己的個人經歷嗎？當然可以！但只限於個人經歷是不夠的，要用更開闊的思路去思考問題。例如，考生不應該說「我認為污染是一個問題，因為會害我咳嗽」，而應該說「我認為污染對這個世界與各個國家來說是一個嚴重問題，因為它會長期影響人們的健康和生活環境」。

在第三部分中，考官對考生的期望是：希望考生對談論的話題有自己的想法和觀點，並能融入到整個討論中。什麼是「融入」呢？考生應該直視考官，聽清他們的提問並回答，愉快地和考官展開觀點的「交鋒」。人與人之間的對話事實上本來不就是這樣嗎？到了西方國家，交朋友、與人溝通。也需要這樣的能力啊。

第三部分討論的話題，都會與第二部分的話題有關。也就是說，如果考生在第二部分描述了某場婚禮，那麼第三部分的討論就會和婚姻有關，可能是婚禮的趨勢或已婚人士的責任，甚至是婚姻對於社會的重要性。考官可能會問：辦大規模的婚禮好，還是規模小的婚禮好？也可能會問度蜜月的趨勢：在你的國家，新婚夫婦喜歡去什麼地方度蜜月？考生回答後，考官可能還會問：這些習俗在改變嗎？本章在後面會舉很多這種例子。

在這個部分，考官也有可能會打斷你的發言。這是因為他認為你在背答案、在重複說過的話或已經沒什麼話可說了，或考生回答的一些內容讓他想起了另一個問題或話題的另一個角度。而且，考官也想看看考生會如何應對考官的干擾、能不能快速接上新的話題。

最後，別忘了在第三部分中，最重要的是要表現出充沛的活力，要有眼神接觸、肢體語言、語調變化、活力和熱情，即使考官似乎已經失去興趣了也要如此。考生可以登錄 www.ieltsyes.net 觀看這方面的影片喔！第三部分非常重要，可以說是成敗在此一刻，大家千萬別忽略它！

第二節 第三部分闖關秘技
10 Ways to Improve Your Discussion Technique

與考官討論時需要什麼樣的技巧、策略和方式？這裡就列出一些你必須具備的能力，讓你能夠融入與考官的討論！

1. **有自己的想法。**在討論中，你要學會表達自己的觀點。可以通過閱讀書籍和瞭解時事新聞來拓寬思維，也可以記錄自己感興趣的話題，和同學、朋友進行腦力激盪訓練，與老師、家人交談想法。

2. **練習如何展開討論。**有很多方法可以幫助你輕而易舉展開討論。你可以談論一個趨勢的利弊，也可以討論一種情況如何隨著時間而變化：過去怎樣，未來又可能如何。你可以對比國內某個地區與另一地區的情況，或對比國內與國外的情況。可以舉例子，也可以預測。

3. **知識面要廣而不必深。**留意身邊發生的事情，注意你就讀的大學、生活的城市和社區或國內正在發生的事情，瞭解其他國家人們身上發生的事情。你不需要深入瞭解，只需知道大概即可。這樣，口語考試時無論遇到什麼話題，你都不會茫然不知所措。

4. **要求考官進行必要的說明。**如果你對考官問的問題不是很清楚，可以詢問考官，請他說得更清楚。例如如果在談論食物，考官說：「你認為食品安全是個很重要的問題嗎？」你可以問：「你是說在國內嗎？」然後考官可能會說：「是的，在國內，但也可以說說普遍現象。」這樣你就可以在國內的食品安全方面展開敘述，也可以大致談談食品安全對各國人民的重要性。

5. **回答要有原創性。**西方的教育體系非常重視原創性、創造性和想像力。在雅思口語考試中，你自己的想法所展現出來的價值遠遠超過你從書上讀到或背下的內容。

6. **為自己的觀點辯護。**你不僅僅需要表達觀點，還要能夠為自己的觀點辯護。討論中總會出現不同的觀點。考官可能會質疑你的觀點，或提到與你的觀點相反的內容。不要認為這是人身攻擊，相反，這是你展開討論、承認考官的某些觀點的絕佳機會。不要屈服，堅持自己的觀點，進一步展開論述，也可以舉出你熟知的例子或你的親身經歷。

7. **擴大詞彙量。**有想法是一回事，能用英語把自己的想法有效表達出來是另外一回事。多練習閱讀各種觀點和詞彙，以增加你的詞彙量。

8. **爭取時間。**開始回答前可以使用一些語氣詞，比如 well, actually 或 mmmm。在現實生活中，人們對話時也經常會用這些語氣詞。考試時，使用這些詞可以給你爭取一點考慮的時間。你也可以說：「That's quite a difficult question」或「That's a tricky question」或「Well, in my opinion...」但不要用太多次。

9. **如果你實在無話可說……**考試過程中你可能突然詞窮或無話可說，而感到尷尬。遇到這種情況，可以使用以下說法：

- Does that make sense?
  我這樣說你大概懂了嗎？

- Can you follow my reasoning?
  你懂我的意思嗎？

- Are you with me?
  你有聽懂嗎？

- Am I making myself clear? Not really? OK, let me try again...
  我說清楚了嗎？沒有？好的，我再說一次……

- Maybe I didn't express myself very well. What I mean is...
  可能我表達得不是太好。我的意思是……

- Basically, what I'm saying is that if I were in a situation like that...
  基本上，我想說的是如果我遇到那種情況……

10. 要有活力。希望考試前你睡了一個好覺，精神抖擻、活潑自信。將你的活力融入肢體語言中吧！坐直，姿態端正；眼睛直視考官；微笑，腦袋不要一動不動；要會利用手勢，語調要富有變化；如果你想大笑或微笑，那就笑吧。

在第三部分中，考官提問題的角度大致可分為以下四個類型。每個問題下面都給出了一位考生的回答供參考。這些回答都是高分回答，無論是在思路還是文法、詞彙方面，都有值得學習之處。請認真學習和練習，切忌全段背誦！

第三節 雅思考官最常提問的「四大角度」答題秘訣
Types of Question in Part Three

第一類問題：
社會和商業趨勢：過去、現在和將來
Social and Business Trends: Current or Past Situations, Predictions about the Future

考官：**You said that a lot of people have migrated to cities in China over the last two decades. Will this trend continue in the future or will people start to move back to the countryside?**

你提到在過去的二十年中，中國有很多人遷移到了城市。請問這種趨勢將來會持續下去還是人們會開始遷回農村？

考生：Well, I am no expert in urban planning or demographics or anything, but I can't see why this trend will stop. I mean, all over the world, countries are becoming more urbanized, I guess because there are more opportunities in the cities, and resources are concentrated there. Take education, for example, which is very important to Chinese people. The educational opportunities are much better in the cities than in the countryside. So I think people from the countryside will continue to migrate to the cities in China. Basically, they are in pursuit of a better life, and they associate better living with being in a city.

考官：**These days more and more Chinese students are going overseas to study. What are the reasons for this trend? Will it continue in the future?**

如今有越來越多的中國學生去海外留學。這一趨勢的原因是什麼？未來還會繼續下去嗎？

考生：Well, I think there is a general perception among Chinese students that universities in the West are often better places to study. The educational methods are different. They leave more space for creativity and personal responsibility. And of course students in foreign countries get a fantastic opportunity to improve their English. As for the future, well, I think this trend is going to continue for quite a while... It's such an eye-opening experience for students to live abroad for a few years.

考官：**You said that advertising is present everywhere in China. Do you think this situation will change in the future?**

你提到中國現在到處都是廣告。你認為這種情況將來會改變嗎？

考生：I guess it is possible that it could change because last year, for example, the Government banned advertising from soap operas on TV at certain times. But I'm not really sure that it will change much. I think modern technology makes it much easier for advertisers to target people: you get SMS messages on your phone, people ring you at home, and there are billboards everywhere, even electronic ones in the subway, so it is really hard to get away from advertising. I think it is increasing, in fact.

考官：**With the rise of e-books, do you think that paper books will eventually disappear?**

隨著電子書的興起，你認為紙質書會逐漸消失嗎？

考生：I suppose one day they will but it will take a while! Lots of people I know, and not just old people, really like to handle a real book, I mean a book made out of paper. They find it more satisfying in some way. They like holding a book in their hands when they are reading in bed. But I guess e-books are definitely the future. Already so many people read on iPads and stuff like that, or on their phones, so I guess if we look fifty years from now, there will be very few people reading books, and they will all use some kind of electronic gadget.

第二類問題：
產生原因和解決方法
Problems: Causes and Solutions

考官：**What are the main causes of traffic congestion in cities? What can governments do to reduce these problems?**

城市交通壅塞的主要原因是什麼？政府可以採取哪些措施來緩解這些問題？

考生：Well, in Beijing, the main cause of congestion is that we have too many cars! I read somewhere that the number of cars in Beijing has doubled in just five years! And I guess the roads are just not adapted to all these extra cars... It's really a problem. You know, the Beijing government keeps extending the subway system. There's lots of new lines, but that doesn't completely solve the problem because there are just too many people in Beijing. I think the government has to institute some kind of tax on cars, or make people pay to drive in the city centre or something, otherwise the problem will just get worse.

考官：**You said that the population of China is getting older. What are the consequences of this trend? What problems does it cause?**

你提到中國人口正在老齡化。這一趨勢會帶來什麼結果？會產生哪些問題？

考生：In a way, having so many old people is a burden on the country. I mean, old people consume more healthcare, for example, and they are not productive, at least not in economic terms. That is one of the main consequences. The Government has to spend more money to look after all the old people which means that there is less money for other things. But, on the other hand, old people spend money — for example on travel — so that helps the economy.

考官：According to Government statistics, there are more and more overweight people in China. What are the reasons for this? What can the Government do to combat this trend?

根據政府的統計資料，中國的肥胖人口越來越多。造成這種情況的原因是什麼？政府可以採取哪些措施來阻止這一發展趨勢？

考生：I think one of the main reasons for this is Western fast food, like McDonald's and KFC. A lot of young kids are kind of addicted to that kind of food, which is not healthy, and it makes them fat. Also, kids are so busy studying that they don't do enough sport. I know it's not just children that are putting on weight, but I think they are the group we should pay most attention to. I think the Government should introduce nutrition classes in school and I also think they should ban advertising for unhealthy food like McDonald's and KFC.

考官：You pointed out some of the negative aspects of the Internet. So, overall, is the Internet a force for good or not?

你指出了網際網路的一些弊端。因此，總體而言，網際網路是好還是不好？

考生：I think that, overall, the Internet is a force for good. I mean, it does make us less active, and people get kind of hooked on it, but it also lets people stay in contact with each other even when they are far away, work together, create things together. There are some fantastic resources on the Internet, plus the possibility to download music and movies and things like that. And, these days, scientists and researchers communicate a lot via the Internet, and often on subjects that can have a huge impact on people's lives.

第三類問題：
推測
Speculation

考官：**When a society changes very quickly, what are the effects on people?**

社會變化太快的話，會對人們產生哪些影響？

考生：They start to feel nervous and anxious. They can't adjust their rhythm to the changes. I mean, the first time there is some kind of change in your environment, you can adjust to the new situation after a while, even if it's a bit awkward. But when the environment then changes again, and again, quickly, each time you try to adapt to it, but you find yourself becoming progressively more exhausted. It is as though you are being left behind, or getting exhausted as you run to catch up.

考官：**In your opinion, what are the major issues facing China over the next twenty years?**

在你看來，中國在未來二十年會面臨哪些主要問題？

考生：Well, I think there are several key issues. Pollution is one. We have very serious air pollution here in Beijing, and the situation is not getting better. The Government publishes information about blue sky days but people can't see the situation improving. Then there are the effects of the economic slowdown. I mean, here in China, in 2008-2009, the Government spent so much money on infrastructure projects... So they have less money now for other things. The Government needs to keep the numbers of unemployed people down by creating more jobs.

考官：The status of women has changed a lot in China since the founding of New China. What are the effects of this change?

新中國成立後，中國婦女的地位發生了翻天覆地的變化。這種變化會帶來哪些影響？

考生：I think women are much more independent now. They work; they have their own careers; they can go to university; they can choose their own husbands. You know, my grandma never worked. My mum has quite a good job as a buyer in a company, but in fact she never went to university and she didn't travel abroad until she was in her forties. My life is so different from theirs. Last year, I spent three months in Ireland—from their point of view, it was something amazing.

考官：Do you think people's personalities are inherited from their parents?

你認為人們的個性是遺傳自父母嗎？

考生：Yeah, I think so. I mean, it is your parents that educate you—you know, in China we say that parents are a child's first teachers—so of course they transmit to you their own values, their own ideas about what is right and wrong, and even their habits. For example, I am a very organized person, and I get that from my dad. And I sometimes make judgements about other people too quickly, and I also get that from my dad. But I am also gentle and open with other people, and I get that from my mum.

第四類問題：
比較
Comparisons

考官：**How much do people show their feelings in Chinese culture? In your opinion, is it different from the West?**

在中國文化中，人們會在多大程度上表達自己的感受？你認為這與西方文化有差異嗎？

考生：Well, in China, I think it depends first of all who you are showing your feelings to. I mean, if it's your parents, then it's not so common to show your feelings. You know, in China, it's not easy for parents to use words like "I love you" or "It hurts" and I guess that is different from the West. In China, kids take it for granted that their parents will do things for them and, when they are teenagers, they don't want their parents asking them too many questions. They want to have a private life. As for expressing your feelings to your boyfriend or girlfriend, for our generation this is not a problem. I guess we are similar to Westerners for that.

考官：**What are the advantages and disadvantages of online shopping compared with traditional shopping?**

與傳統購物方式相比，網路購物有哪些優缺點？

考生：Well, with online shopping, you can find things more quickly for one thing. There is more choice online, and the prices are lower. As for disadvantages, well, there is the risk that the stuff you ordered never arrives, or arrives late, or that you don't like it when it gets there. Another thing is that with online shopping you can't try things on, and you don't have the pleasure of being in the shop and looking at things, handling them, comparing them. For a girl that is really important.

考官：Do you think young people these days have a healthier lifestyle than their parents had?

你認為現代年輕人的生活方式比他們的父母更健康嗎？

考生：No, I don't, and the main reason is computers. These days, young people spend a lot of time surfing the internet or doing stuff on the computer, chatting or whatever. I mean I have my own computer and I am sort of chained to it in the evenings. But, before, for example when my parents were young, they had to go outside to play. My dad told me he played outside every day after school for hours. And, back then, there were fewer fast food restaurants, and the quality of food was probably better. Oh yeah, and I think they did more sport than we do. So I guess they had a healthier lifestyle.

考官：Is the way that people develop their careers today in China very different from the way they did it in the past?

現代中國人的職業發展生涯與過去相比有很大的不同嗎？

考生：I think so. In my father's generation, people mainly worked for state-owned companies and they just had to be present in the office from 9 am to 5 pm. They had a very stable life. In those days, companies were more affected by politics than by economics. But now it's different. As China's economy has opened up, companies have had to become more competitive, and so the staff have to be more competitive too. There are more opportunities for us these days, and we are influenced by Western culture. But not everyone is like this! People in the big cities like Shanghai or Beijing want to move and be competitive but in some small cities, like Nanning my hometown, some of my friends are just like the generation of my parents—they want to be stable, rather than explore the wonderful world!

第四節 取其精華，去其糟粕：考官為你點評真實案例
Case Studies

一、前車之鑒——考生表現不佳的案例分析
Learning from Others' Mistakes

考生在考試中會犯一些較為典型的錯誤，下面的回答就是一些例子。請仔細看點評部分，避免犯此類錯誤喔！

話題：婚禮與婚姻

考官：We've been talking about a wedding you went to, your sister's, and now I'd like to ask you some more general questions related to this. Let's look first at marriage... Do you think there's an ideal age to get married?

我們已經討論了你參加過的一個婚禮，是你姐姐的。現在我想再問一些關於這方面的問題。首先我們來討論一下婚姻……你認為結婚有沒有一個理想的年齡？

考生：Well, I think when you get married it's a very important day... for you and your husband and also your family. In China the woman usually wears red, you know, and there are a lot of customs that Chinese people respect at a wedding.

考官講評 在文法方面，這個考生的回答沒有什麼大問題，也用了一些好詞，如 wear、customs 和 respect。考生的語言相當流利，但沒有回答考官提出的問題，因此在連貫性上會失分。

考官：OK, but do you think there's an IDEAL age to get married?
好的，那你認為有理想的結婚年齡嗎？

> **考生：** Well, a lot of my friends are married. Some of them are just 25 but most of them were... 28 or maybe 30 when they got married. And one of my friends is getting married soon. It's very exciting. She and her boyfriend made some photos in Hainan.

考官講評 由於考生沒有正面回答問題，所以考官又問了一次，還特別強調了 ideal 這個詞。這一次，考生回答得依然很流利，文法方面也把握得很好。但她回答得很含糊，然後就把話題轉移到自己朋友的身上，跟考官的問題沒有直接聯繫。made some photos 應改為 took some photos，但事實上更準確的説法是 had some photos taken。

考官：Let's talk a little about responsibilities inside a marriage. Do you think men and women should share responsibilities equally inside a marriage?
我們來討論一下婚姻雙方的責任吧。你認為男人和女人在婚後應承擔同樣的責任嗎？

> **考生：** Yes, definitely. I think both people should be responsible because otherwise how can their love last forever? That's the question for them. I think they have to love each other truly and make... err... make compromises. I think that is being responsible.

考官講評 考生雖然以 "Yes, definitely." 開始回答這個問題，但隨後的回答更多是關於婚後的愛情而非雙方的責任。這一次又沒有直接回答問題。

考官：Yes but, for example, should they both be responsible for raising the children? Should they share household tasks? What do you think about that?

是的，但舉例來說，他們都有責任撫養兒女嗎？他們應該分擔家務嗎？你是怎麼看的？

考生：You know, in China, men don't like to do housework and things like that. But I think nowadays they must change because the world has changed. You know in China everything is changing very fast, the economy, everything in the society. And so people have to be responsible both. But in China a woman will mainly look after the child because that is her role.

考官講評 考官開始以 "Yes, but..." 的說法來表示他或她對考生的回答不滿意。隨後舉例時提到撫養子女及承擔家務是為了鼓勵考生回答得更具體一點。And so people have to be responsible both 應改為 Everyone has to be responsible，society 前不必加 the。

考官：What about if the woman has a job? Can she share the responsibility for raising the child with her husband?

如果妻子有工作呢？她還能與丈夫分擔養育孩子的責任嗎？

考生：The grandparents, they can help a lot. You know, nowadays women have to work because the price of the living is so high now. Maybe you noticed that too, right? To buy an apartment or for the education, or just for the living. So a woman has to have a job, and so it's not easy to balance the life and the marriage with her husband. Because her husband wants her to be beautiful, and then she have to go on business trip, like my sister, and so she is not always to look after the child, so most couples will have to ask their parents or their ayi to do that.

考官講評 這個回答有所改進，但仍然不太切題。文法方面把握得不太好，如 education、living、life 和 marriage 前面不必加 the。price 應改為 cost；have to go on business trip 應改為 has to go on business trips；always 後

面應加 able。提到生活成本並沒有使她的回答顯得更合理。如果考生這樣回答可能會更好一點：

Yes, I think that both parents should share the responsibility for raising the child. Maybe the mother will do more, because it is in her nature to do so, but the father's input and presence is crucial too. And this is even more the case if the woman is working. The couple need to work out some arrangement so that they can both work and develop their careers while still spending time with their child and helping their child to grow and develop.

（是的，我認為父母雙方都有義務撫養孩子。可能母親會付出得多一點，因為這是她們的天性使然。但父親的付出和存在也很重要。如果母親有工作的話，父親就顯得尤其重要。夫妻雙方需要做一些計畫，這樣他們既能好好工作、發展事業，也能花時間陪孩子，幫助孩子成長和進步。）

考官：Uh-huh. Do you think it's better to have a big wedding or a small wedding?

嗯。你認為舉行規模大的婚禮好還是規模小的婚禮好？

考生：For me, I like big weddings! You know, like I said before, when my sister got married with her husband, there were almost 200 people there. That's quite common in China, to have a lot of guests. And everyone was so happy for her. She looked so beautiful that day; it made me cry. You know, she threw the flowers and I was the one who catched them! Everybody wanted to make her and her husband a toast. You know in China at a wedding you have to drink with every table of guests, to be polite. But usually the woman doesn't have to drink baijiu with everyone. It's too much. Yeah, that would be crazy. And her husband said some words and held her hand. It was so beautiful. It was sad; really it was lovely. You know, I hope I can have a big wedding like her.

考官講評　該考生的文法能力還說得過去，有幾處明顯的錯誤：

1. catched 應該說 caught，to make her a toast 應改為 to drink a toast to the couple 或 to propose a toast to the couple，married with 應改為 married to。從她的表現可以看出她既能處理簡單的句子也能運用複雜的句子。

2. usually 發音錯誤。

3. 還有就是連貫性的問題：考生説了她喜歡大型婚禮，雖然沒有明確表示大型婚禮更好，但在某種程度上回答了這個問題。但之後她又説了一堆關於她姐姐婚禮的事，而這些內容她在第二部分已經講過。嚴格來説，她的回答並不切題，表示她很難對抽象的事物展開討論，更善於談論個人事情。

考官：Thank you very much. That is the end of the Speaking Test.
非常感謝。口語考試到此結束。

考官總評

考官給這位考生的詞彙、文法和發音打了 6 分，但在流暢度和連貫性方面只打了 5 分。考生的語言流暢度還可以，但連貫性欠佳。

二、見優思齊——考生表現良好的案例分析
Learning from Others' Success

話題：飲食與健康（考生 A）

考官：Well, we have been talking about a restaurant you enjoy going to and now I'd like to ask you some general questions in relation to this. Let's consider first of all types of restaurant. Which restaurants are most popular in China — traditional restaurants or fast food restaurants?

嗯，我們已經談論了你喜歡去的餐廳。現在我想問幾個這方面的問題。首先討論一下餐廳的類型。哪一種餐廳在中國最受歡迎：傳統餐廳還是速食店？

考生 A：Actually, they're both popular. Fast food restaurants are popular with young people, and kids, or families with young kids — that's why you see so many overweight kids these days! And I guess that traditional restaurants are popular with everyone.

考官講評　該考生思路清晰，回答問題積極主動，還帶著一絲幽默。

考官：**What makes people decide to go to a fast food restaurant rather than a traditional restaurant?**

人們決定去速食店而非傳統餐廳的原因是什麼？

> **考生 A**：Well, they might be pushed for time. You know, if they're in a hurry, they can pop into a McDonald's or a KFC and pick up a burger or some chicken nuggets or something very quickly. Or it might be for the atmosphere, quite a lot of young people like to hang out at McDonald's, they feel comfortable and relaxed there.

考官講評　語言流利連貫。考生說了兩個原因，並分別舉例說明。詞彙用得好，片語 pop into、pick up 及 pushed for time 令人印象深刻，片語 chicken nuggets（炸雞塊）也用得很好。

考官：**What about traditional restaurants? Are they becoming less popular?**

傳統餐廳呢？它們不如以前受歡迎了嗎？

> **考生 A**：No, I don't think so. You know, food is incredibly important in Chinese culture. We have a saying that goes "Min yi shi wei tian". It means that Chinese people attach a huge amount of importance to food.

考官講評　再次非常清晰、直接地回答了考官提出的問題。用到的文法雖然簡單，但使用正確，還用到了副詞 incredibly。考生引用了中國諺語「民以食為天」。雖然他不知道該諺語的確切翻譯，但他用自己的話對其進行了解釋，也是一種很好的表達方式。

考官：**You mentioned that there are more overweight children these days. Is that partly because of fast food restaurants?**

你提到如今肥胖兒童增多了，部分原因是因為吃速食店的食品嗎？

考生 A：For sure. If kids eat McDonald's or KFC regularly or Chinese street food, their health is going to be affected. Personally, I hardly ever go to fast food restaurants because I don't want to get fat. I saw an amazing film called *Super Size Guy* or something like that about a guy who goes to McDonald's every day for a month. He only eats McDonald's food. It's really horrible. He gets so fat... and weak as well. I know that some fast food places are trying to improve their menus. But still, the food is too fatty. It's too rich in calories. There's too much sugar. In my opinion, if people want to stay healthy — kids especially — they should eat more fruit and vegetables. And do exercise, of course.

考官講評 在此之前，考生的回答都比較簡短，現在開始用長句了，非常好。該考生的回答在多個方面都非常優秀：語言流暢度、連貫性、詞彙和文法。在文法方面主要用了一般現在式，但也有一處過去式和兩個子句。介系詞和代名詞用法正確，在詞彙方面用詞豐富、貼切。

考官：**Do you think that children should be taught about nutrition at school?**

你認為學校應該教兒童營養知識嗎？

考生 A：Yeah, definitely! It would be great if children could learn the basic facts about nutrition at school because then they would find it easier to keep themselves healthy and they would be encouraged to develop some good habits as far as food goes. You know fast food is linked with various diseases, ummm, for example... diabete or diabetes, something like that... and heart disease. I think teachers should tell kids about that. The problem is that at school in China everyone is so focused on exam scores that we never get a chance to look at issues like obesity, or things like that. It's a pity.

考官講評　又是一個精彩的回答。在文法方面，複合句使用得遊刃有餘，還使用了子句。在詞彙方面，使用了一些不太常用的詞彙和表達，如 nutrition、focused、obesity、develop habits，甚至還用上了 diabetes（糖尿病）一詞。回答的開頭和結尾都提到了學齡兒童，整體內容非常連貫。

考官：Do you think that the health of children in China is improving?
你認為中國兒童的健康問題正在改善嗎？

考生 A：Well, maybe. Actually, I'm not sure. I mean, we have much better access to food than our parents or grandparents had. That's for sure. But on the other hand, there are problems like obesity, and also a lot of eye problems, eyesight problems. You know, in the big cities like Shanghai and Beijing, almost all school kids have to wear glasses — like me! I guess it's because we spend so much time looking at computer screens and game consoles and stuff like that. Also, kids don't do enough exercise. They sit around too much. It's not good for their health.

考官講評　語言通順、連貫，用詞恰當，文法正確。使用了 on the one hand, on the other hand 來加強前後的連貫性，而 also 起到了補充說明的作用。在詞彙方面，用詞非常標準，出彩的表達有 consoles（遊戲機）、obesity 以及動詞片語 sit around。在文法方面，語氣詞用得很到位，熟練運用了動名詞：they spend so much time looking。

考官：Does this mean that people from your generation might have health problems when they get older?
這是不是意味著從你們這代人開始，人們上了年紀就會出現健康問題呢？

考生 A：I guess it does! It's horrible! What a horrible prospect!

考官講評　回答得很好。

考官：**So what can the Government do about the situation?**

那麼政府該如何應對這一狀況呢？

考生 A：I think the Government should organize more health awareness campaigns, put ads on TV and send health workers to schools and communities, to make people aware of the consequences of eating fast food, or not doing exercise, or other bad habits. Otherwise, I'm afraid the hospitals are going to be completely overloaded in a few years!

考官講評 語言通順且連貫。考生採用句型 the Government should 開頭，引出建議政府要做的事，然後用 otherwise 引導出不採取以上措施的結果。文法知識掌握得很好，特別是開頭的長句。用詞準確，使用了如 health workers、consequences 和 communities 之類的好的說法。

考官：**Thank you very much. That is the end of the Speaking Test.**

非常感謝。口語考試到此結束。

考官總評 根據考生在流暢度、連貫性、詞彙、文法和發音方面的綜合表現，考官會給這位考生打 7 分。

話題：企業及其領導者（考生 B）

考官：**Well, we have been talking about a successful small business that you know and now I'd like to ask you some general questions in relation to this. Let's consider first of all working in a company. Is it better for young people to work in a big company or a small company?**

嗯，我們已經討論了你瞭解的一家成功的小公司。現在我想問一些這方面的問題。首先我們來談談在公司中工作。對年輕人來說，是進大公司工作好還是進小公司好？

考生 B：Actually, that's a difficult question. Usually, in China, young graduates prefer big companies because they feel they can get better trainings there and that a few years in a famous company will improve their CV. And people usually feel more safer in a big company. But I think a small company can have some advantages too, if people are OK to go there!

考官講評　考生回答問題的思路非常清晰，解釋了為什麼年輕人更喜歡大公司。在文法方面，總體上文法知識掌握得不錯，但有幾處小錯誤，比如 more safer 應為 safer，且 trainings 應為 training。在用詞方面，用詞得當。在最後一句中，用單字 bold（勇敢的）代替 OK 會更好一些。

考官：**So, what are the advantages of working in a small company?**
那麼，在小公司工作的優勢有哪些？

考生 B：Well, I think you can get promoted more rapidly in a small company. There are less staff so you have to be good at several things. You have to multitask, and you quickly get asked to take on different kinds of responsibility. I have a cousin who went to work in a small computer company in Xiamen and he never regret it. He became Sales Manager after just one year there.

考官講評　這一回答通順、連貫，且考生用自己的個人經歷（a cousin）來論證了自己的觀點。在詞彙方面，用了 regret、multitask 及 to be good at something 等一些好的說法。在文法方面，使用了被動結構 you can get promoted 和 you quickly get asked。但動詞 regret（應用 regretted 或 has regretted）的錯誤使用影響了整體的文法分數。

考官：**You mentioned training. Do companies have a responsibility to provide training for new recruits?**

你提到了培訓。公司是否有義務培訓新員工？

> **考生 B：** Yes, I think they have to do that because otherwise those new staffs won't be very efficient on their work. Maybe their knowledge comes mainly from books and they need some explanations from the experienced people and the trainers. And if the company does not give them any training, they might hate the boss because their friends in other companies are doing that. Also, if they do a training they can understand the company better. So it is good for the staffs but it's in the company's interest as well.

考官講評　總體來說，考生的回答連貫，但用詞不豐富，文法和詞彙的錯誤影響了整體的分數。在用詞方面，staff 在英語中是不可數名詞，所以不可能加 s。training 也一樣，你可以說 a training course，但如果不是特指的 training，前面是不加 a 的。efficient 後應加 in。在文法方面，現在進行式（are doing that）用得很恰當，但 won't be very efficient on their work 應該是 won't do their work very efficiently。

考官：**Let's move on to talk about business leaders. What qualities does a person need to lead a company?**

現在我們來談一談企業領導人。領導一家公司的人應具備哪些素質？

> **考生 B：** Well, they have to be good communicators. That's for sure, but even before that, they have to have an idea—for their product—and a method for developing it and bringing it to market. And I think they need to be able to inspire their workers. That's what I mean by being a good communicator. Take Steve Jobs for example. I think the people at Apple were proud to work for him because he always had new ideas and he was a kind of, mmmm, how do you say it? Yeah, a perfectionist.

考官講評　回答得很好。考生明確提出了領導人的幾種重要素質：溝通技巧、激勵他人的能力和創新意識。舉史蒂夫·賈伯斯（Steve Jobs）的例子和問題相關，也很合適。文法方面的表現都非常好。用到的一些好詞彙有 inspire、method、proud 和 perfectionist。

考官：You mentioned new ideas. Do you think that innovation is very important in business?

你剛才提到了創意。你認為創新對於企業很重要嗎？

> **考生 B：** Definitely! Our professor always quotes that guy Peter Drummer who says that innovation is the most important function of a business. Take Apple. The iPhone is very innovative, and so it's very fashion. And Apple keep doing it. They always seem to be one step ahead of the competition. There are some Chinese companies that are really good at innovation too, like Lenovo. Their new laptops are really cool, and so they are growing really fast.

考官講評　該考生為商學院的學生，所以對這個主題駕輕就熟。他不僅會使用這方面的詞彙，在討論時也非常輕鬆。他能夠引用彼得·德魯克（Peter Drucker）的話（名字說錯了，但考官不會因此降低他的分數）。有一處詞彙錯誤，fashion 應該是 fashionable。在文法方面，很好地使用了現在進行式：they are growing really fast。

考官：Do you think that Chinese companies like Lenovo will concentrate on the Chinese market or look to expand in other countries?

你認為聯想之類的中國公司會專注於中國市場還是會把業務擴展到其他國家？

> **考生 B：** I think they are already quite well-established in other countries. You know, Lenovo bought a lot of patents and licences and even the brand name from IBM and they took over some of IBM's designs so they were already recognized in Western countries. They have a good manufacturing base like the companies in Taiwan. And similar costs. That's why innovation is so important for them.

考官講評 關於 Lenovo 電腦的討論還在繼續，因為考生在這方面非常有自信，所以還是表現得很好。在詞彙方面，他能夠使用像 patents、licences、manufacturing base 這樣的高級詞彙。在文法方面，他用了過去式（bought、took over、were recognized）和一般現在式（think、are established、have、is），準確且恰當。

考官：**What about other Chinese companies? Will they expand overseas in the next decade?**

那麼其他的中國公司呢？他們會在未來十年內把業務擴展到國外嗎？

考生 B： I hope so! But I think it is still controversial. You know, a couple of years ago, Sinopec wanted to buy a petrol company in the US, but the US government wouldn't agree to it. And then there was a guy who wanted to buy land in Greenland but he got refused also. It's not really fair. The Western countries are a little afraid of China, I think. Sometimes the foreign media are criticizing China and Chinese companies, even though there are so many Western companies here in China. But I still think it will happen. As they get stronger, more and more Chinese companies will have the money to develop abroad.

考官講評 語言通順、連貫。考生舉例說明了自己的觀點，並在結尾處進行了觀點明確的總結。在文法方面，整體把握得不錯，除了 are criticizing 應改為 criticize。在詞彙方面，用到了 controversial、rejected 和 criticize。但請注意，petrol company 這一表達不夠準確，應該是 oil company。另外，應該用 allow it 而不是 agree to it，應該用 turned down 來代替 refused。

考官：**Can you explain a bit more? What are Western countries afraid of?**

你能再解釋一下嗎？西方國家害怕什麼？

考生 B： Well, in my opinion, the Western countries do not want to lose their domination. So, when they see that China keeps getting stronger, they feel a little afraid of it! I guess the Western countries realize that they are not as strong as they were before. Take Europe for example. China gave money to help save Greece because Europe does not have enough ability to do that. But, if China does that, the Western countries should be more understanding with China. I mean, lots of Western companies like McDonald's and Apple operate here in China, even oil companies. So I don't see why Chinese companies can't operate in Western countries. Everyone should cooperate together.

考官講評 考生的回答仍然通順、連貫。用詞不錯，儘管 dominance 可能比 domination 更恰當一些。用 a little afraid 就可以了，沒有必要在後面加上 of it。用 as they used to be 比 as they were before 好一點。同樣，用 sufficient resources 或 enough resources 比用 enough ability 更好。cooperate 已經包括 together 的意思了，所以 together 是多餘的。

考官：**Thank you very much. That is the end of the Speaking Test.**
非常感謝。口語考試到此結束了。

考官總評

　　考官願意給這位考生在流暢度、連貫性、文法和詞彙方面打 7 分。考生有一些文法錯誤，而且有一兩處是基本錯誤，但正確的句子還是多數，並且展示了他對簡單句和複合句的把握能力。因此，在這一天考試結束時，這位考生拿到了 7 分。

第五節 六種遊戲幫你練口語！
Six Games to Develop Ideas and Fluency for Part Three

▶ 1. 圍圈圈談論球上的主題

　　參與者坐下來圍成一圈，選擇一個討論的主題，把主題寫在球上。參與者要拿著球談論這個主題，表達自己的觀點，其他人則認真聽。發言者說完自己的觀點，便將球傳給旁邊的人。此遊戲能幫助你透過練習口頭表達和傾聽他人看法來開拓思路，提高語言流暢度。

▶ 2. 圍成兩圈談論球上的主題

　　參與者坐成兩圈，裡面一圈，外面一圈。內圈的同學進行討論，規則如上，持球的人發言，外圈的同學則負責聽。等內圈所有人都發完言後，或規定的時間到了，內外圈的同學交換位置。坐在外圈的同學換到內圈，成為活躍的發言者。這樣每個人就都有機會聽到更多人的想法。

▶ 3. 講故事

　　參與者圍坐成一圈。提前準備好的人可以談論以下內容：

* 讀過的一本書

* 看過的一部電影

* 看過的一部電視劇

* 一則新聞故事

　　這些書或電影可以是英文作品，新聞故事也可以是發生在國外的。但參與者也可以討論中文作品和發生在國內的事情。介紹書或電影的同學可以對書或電影進行簡單的介紹、讀一段有趣或精彩的內容、播放電影的一個片段、甚至扮演成故事中的人物。其他參與者則可以對書或電影提出問題。

假設有一個學生決定介紹道格拉斯·亞當斯寫的《星際大奇航》（*The Hitch-hiker's Guide to the Galaxy*）一書。這本書被一些書迷稱為 HHGTTG 甚至 H2G2，以地球的毀滅開始講起。主角亞瑟·登特（Arthur Dent）是在地球毀滅後生存的兩個地球人之一。在漫遊銀河系的時候，他遇到各種生物，包括一台名為「沉思」（Deep Thought）的超級電腦。「沉思」的目標是計算生命、宇宙及一切事物之終極問題的答案，最後計算出的結果為 42。學生可以挑戰介紹亞當斯的一些幽默語錄，但幽默是一種文化，很難解釋，所以對學生來說，介紹這類書真的會是很大的挑戰，因為英語國家的人覺得有趣的東西，東方人不一定覺得有趣。

另外，學生還可能會選擇介紹一本中文書籍，比如《紅樓夢》。用英文介紹這類書也是個挑戰，但也是擴展詞彙量、準備雅思考試的最好方法。

▶ 4. 角色扮演

由一位學生扮演考官，另一位學生扮演考生。扮演考官的人應該提前準備好問題及第二部分的話題。如果條件允許，可以準備一台錄影機，這樣就可以把整段會話錄下來。錄影機對準考生，而非考官。同時要準備一個計時器，這樣才能確保時間不超過 14 分鐘。

兩人開始談話。「考官」向「考生」提出問題，「考生」回答。談話結束後互換角色，重新來一遍。然後觀看影片，一邊看一邊聽發音和文法錯誤，聽語言是否流利和連貫，聽詞彙是否有趣，順便再看看考生的肢體語言是否生動。

▶ 5. 十二個單字的遊戲

這個遊戲的目的是讓學生通過感受語言的趣味性和互相學習來拓展詞彙、培養創造力和想像力。參與者不要超過 12 個人，總共要說出 12 個單字，要包括：

- 2 個介系詞
- 3 個名詞
- 3 個形容詞
- 4 個動詞

然後用這些單字來造句。例如，參與者可以説出：

介系詞 by（通過、以）、behind（在……後面）

名詞 cowboy（牛仔）、window（窗戶）、turtle（烏龜）

形容詞 smart（聰明的）、gorgeous（非常漂亮的）、incredible（難以置信的）

動詞 turn down（拒絕）、betray（背叛）、lift（舉起）、shoot（射）

然後參與者進行單獨練習或小組練習，用這些單字來造句，要做到沒有文法錯誤。例如：

As the gorgeous turtle came into view, the cowardly cowboy stepped up to the window behind her, lifted his rifle and shot her. He was angry because the turtle had turned down his incredible gift. She had betrayed him by eloping with a smart jellyfish.

隨著魅力四射的烏龜映入眼簾後，懦弱的牛仔踏上了她身後的窗戶，舉起步槍擊中了她。他很生氣，因為這隻烏龜拒絕了他那令所有人驚歎的禮物。她背叛了他，與一隻聰明的水母私奔。

▶ 6. 集體討論

集體討論的目的是促使遊戲參與者主動預測第三部分可能會問到的問題。如果參與者能夠想到可能會考什麼問題，就能做好充分的準備。任何一個話題都可以通過集體討論得出十個與其相關的問題。假設第二部分的話題是你過去的一次旅行。第三部分就有可能討論有關交通的話題。考官會問一些什麼樣的交通問題呢？比如考官可能會問下列十個問題：

1. What types of transport are used most often in cities in your country?
   你們國家城市中最常用的交通工具是什麼？

2. Has the use of bicycles declined in cities in recent years? If so, why?
   近年來城市裡騎自行車的人減少了嗎？如果減少了，為什麼？

3. Has the transport system in your city or town changed in the last ten years? In what ways?
   在過去十年中，你所住的城市或城鎮的交通系統有變化嗎？有哪些方面的變化？

4. Is public transport in your country improving?
   你們國家的公共交通狀況改善了嗎？

5. Are traffic jams common in your city? What are the reasons for them?
   你住的城市中，塞車常見嗎？塞車的原因是什麼？

6. What can governments do to combat traffic congestion?
   政府可以做哪些事情來改善塞車？

7. Cars emit pollution. How dangerous is this pollution for people's health?
   汽車會排放污染氣體。這些氣體對人們的健康有什麼危害？

8. Should cars be banned from the city centre in order to combat pollution?
   為了治理污染，城市中心應該禁止汽車通行嗎？

9. Does your country have a big car industry? Is it important to the economy?
   你們國家的汽車行業發達嗎？這對經濟發展來說重要嗎？

10. How do you think the traffic situation where you live could be improved?
    你認為應如何改善你居住的地方的交通狀況？

第六節 黃金法則
Dos and Don'ts

▶一定要…… Do...

▸▸關注新聞報導中的事件，無論是發生在國內的還是其他國家的。可以和朋友對這些事件進行討論，這樣到了考試的時候，在第三部分你就有很多話可說。

Stay up to date with what is happening in the news, both in your country and in the rest of the world. Talk about what's happening in the news with your friends so that when you get to Part 3, you have lots to say.

➡️ 不要害怕自信地表達你的觀點。如果考官不同意你的觀點，這可能是個好兆頭，因為這意味著考官在很認真地聆聽。可以承認考官的觀點有道理，但仍然要堅持自己的觀點。

Do not be afraid to express your opinion confidently. If the examiner appears to disagree, this is probably a good sign. It means the examiner is listening closely. Acknowledge the examiner's point of view but continue to express your idea.

➡️ 如果在考試前一年，你很認真地準備了，那麼你在改善詞彙和語言流暢度方面所付出的努力終於要有收穫了。當你要表達自己的想法時，豐富的詞彙自然就會脫口而出。

If you have worked hard over the previous year, this is the time when all that vocabulary and fluency work will really pay off. As you seek to express your idea, vocabulary will come naturally to you.

➡️ 記住，考官很樂意與你進行思想的交鋒。不要害怕爭論，也不要害怕用例子來論證你的觀點。

Remember that the examiner will enjoy confronting viewpoints with you. Do not be afraid to disagree or to point out evidence that supports your view.

▶千萬別⋯⋯ Don't...

➡️ 不要背答案。如果你事先已經「排練」過了話題，考官是能辨別出來的。

Don't learn answers off by heart. The examiner can tell when topics have been rehearsed!

NOTE

"第5章"

雅思考官評估考生的「四大標準」！
讓你一一突破考官心防，輕鬆滿分！

第一節 標準一：語言的流暢度與連貫性
Fluency and Coherence

☞ 一、讓考官告訴你：如何練就流暢連貫的語言
☞ 二、40 個流暢度練習
☞ 三、第一部分：展現流暢連貫的語言
☞ 四、第二部分：流暢連貫地聊電影
☞ 五、第三部分：融入與考官的討論之中
☞ 六、黃金法則

語言的流暢度和連貫性（Fluency and Coherence）是雅思口語考試的關鍵評分標準之一，通常被考官們簡稱為「FC」。在本節中，我們將通過分析「電影」這一話題，向你展現如何使語言更流暢和連貫，以及需要避免哪些錯誤表達。

流暢度指的是什麼？

流暢度在一定程度上關乎說話的速度，同時也考核你運用語言的熟練程度，還要看說話時是否會出現停頓和卡住。事實上，這三方面的情況都和「流暢」的定義有關。在考試中，如果你努力回想某個具體的單字，你就會很自然地放慢語速並出現停頓，考官們通常把這種情況稱為 noticeable pause（明顯停頓），也就是口語中說的 hole，就是指你在試圖回憶單字或之前提過的內容時，出現卡卡的情況。

這種由於單字量不足導致的問題是可以克服的，可以換種說法表達詞義。例如，如果考生想說「門被鎖住了」，但是想不起「鎖住」（lock）這個單字怎麼講，於是就說 the door was closed...with a key（門被鑰匙關上了）。就這樣，問題就解決啦！但是如果他連「鑰匙」這個單字都想不起來，那就比較麻煩了，單字量小的問題一定也會降低他在流暢度方面的得分。

連貫性又是什麼意思呢？

整體來說，連貫性就是指你的表達要意思明確，可以理解為對問題要進行正面回答。換句話說，連貫性就是以一種自然連貫的方式把語句組織起來回答問題。聽起來好像有

點不太好懂，但不要擔心，在後面的例文中你就會有直觀的瞭解。當然，運用一些 but、and、however 之類的連接詞也是語言連貫的標誌之一。

一、讓考官告訴你：如何練就流暢連貫的語言
Being Fluent and Coherent

有些考生詞彙量很豐富，表達很準確，用到了多種動詞時態，內容也很有意思，但是就是缺那臨門一腳：不夠流暢。這些考生的語速比較慢，中間的停頓太多，卡住的地方也太多。在日常對話中，當你與別人分享觀點和想法時，對自己想要表達的內容進行思考是很自然和正常的事情。但別忘了，在口語考試中，作為應試者，你不能花太多時間考慮如何回答，這會讓考官覺得你的語言表達能力有限。長時間的停頓會讓考官產生疑慮，不知道你是在思考回答的內容，還是在語言表達上有困難。如果他認為是後者，那麼你在流暢度方面的得分就會降低。

那該怎麼做才能說得更流暢呢？有兩種辦法。第一，經常練習各種口語話題。多練一些話題，把自己說的話錄下來，從中挑出一些關鍵字並寫下來，然後強迫自己說得更快，不要有任何停頓，力求在更短的時間內說出所有重點。第二，練習做筆記。如果你一分鐘內可以快速寫下一些關鍵字，這樣不僅能準備好第二部分所需要的詞彙，還可以搭建起一個思路框架，這樣就可以一個接一個地運用那些詞彙來完成陳述。所以你必須練習快速寫下詞彙的能力，寫下可以幫助你完成兩分鐘表達的詞彙。可以計時看看，只給自己 50 秒來寫詞彙。這樣到了正式考試時，思路會變得比較清晰，就不會因為想不出該講的內容而講不快，害得考官以為是你英文不好才說得這麼慢。

不過，雖然不能說得太慢，但說得太快也不見得是好現象。有些考生語速確實很快，沒有任何停頓，但他們的問題是會不斷重複相同的內容，反覆表達同一個意思，這樣也會在流暢度和連貫性上失分。想表達流利，需要有自己的想法、有足夠的詞彙、還要避免卡住。

說完了如何達到「流暢度」，我們再來說說如何達到「連貫性」。語言連貫是指你表達的內容具有邏輯性。這並不是說你的表達要很機械化，而是說你要很清楚自己要表達什麼。你可以運用一些諸如 however、also、besides、but、I think the other reason why...、it was the moment when... 等詞彙和表達來展現你的回答的邏輯性。而且別忘了一定要切題喔！你可以說出有創意的回答，但決不能離題！如果考官要你談談自己認識的長輩，你就不能從你和朋友打籃球說起！語言連貫也表示你要正面回答問題。

二、40 個流暢度練習
Fluency Game

以下這些問題類似於第二章的 60 個通關問題。這次的練習目標是連續陳述兩分鐘，也就是說，你需要像回答第二部分那樣來回答下列問題。

從 1~40 中隨意選擇一個數字，在下面找到相應的問題，針對該問題連續回答兩分鐘。如果可能的話，錄下你的回答，然後看看在詞彙、文法、思路或創意方面還可以如何提高。

1. What's so great about children?

2. Describe the ideal wedding.

3. Cats are too selfish to be nice — agree?

4. What's so great about swimming?

5. What's so great about love and romance?

6. How has your life changed recently?

7. Tell us a story.

8. Tell us about your mum.

9. Is it more important to be physically strong or mentally strong?

10. What can we learn from failure?

11. What's so great about TV?

12. What's the best job in your country?

13. Who attracts you more? Someone who is good-looking or someone who is funny?

14. Is advertising good or bad?

15. What's so great about mobile phones?

16. What makes your family members happy?

17. Cars: a blessing or a curse?

18. Do people spend enough time outdoors these days?

19. What's the best country in the world?

20. Tell us your favourite memory of your schooldays.

21. What's so great about going to university?

22. What's so great about nature?

23. Young people shouldn't listen too much to their parents' advice — agree?

24. What's the best movie ever? Describe it.

25. What kind of clothes do you like?

26. Should people go to university straight after high school? Or travel or work first and get some experience?

27. What's the best job in the world? Describe it.

28. What's so great about the seaside?

29. Tell us about your dad.

30. Tell us about a person you admire.

31. People who are well-organized are more successful. Do you agree?

32. Will our planet survive?

33. Are dogs great? Or a nuisance?

34. Guys have to be ambitious and women have to be understanding — agree?

35. Is fashion important?

36. Tell us about the best weekend you ever had.

37. You can tell a person's personality from the clothes they wear — agree?

38. English is more useful than Chinese — agree?

39. Coffee or tea — which is better?

40. Who's the greatest person in your country? Describe that person.

三、第一部分：展現流暢連貫的語言
Fluency and Coherence in Part One

在第一部分，語言的流暢度重要嗎？答案是肯定的。雖然和第二、第三部分相比，第一部分沒有那麼重視考核流暢度，但依然是很重要的一個考查方面。我們來看看下面這些考生的範例。

考官：Let's move on to talk about movies or films. Do you like the same kind of films now as you did when you were a child?

考生 A： When I was a kid, I really liked cartoons, and in fact I still like them. *Kung Fu Panda* was great for example, and some people like the sequel better than the first one. Actually I disagree because...

考官點評 語言比較流暢但不夠連貫，因為考生只關注於電影《功夫熊貓》本身，而沒有解釋為什麼喜歡這類電影。

考生 B： Not really. When I was a kid, I really liked, um, er, cartoons. I remember, um, I was sitting, I was sitting on the, on the... floor and watching *Yue Fei*. It was... great. I used to watch it every, every week at my grandmother's...

考官點評 這個回答是連貫的。not really 是對問題的正面回答。但是回答過程中出現了猶豫和停頓，所以不能算流暢。

考官：**What kind of films do you like most?**

> **考生 A：**I like action movies. Actually Schwarzenegger's *True Lies* is my favourite movie of all time. The opening scene, where Arnie goes underwater to get to the party, and then dances with the evil lady, is terrific...

考官點評 同時做到了流暢和連貫。該考生的回答不僅清晰而且詳細。

> **考生 B：**I like comedies, especially foreign ones. I really liked the movie *Little Miss Sunshine*. It's about a family in the US who travel to a beauty pageant and all sorts of things happen, like the granddad dies for example and they have to smuggle his body out of the hospital...

考官點評 回答既流暢又連貫，而且考生也展現出了豐富的詞彙，比如 pageant、smuggle out 等。以一種很自然的方式用到這些詞彙是流暢度的又一種展現。

> **考生 C：**I like romantic movies, like *Titanic* and *P.S. I love you*. In *Titanic*, Jack is so handsome and the romance between him and Rose is very touching and the final scene, when he gives his life to save hers, wow, it's incredible... And *P.S. I love you* is really amazing too. It's about a woman who receives letters from her dead husband.

考官點評 考生舉出了很好的例子，用到了 moving、incredible 等一些很好的詞彙，而且句子結構一直能保持完整。

考官：**Do you prefer watching movies at home or in the cinema?**

> **考生 A：**At home? Or in the cinema? Umm, for me, it depends. If it is a film action, I mean action movie, an action movie, I like watching, I like to watch the cinema, I like to watch in the cinema... The cinema is at, umm, you can watch with others. Other people can go there.

考官點評 出現了多處重複和猶豫的情況，不夠流暢，但內容還算比較連貫。

> **考生 B**：I prefer watching movies at home because it's more cheap and also more cosy. My dad bought a really comfortable couch and I can stretch out there with some cushions and watch movies on my laptop. Sometimes my mum brings me chocolate. It's really happiness.

考官點評 有明顯的文法錯誤，如 cheap 的比較級是 cheaper，而不是 more cheap。另外，最後一句應說 it's a really happy feeling 或者 it's a really happy moment。不過這個回答在流暢度和連貫性方面還算不錯。

考官：**Now I'm going to give you a topic and I would like you to talk about it for one to two minutes...**

考官點評 有時候考官雖然這樣講，但並不會讓你講這麼久。他們會隨時打斷你，問你其他問題。不要讓這一點動搖你！

四、第二部分：流暢連貫地聊電影
Fluency and Coherence in Part Two: Movies

在第二部分中，考生必須要進行兩分鐘的陳述。考官可能在兩分鐘快要結束時以一個過渡性問題來打斷你，但你必須具備能說兩分鐘的語言能力。換句話說，在這一部分中，流暢度和想像力是考查的重點。一些考生沒有足夠的觀點和能力可以一直講兩分鐘，這就表示他們會在流暢度方面失分。

另外，雖然一些考生可以說足兩分鐘，卻無法連貫地表達出一條清晰的理由或原因。而最常見的情況就是文不對題！比如說，要表述的話題是「描述一個你認為可以讓世界變得更好的工作」，但考生卻不停地說他有多麼喜歡籃球；或者話題是「描述一個你將來想去的地方」，考生卻談及自己去年去海南的經歷。

除此之外，如果考生沒有組織好語言、讓聽者無法理解，也會失分。以「電影」這一話題為例，如果想有好的表現，那麼流暢的表達就至關重要。要做到流暢，你需要有足夠多的詞彙和觀點，而且還要努力避免卡住，減少在腦海中尋找合適詞彙時所出現的停頓。

讓我們先看一個考生對這一話題的回答。

1. 流暢例文：讓子彈飛

Track 002
聽聽看！別的考生都怎麼說？

I like the[1] action movies... and the recent movie that I watched... is *Let the Bullet Fly*[2] and in fact the box office of this movie is really good and my friend[2] around me went to, went to the cinema to watch that movie and they all think this movie is fantastic and very good and I was encouraged by them to go to the movie to watch that film and what impressed me most is the philosophy of that movie and the wisdom and the humour that the disaster bring by this movie[3] and the words, the subtitles[4] is very sarcastic[5] and the plot is quite intrigue, intriguing[6]. It is about a competition and a fight about[7] a bandit[8] and the landlord[9] and at last the bandit takes the landlord down by the power... of the public. At first the people... in the city are scared of that landlord because he's really powerful and he's the real power behind the scene[10] ...and he also had a... substi, substi, substi, substitute...[11] but the bandit, but the bandit kill[12] the substitute and then the people in the city think the landlord, the real landlord in the city is killed and so they rose up and take the gun to pull down this government, or this ruler, and um... what struck me most is the, is the characters in that movie. They are really strong and have beautiful muscles and so they attract all of[13] boys and girls...

考官評價

　　雖然存在發音錯誤，但整體來看發音比較清晰而且不影響理解。節奏和語調掌握得都不錯，文法的運用也得當。後面出現了現在式和過去式表達不一致的問題，但這不是一個嚴重問題。用到了一些讓人印象深刻的詞彙，如 sarcastic、intriguing 和 behind the scenes 等。同時，流暢度方面的表現也很好。第一句話很長，甚至長於在書面語中的表達，但這一點在口語中不是問題。真正重要的是考生要表達流暢，且沒有停頓！而這位考生就可以輕鬆地在兩分鐘裡不間斷地表達自己。

　　整體來看，該考生的表達流暢且連貫。詞彙比較豐富，對文法的控制也很好。考生在如此長時間的表述中保持了很好的連貫性，偶爾有停頓也是為了找到合適的詞語。因此，她在流暢度方面可得 7 分，連貫性方面可得到 8 分。

文法重點

1. 沒有必要加冠詞 the，改為 I like action movies。

2. 名詞單複數用得不合適，Bullet 應改為 Bullets，friend 改為 friends。

3. 此處考生表達的意思過於含糊，不夠清楚。

4. subtitles 發音錯誤，聽起來像 substitles。

5. sarcastic（諷刺的，嘲諷的）用在這裡很合適，會給考官留下深刻印象。

6. intriguing 一詞發音錯誤，應為 [ɪnˋtrigɪŋ]。

7. 這裡的介系詞應該用 between，而不是 about。

8. 該考生在提到 bandit 時都發錯了音，聽起來像是 bandidit。

9. 在首次提到電影中的角色時，可以說 a bandit 和 a landlord，再提到他們時才用 the 去修飾。

10. behind the scene（幕後的）在這裡是個可以增分的表達。

11. 雖然遇到了發音卡住的問題，但考生及時找到了正確的詞語，回歸到了正常語速。

12. 出現了主詞、動詞型態不一致的嚴重文法錯誤，應該把 kill 改為 kills，因為句中用的是一般現在式。

13. 不必加 of，改為 all boys and girls，但如果能說 people from both sexes 就會更好，畢竟這是一部給成人觀看的電影。

翻譯

　　我喜歡看動作片，最近看過的一部電影是《讓子彈飛》。事實上，這部影片的票房很不錯。我周圍的朋友都去電影院看了這部電影，而且都覺得很棒。我被他們鼓動著也去看了。我發現這部電影讓我印象最深刻的地方是它傳遞出的哲學思想、智慧和幽默。影片的名稱和臺詞都很有嘲諷的意味，情節的設計也很巧妙。它講的是一個土匪和一個地主之間鬥爭的故事，最後那個土匪利用民眾的力量把那個地主打倒了。起初城裡的人們很害怕地主，因為他很強勢而且是真正的幕後主使，此外他還有一個替……替……替身。但是後來土匪殺死了替身，這讓城裡的人們相信真的地主已經被殺死了，於是他們拿起槍推翻了政府和統治他們的人。最吸引我的是電影中的角色，他們身體強壯、肌肉強健，吸引了很多的男孩和女孩……

2. 看看考官會如何作答

（1）搶救雷恩大兵 *Saving Private Ryan*

Track 003

聽聽看！考官都怎麼說？

Well, actually[1], the kind of films I like best are probably[2] the older ones. For example[3], one of my favourites is *Saving Private Ryan*. I think I like war movies and I particularly like that one, I suppose[4] because[5] the acting is excellent with Tom Hanks[6] and a bunch of other people who are really really good. It's a good story but I suppose the thing that is most impressive for me is that initial opening scene where the troops are actually landing in Normandy on the beaches. It's very meaningful for me because my dad was in the Second World War and also because I visited those beaches in Normandy[7]. It's easy for me, having been there[8], to imagine what those guys were actually facing as they came off the landing craft and had to face a hail of bullets from the German machine gun posts. And I think the other reason I really like that film is because it represents America when America was great, when America was at its best. Around the time of the Second World War, I think America was a beacon for many countries. It seemed to be freer, and more powerful, more hopeful, more optimistic as well as gutsy[9]. It seemed to offer more pleasure for human beings as a nation and to be less cluttered up by old traditions that weren't very useful any more. So I think that's one of the reasons I really like that film[10] because it represents the best of the US whereas now I guess the US is a bit more in decline.

學習要點

1. 控制好說話的節奏，給自己留出思考的時間。
2. 使用副詞可以增加表達的準確度，所以不要吝嗇使用。
3. for example 就像一個符號，表示你即將舉出具體的例子。
4. 用 I suppose 代替了 I think。平心而論，後者我們已經用得太多了。
5. 「因為……所以……」是表現思想邏輯的最基本形式。
6. 如果能夠熟練說出幾個外國名人的名字，就能給考官留下一個更好的印象，也使得你的回答更具有個人特色和可信度。
7. 將話題與個人經歷聯繫起來，增加了真實性和故事性。
8. 分詞片語作插入語，使得語言的節奏感和靈活性躍然紙上，希望你能重點模仿！
9. 通過這種排比式的強調，既可以使語言更有說服力，又可以展現豐富的詞彙。
10. 回答要有頭有尾！不必進行過多描述，但保證完整性是有效交流的必要原則。

翻譯

　　事實上，我最喜歡看的是些老電影，比如《搶救萊恩大兵》。我想我比較喜愛戰爭片，尤其是這一部，可能是因為湯姆‧漢克斯的精湛演技和其他一些演員的精彩表現。這部電影的故事情節很不錯，但我想讓我印象最深刻的是影片剛開始的那一幕，也就是士兵們在諾曼第海灘登陸的那個場景。這個場景很感動我，因為我父親曾經參加過第二次世界大戰，而且我本人去過那裡的海灘，所以我能身臨其境般地感受到那些士兵面臨的境遇：從登陸艇上下來就遭遇德軍機槍掃射出的槍林彈雨。我喜歡這部影片的另一個原因是它展示了當時最強大的、處於巔峰時期的美國。二戰期間，美國是其他很多國家的引領者。是個比較自由、比較強大、比較有希望、比較樂觀和勇敢的國家。這個國家在那個時候似乎能給人民帶來更多的快樂，而且還摒棄了很多已經失去意義的陳舊傳統。所以這是我那麼喜歡這部電影的原因之一，因為它代表了全盛時期的美國，而我感覺現在的美國有點趨於衰退。

考官想跟你說

　　電影是故事，也是很多人的夢。在成長的過程中，你一定會看過幾部電影，所以一定會有一到兩部你喜歡和周圍的親朋好友津津樂道的影片。好好想一下吧！你需要弄清楚的是你為什麼認為這部電影很吸引人。從這方面來看，學習過的詞彙就能派上大用場了，比如 incredible、memorable、impressive、amusing 等詞彙應該可以隨時脫口而出。而且你需要具備描述一個場景的能力。請將你自身對電影的體會和對一些細節的描述結合起來，這樣就可以呈現出一種生動有趣的表達方式。

（2）大紅燈籠高高掛 *Raise the Red Lantern*

Track 004

聽聽看！考官都怎麼說？

Talking about Chinese movies[1], what actually comes to mind for me first of all is Gong Li because I suppose to me she's the most beautiful and expressive Chinese actress. When I imagine her[2], I can remember her from *Red Sorghum* and also a gangster movie made in the US but probably the scene that most sticks in my mind is from *Raise the Red Lantern*, where she becomes the concubine of a powerful guy[3], and it's that scene where she sits there silent, with her mother, before she leaves home forever. She is dressed in very formal beautiful clothes, and her face is impassive, and then a tear rolls down her cheek[4].

I found that scene very moving, very memorable, because she is such a beautiful young woman and she is off to the slaughter in a way. In the movie one of the concubines ends up committing suicide. There is this beautiful grey stone architecture and beautiful lighting but for the women there is a great deal of psychological suffering[5].

學習要點

1. 以分詞片語開頭，表達會顯得更加靈活。

2. 很自然的過渡，説明來自於個人的實際體驗。

3. 用非限定性定語子句起解釋説明的作用，使兩句話之間的聯繫不會顯得刻意。

4. 細節的描述會使你的表達更為生動。

5. 在話題中融入個人的思想，使整個回答更具有吸引力。

翻譯

　　談到中國電影，我首先想到的就是鞏俐，因為在我看來，她是中國女演員中最漂亮、最具表現力的。當我想起她時，映入腦海的是她在電影《紅高粱》中的形象，還有美國警匪片中的角色，但我印象最深的還是她演過的《大紅燈籠高高掛》。在那部電影裡，她成了一個有權有勢的男人的小妾。我印象最深的是她在離家前和母親相坐無語的那一幕。她穿著一身很漂亮的衣服，表情木然，一滴淚水順著她的臉頰滑落下來。

　　那一幕很觸人心扉，讓人難忘，因為一個如此美麗的年輕女人就這樣走向人生的囚牢。電影中還有一個小妾自殺了。裡面有很美觀的灰色石頭建築和美麗的光影。但是對於那些女人來説，卻只有心理上承受的巨大苦難。

考官建議

　　在個人表述中，可以加入自己的情感體驗，這樣更容易使聽者產生共鳴。細節的描述不僅可以有效説明你對話題的熟悉程度，也能增添許多鮮活的元素。

3. 流暢度訓練

　　下面是如何就「電影」這一話題完成流暢度訓練的一個範例。

　　首先準備一張紙和一支筆，在一分鐘的時間內寫下你能想到的和電影有關的所有資訊。由於時間較短，可以以詞彙的方式記錄。注意最好別通過畫圖來代表！因為你可能會在隨後的陳述時忘記相應的詞彙。

電影話題詞彙

opening scene 開場	sticks in my mind 讓我印象深刻
action movies 動作片	thought-provoking 令人深思的
special effects 特效	bullet 子彈
memorable 難忘的	actor 演員
Gong Li 鞏俐	meaningful 有意義的
traditions 傳統	box office 票房
represents 代表	beautiful 美麗的
future 未來	

考官建議

1. 用你熟悉的詞或片語來開頭，如果對英語詞彙確定的話就只用英語記錄。

2. 如果對英語詞彙不確定，寫中文也可以。

3. 在空白處寫出你喜歡的詞彙和片語。

4. 把自己想說的話錄五分鐘。

5. 聽錄音，將其中用到的關鍵字記錄下來。

6. 努力用兩分鐘將全部內容說出，注意語言的流暢度，並盡可能多用你已掌握的詞彙，這種方式可以幫助你提高語言流暢度。

7. 將這一頁的內容抄到筆記本上。

8. 一週之內，繼續在筆記本上添加新的話題和相關的詞彙。

4. 如何構建思路和詞彙

　　首先和你的同學或老師討論下面的語錄。你能理解它們的意思嗎？你是否同意他們的觀點呢？

　　當你思考時，記錄下可以幫助你談論這些內容的英語詞彙。還有沒有其他一些類似的語錄讓你很感興趣？也可以記錄下來。

Life is a tragedy when seen in close-up, but a comedy in long-shot.

—Charlie Chaplin, British actor, 1889-1977

特寫鏡頭下的人生是悲劇的，但如果用遠鏡頭來看，它會是個喜劇。

——英國演員查理‧卓別林（1889 年～ 1977 年）

考官點評

What is Charlie Chaplin saying here? We can paraphrase his remark by saying that, when you look very closely at the details of someone's life, it may seem tragic, because of the pain they suffer, the disappointment, the frustrations, the heartbreak... For example, my friend Zhi got a disease, or maybe my friend Kate had a very painful break-up with her boyfriend, or maybe she realized one day when she was 32, and already had a baby, that she had married the wrong man. These things can make life seem tragic. But when you stand back from the events of individuals, and observe people — being born, growing up, sometimes failing or getting hurt but picking themselves up, having a laugh, trying again, and the generations renewing themselves over and over — then life is more of a comedy. Life goes on!

怎樣理解卓別林的這句話呢？我們可以嘗試著這樣理解：當你過於關注一個人的生活細節時，會發現人生因為要遭受痛苦、失望、挫折和傷心，看起來似乎是個悲劇……比如，我的朋友阿志得了病，或者我的朋友凱特跟她男友分手分得轟轟烈烈，或她在有了一個孩子以後，32 歲的她才意識到自己嫁錯了人。這些事情會讓生活看起來是一場悲劇。但是如果你遠離這些個人的生活，從整體上審視人類的生命：孩子出生、成長，有時經歷失敗和傷痛但仍能鼓起勇氣站起來，微笑著再次嘗試，還有一代接一代的生命更迭，會覺得生活更像是一場喜劇。生命不息！

Cinema in India is like brushing your teeth in the morning. You can't escape it.

—Shahrukh Khan, Indian actor, born 1965

在印度，電影就好像每天早晨要刷牙一樣，你躲都躲不掉。

——印度演員沙魯克汗（生於 1965 年）

考官點評

What is Shahrukh Khan saying here? First of all, he is saying that, in India, films are everywhere. They surround you. You can't get away from them. After all, India produces more films each year than any other country! The US is no. 2, and China is no. 3. Indian films are produced in more than 20 different languages. The Indian film industry is often referred to by the name "Bollywood" as opposed to Hollywood. The *B* in Bollywood refers to the city of Bombay—or Mumbai—on the west coast of India, the center of the Indian film-making industry. Have you ever seen a Bollywood film?

沙魯克汗的話到底是什麼意思呢？首先，在印度到處都可以看電影。電影就在你的身邊，你躲都躲不了。畢竟，印度每年製作的電影數量都比其他國家多多了！美國排第二，中國排第三位。印度電影還被製作成 20 多種不同語言的版本。印度的電影業常被人們稱作「寶萊塢」（Bollywood），與「好萊塢」相對應。在 Bollywood 一詞中，B 代表位於印度西海岸的孟買（Bombay），那裡是印度電影業的中心。你看過寶萊塢的電影嗎？

I pity the French Cinema because it has no money. I pity the American Cinema because it has no ideas.
—Jean-Luc Godard, French-Swiss film director, born 1930
我為法國電影感到可憐，因為它們沒有資金。我為美國電影感到遺憾，因為它們沒有思想。

——法裔瑞士籍電影導演尚呂克‧戈達爾（生於 1930 年）

考官點評

Jean-Luc Godard is a typical French intellectual, who thinks that French films are necessarily superior to dumbass American blockbusters! He's an elderly gentleman now but his opinions haven't changed! For him, American movies have few ideas, but big budgets and huge audiences all around the world, whereas French films are underfunded masterpieces full of ideas and artistry! The only problem is that not many people see them! What about Chinese films? Chinese filmmakers are big on historical dramas that sometimes seem like they have all been produced from the same recipe book, but they also produce whacky, original comedies like *Crazy Stone*...

　　尚呂克・戈達爾是一個典型的法國知識份子。他認為法國電影毫無疑問地要比愚蠢的美國大片優秀！現在的他已經上了年紀，但他的想法從未改變過！對於他來說，美國電影除了有大量資金和遍佈世界各地的觀眾，幾乎毫無思想可言；而法國電影卻是具有豐富思想內涵和藝術性的資金不足的傑作。但唯一的問題是沒有太多的觀眾觀看！那麼中國的電影又是什麼情況呢？中國的電影人熱衷於拍歷史劇，使得這些作品有時候看上去好像都是按照同一個劇本拍出來的，但他們也可以製作出像《瘋狂的石頭》那樣新奇的原創喜劇。

5. 詞彙擴展

　　詞彙的重要性不言自明。為了儘量避免找不到合適的詞來表達自己的想法，從現在就開始收集和記憶單字吧！

　　下面依然以電影為例，列舉出了一些可以用於談論電影的詞彙。請在你的話題書中填入更多的相關詞彙和片語。

動詞 VERBS		
1	to shoot	拍攝
2	to shock	使震驚
3	to touch	感動，觸動
4	to describe	描述，敘述，形容
5	to disappoint	使失望
6	to act	演出
7	to represent	代表
8	to symbolize	象徵
9	to make a lasting impression	留下永久的印象
10	to suppose	認為，猜想

形容詞 ADJECTIVES		
1	particular	個別的；特殊的
2	fascinating	吸引人的，迷人的
3	impressive	給人以深刻印象的
4	amusing	有趣的，引人發笑的
5	entertaining	使人愉快的，有趣的
6	amazing	驚人的，了不起的
7	subtle	難以捉摸的，微妙的
8	scary	可怕的，恐怖的
9	bizarre	古怪的，奇異的
10	mainstream	主流的，主要的
名詞 NOUNS		
1	a director	導演
2	a hero	男主角
3	a villain	反面人物，反派角色
4	a scene	片段，場面
5	a close-up	特寫
6	a comedy	喜劇
7	some footage	片段
8	a plot	故事情節
9	an action movie	動作片
10	special effects	特效

6. 加分的說法

　　以下的説法很可能會給考官留下深刻的印象。請認真學習並反覆演練，並嘗試在下一次和別人用英語交流時運用到其中的一些説法，相信你自己一定可以感覺到變化！請特別注意套色的地方，都是一些很道地、很加分的用法喔！

1	All my friends were raving about the movie and telling me that I had to go see it, so I did, and I also thought it was fantastic.	我所有朋友都對這部電影讚不絕口，並告訴我必須去看。所以我去了，而且我覺得確實很不錯。
2	One of the things that really impressed me in that film was...	這部電影讓我印象深刻的一點是……
3	I really go for/like action movies because they are so exciting/ fast-moving/ spectacular.	我的確很喜歡看動作片，因為它們確實讓人興奮／節奏很快／扣人心弦。
4	Well, actually, what puts me off is the price of tickets. I mean at some cinemas now you have to pay 120 yuan to see a movie, and it really is a rip-off!	嗯，事實上，真正阻礙我去電影院的是票價。我是説，現在在有些電影院，你必須花120元才能看場電影，這簡直就是剝削。
5	I think that one of the reasons I really like that film is because it represents some of the best aspects of Chinese culture.	我喜歡這部電影的原因之一是它代表了中國文化很多優秀的方面。
6	Everybody recognizes that films change people's lives, and provoke strong emotions.	大家都認為電影可以改變人們的生活，並且可以激起強烈的情緒。
7	If you think about the legendary films of the last few decades, you're gonna find that they all had great directors, a great storyline and great actors.	如果你回想一下過去幾十年中最著名的電影，你會發現它們無一例外都有很了不起的導演、很棒的故事情節和出色的演員。

8	Well, I've never really thought about that in detail, but one thing I do know is that...	嗯，我從未仔細考慮過這個問題，但我的確知道……
9	Some people say that *Hero* is crap, and they say there's no real plot, just special effects and strong colours, but I think it's really moving. I loved the character Moon played by Zhang Ziyi. She is so deep and her hair is so gorgeous...	有人認為《英雄》是部爛片。他們認為它沒有故事情節，只有特效和強烈的色彩。但我卻覺得很感人。我很喜歡裡面章子怡扮演的如月，深藏不露而且頭髮很美……
10	Talking about movies, what immediately comes to mind for me is...	說到電影，首先映入我腦海中的是……

五、第三部分：融入與考官的討論之中
Engaging in the Discussion with the Examiner in Part Three

第三部分依然要考語言流暢度和連貫性。考官會檢閱你的詞彙水準、對文法結構的控制，會看你能否流暢地表達自己的觀點，能否展開論證，對於考官提出的不同意見是否可以應對自如。這些都是第三部分考核的重中之重！

要想在第三部分展現出流暢和連貫的語言，必須注意以下三個方面：

- 你必須有想法。雖然雅思考試是考核語言能力的考試，但要是你沒想法到連用中文都沒辦法談論話題，那你當然也不可能用英文談論了。

- 你必須會豐富的詞彙。

- 你必須能融入與考官的交流之中。換句話說，就是要投入到討論中，和考官要有互動。

以電影話題為例，如果要以一種具有邏輯性和描述性的方式來闡述，你表達的內容就需要有細節支撐。如果你能記得和描述一些電影場景、在哪裡和誰看的電影，還有你的看法的話，你的回答就會更充實有趣。

細節非常重要，但細節不是全部。投入到和考官的討論中就表示要準備好表達自己的想法，為自己的觀點辯護。請看下列考生的回答範例，為迎接第三部分的挑戰做好準備，並仔細閱讀點評部分吧！

考官語錄

Engaging in a discussion with the examiner means being prepared to express ideas and defend a viewpoint.

考官：**How much impact do films have on young people?**

考生 A：I think films affect young people a lot because we are at the age where we're thinking a lot about our future, and about who we are, and stuff like that. Films entertain us, and move us, and make us laugh, and they also sometimes make us aware what we have and what we sometimes overlook. They remind us that love exists, as well as conflict... for example, in *Kung Fu Panda 2*, the love of the goose for his son—the panda is a bit soppy and sentimental, but it makes us think about our own parents and what they mean to us. And, you know, I think that if people are depressed, a film with positive values and a positive spirit can inspire them to go on fighting the frustrations in life. If people have an active attitude, very likely the future can be changed. I really believe that...

考官點評 該考生的語言連貫性很不錯，清楚描述了電影的影響力，同時還舉例闡明了自己的想法。只看文字看不出語言是否流暢，只能通過錄音來瞭解。瞭解時要看表達過程中是否有停頓，是否有猶豫不決的情況。

其實很多能給人們帶來影響的事物都會給人們的生活和生活態度帶來改變。所以當遇到這樣的問題時，就可以從我們周圍的生活說起，這樣就不用擔心沒有內容可說，而且有可能會滔滔不絕呢！

考官：To what extent do films influence the values and ambitions of young people?

考生 B：Well, let me think about it. I think, err... young people are good at, at, umm... at imitating things and imitating people... I mean they are at a period... of their lives where they have a lot of dreams and, and aspirations, and when they see something very nice, very attractive on the screen—someone living in an amazing department or, or, or a really move, really moving love story, or maybe an... errr, an incredible lifestyle—they will want to have that kind of life themselves so... they will make that, that kind of life their goal and... they will strive for that, so I think they can be affected a lot... This also explains why more and more youngers all want to be rich or to try something new...

考官點評　語言基本還算連貫，但表達時出現了很多的 er 和 umm 以及語言的重複，這對他來說是個問題。考生提到了 younger，這是個形容詞比較級，所以應改為 young people。再就是不要把 apartment 和 department 弄混。動詞 strive 用在這裡非常合適。

考官：You said that more and more young people want to be rich. Do you think that today's society is too materialistic?

考生 C：Well, actually, I think that everyone is materialistic really. I mean we all want iPhones and iPads and BMWs and things like that. In China, family is very important too, and loving your country, but in the family, we are always pushed to succeed, and for most parents success means a good job and a house and a car and stuff like that. You know, things are more and more expensive every day. Inflation is rising. Just look at the newspaper headlines, and so everyone has to think about financial security and that means we are materialistic. Also, in China, the older generation remember the period when people were poor and nobody wants to go back to that...

考官點評 語言流暢且連貫，文法和詞彙運用方面表現良好。考生在開始回答時用到了 materialistic（物質的）這個詞，隨後在提及成功、通貨膨脹、金融危機的過程中顯示出了她對「物質」的準確理解。同時，考生在討論過程中的投入給人留下了深刻印象。換句話說，在表述過程中，她一直堅持自己明確的觀點。所以最好不要 sit on the fence（不選邊站；態度不明確）。

現在，請嘗試自己回答上面的問題。錄下自己的表述並聽一聽錄音的效果。

六、黃金法則
Dos and Don'ts

▶一定要…… Do...

▸▸ 緊密圍繞話題展開對話，但不必受制於話題本身，可以靈活地將話題引向自己感興趣的領域。

Definitely do keep to the topic but don't feel constrained by it; feel free to use the topic to move into areas that interest you.

▸▸ 注意重音和語調。

Use stress and intonation.

▸▸ 聲音要有力。

Put energy into your voice.

▸▸ 用個人經歷來舉例說明。

Do use personal examples.

▸▸ 廣泛使用豐富的詞彙。

Do use a range of vocabulary.

▸▸ 至少使用三種不同的動詞時態。

Do use at least three different verb tenses.

▸▸ 考前要進行大量練習。

Do practise a lot before the test.

▶千萬別…… Don't...

▶▶┃ 不要談論和話題卡上的話題毫不相關的內容。

Don't talk on a completely different topic from the one on the topic card.

▶▶┃ 在陳述過程中，不要有長時間的停頓。

Don't leave big holes when you are speaking.

▶▶┃ 不要過度關注句子結構。

Don't worry too much about sentence structure.

第二節 標準二：足夠的單字量
Lexical Resource

☞ 一、讓考官告訴你：單字量小，就沒有說服力！

☞ 二、幫你拿到 5 ～ 8 分的重要單字

☞ 三、說文解字：瞭解單字詞源

☞ 四、100 個讓分數步步高升的副詞

☞ 五、錦上添花的俚語

☞ 六、幫你拿到 7 分的動詞片語

☞ 七、告別老掉牙詞彙：學習近義詞和反義詞

☞ 八、告別老掉牙話題：舊題新說

☞ 九、黃金法則

考官語錄

在剛開始學習一門語言時，與學習詞彙相比，更重要的是要熟悉這門語言的語音體系和文法結構。但在掌握了基本的語音和文法知識後，詞彙的學習就成為當務之急。如果詞彙量不夠，我們在表達自己的想法時就只能泛泛點到，而且還有太多話題我們會無法談及。換句話說，詞彙就是你表達想法的基礎裝備。

Vocabulary is essential ammunition for expressing your thoughts.

一、讓考官告訴你：單字量小，就沒有說服力！
No Bricks, No Building; No Vocab, No Power

對考官來說，學生的詞彙量有限是很奇怪的一件事。他們會覺得既然要考試，不就應該多會一點單字再來考嗎？不過，看在學習者的角度，則會覺得這有兩個原因：第一，老師沒教學生學習詞彙的正確方法；第二，學生學習詞彙的方法沒有條理。

樓房的高度是由修建它的磚塊的數量決定的，而詞彙就是構建語言的磚塊。沒有詞彙，人們就無法生動準確地表達出自己的意思。所以，學生積累的詞彙當然越多越好，特別是計畫出國的學生更是。擴大詞彙量是所有英語學習者的首要任務！

那麼我們建議學習者該如何學單字、練詞彙？首先，我們認為每個考生都應該有一本中英文對照的詞彙書。可以先把詞彙書瀏覽一遍，用螢光筆把認識的詞、和想要用的詞標出來，並收集需要用的詞彙。那要怎樣實際運用這些收集到的新詞彙呢？就是要積極應用這些詞，例如用它們造句，這有助於熟悉單字在句子中的作用。

閱讀也是「練單字」的一個重要方法！我個人建議考生每天的閱讀量要達到 3000 個單字，這樣才能在上下文中理解詞彙。在閱讀過程中，考生肯定會遇到在詞彙書中見過的詞，這樣就有堅持學習下去的動力了。那該讀什麼書呢？建議你，別只讀教科書和一些短文，也不要只讀像《哈利波特》之類有名的書。其他所有的書也都可以讀讀看啊！閱讀是學習詞彙的捷徑。在我遇見的所有得 8 分的考生中，沒有一個不經常進行英文閱讀的。

詞彙量是這樣累積的！

❶收集詞彙：	❷應用詞彙：	❸閱讀：	❹改善流暢度：
把詞彙書瀏覽一遍，用螢光筆把認識的詞和想要用的詞標出來。	積極應用這些詞，例如用它們造句。每天寫 300 個單字左右，儘量用上所學詞彙。	閱讀是學習詞彙的捷徑，每天閱讀至少 3000 個單字的長度。	記錄下能想到的所有詞彙，然後加以運用。

二、幫你拿到 5 ～ 8 分的重要單字
Words for level 5-8

現在，你已經瞭解了詞彙的重要性。下面我們來看看豐富的詞彙，尤其是多樣的形容詞能給你的口語帶來什麼樣的變化。

1. 設想考生在描述一個他認識的人，而這個人一直喜歡吃大量的速食。

5 分考生會這樣描述：He is too big, too fat. 他塊頭很大，很胖。

6 分考生會這樣描述：He is fat and overweight. 他很胖，超重了。

7 分考生會這樣描述：He is seriously overweight, I mean, way beyond plump! 他嚴重超重。我是說，他可不僅僅是偏胖。

8 分考生會這樣描述：He has ballooned out to an incredible size. He's so fat now he can scarcely walk. 他像吹氣球似地胖了起來，塊頭大得嚇人，胖得幾乎都走不了路。

2. 設想考生在談論周圍環境及全球變暖的威脅。

5 分考生會這樣描述全球變暖帶來的威脅：Now the planet is getting global warming. The weather is not good. 現在地球正在全球變暖，天氣不好。

6 分考生會說：Global warming is a big problem. The ice is melting. 全球變暖是個大問題。冰在融化。

7 分考生會說：Global warming is causing significant climate change. For example, the glaciers are getting smaller and weather patterns are changing. 全球變暖正導致明顯的氣候變化。例如，冰川正在變小，天氣類型正在改變。

8 分考生會說：Global warming is a major threat. Glaciers are dwindling and potentially the sea level could rise and flood many coastal cities. 全球變暖是一大威脅。冰川逐漸縮小，從而可能導致海平面上升，淹沒沿海城市。

3. 設想考生在談論北京的天氣。

5 分考生可能會這樣描述北京的天氣：Autumn in Beijing is nice but the winter is too much cold. 北京的秋天很好，但是冬天太冷。

6 分考生會說：The autumn in Beijing is a nice period, but it gets chilly from late October and the winter is very cold. 北京的秋天是個很好的季節，但從十月底就開始轉涼，而且冬天非常冷。

7 分考生會説：Autumn is lovely in Beijing but the winter can be freezing. Temperatures drop below zero and the wind makes it even colder. 北京的秋天很宜人，但冬天十分寒冷。氣溫會降到零度以下，刮起風來則讓人感覺更加寒冷。

8 分考生會説：Beijingers complain that the autumn is too short. You can understand their point of view because when winter arrives, you really need long johns and gloves and scarves and all the gear because the temperatures can really plummet. 北京人總抱怨北京的秋天太短。這是可以理解的，因為冬天一到，你就非常需要穿保暖內衣、手套、圍巾等來「全副武裝」，因為氣溫會驟降。

4. 設想考生在談論他們自己的個性和性格。

5 分考生會這樣説：I am not good at communicating with people. I do not like to go the party. 我不善於和別人交流，不喜歡參加派對。

6 分考生會説：I am quite shy so I don't often go to parties. 我很靦腆，所以不常參加派對。

7 分考生會説：I am a little introverted. I mean that sometimes I prefer to be alone. 我有點內向。我是説有時候我更喜歡獨處。

8 分考生會説：I guess it's fair to say that I'm a little introverted. I mean I like parties and people but sometimes I need to spend time alone to recharge my batteries. 平心而論，我是有點內向。我是説我喜歡派對，喜歡和人打交道，但有時我需要獨處，為自己「充電」，補充一下能量。

三、說文解字：瞭解單字詞源
Etymology

　　詞源學是研究詞的來源和發展變化的學科。英語受到過其他多種語言的強烈影響，特別是法語、拉丁語以及希臘語。如果搞懂單字的來源，多學一些字根與字首、字尾的意思，記單字不但更快，看到陌生的單字時也更容易推理出它的意思。

考官語錄

English has been heavily influenced by several other languages, in particular French, Latin and Greek.

　　例如，英語中的 telephone（電話）和 telescope（望遠鏡）就是從希臘單字 tele（遠）、phonos（嗓音）和 skopos（看見）衍生而來。而其他詞也可與 tele 結合成新詞，如 telecom（電信），如下頁的表格所示。

詞源與其意義	詞源與其意義	單字	中文翻譯
tele（遠的）	phonos（嗓音）	telephone	電話
tele（遠的）	skopos（看）	telescope	望遠鏡
tele（遠的）	communicate（交流）	telecom	遠程通信
tele（遠的）	conference（與身在不同地方的人）	teleconference	電話會議

拉丁詞語 ex（外）與動詞 ducere（引導）進行絕妙組合後，就得到了 educate（教育）一詞。換而言之，「教育」就是從人身上引導出事物，而不是往裡填塞！下面是一些拉丁詞與希臘詞構成英語詞語的其他例子：

詞源與其意義	詞源與其意義	單字	中文翻譯
anti（對抗）	bioticus（生命的）	antibiotic	抗菌的
	onym（名字）	antonym	反義詞
aster（恆星）	nautes（水手）	astronaut	太空人
	logia（對待）	astrology	占星學
autos（自己）	bio（生命） graphia（紀錄）	autobiography	自傳
	nomos（風俗）	autonomy	自治，自治權
	matos（思考）	automatic	自動的
	kraos（統治）	autocratic	獨裁的，專制的
bene（好的）	factum（行為）	benefit	利益
malus（壞的）	nutrire（滋養）	malnutrition	營養不良
de（下降）	pretium（價格）	depreciate	貶值
	linere（塗抹）	delete	刪除

demos（人民）	kratos（統治）	democracy	民主
	epi（在……中）	epidemic	流行的
fore（在……前）	casten（策劃）	forecast	預測
	sight（視野）	foresight	預先設想
	tell（告訴）	foretell	預言，預料
in、il、im、ir（不）	maturus（成熟的）	immature	不成熟的
	literatus（文學的，有知識的）	illiterate	不識字的
	posse（有能力的）	impossible	不可能的
	decere（合適的）	indecent	不適當的
pro（向前）	pellere（推動）	propel	推進，驅動
	minere（計畫，規劃）	prominent	突出的，傑出的
scribere（寫）		script	劇本
	circum（圍繞）	circumscribe	限制，約束
solvere（鬆開）		soluble	可溶解的
	dis（分開）	dissolve	使溶解，解散
verus（真實的）	facere（做）	verify	證實
	dicere（說）	verdict	裁決，決定
videre（看見）		visible	可見的，看得見的
	tele（遠的）	television	電視
	re（再次）	revise	修正

四、100 個讓分數步步高升的副詞
Adverbs

1.6 分副詞

用對副詞，就能讓自己所敘述的話更為生動，更令人印象深刻，也更能具體地、強烈地表達出自己的意見，因此考官非常喜歡聽到考生使用副詞。下面我們列出了 30 個最常用的副詞，並搭配例句。例句多數以第一人稱陳述，因為考生在考口語考試時，多半也是用第一人稱來回答問題。想想看，你能將這些副詞用於什麼樣的話題中？

	副詞	中文意思	例句	例句翻譯	可以用在這些話題中！
1	about / around	到處，處處	He ran about/around giving people orders and encouraging them.	他到處發號施令、替人打氣。	A Job You Did; Leadership
2	absolutely	絕對地，完全地	I am absolutely convinced that they will become a big force in the Asian market.	我絕對相信他們會給亞洲市場帶來強大的影響力。	A Small Company You Know
3	afterwards	隨後，以後，後來	Afterwards we might go to a bar.	之後我們可能會去一家酒吧。	How You Spend A Weekend
4	already	已經	We have already decided to go to Thailand for our holiday.	我們已經決定去泰國度假了。	A Trip You Would Like to Take
5	always	總是，一直	They always have new products on display.	他們總會陳列展示新產品。	A Shop You Like
6	away	離開，朝另一個方向	And then he ran away as fast as he could.	然後他快速跑開了。	A News Story; Your Childhood Memory

	副詞	中文意思	例句	例句翻譯	可以用在這些話題中！
7	carefully	小心地，仔細地	So I carefully placed the book back on the shelf and quietly left the room.	於是我小心翼翼地把書放回書架上，悄悄地離開了房間。	An Old Person
8	clearly	毫無疑問，顯然	Going to Australia is clearly the best option.	去澳洲顯然是最好的選擇。	A Country You Would Like to Visit
9	completely	完全地，徹底地；全部地	That's completely ridiculous! You can't marry him if you don't love him!	這簡直太荒唐了！你不愛他就不能嫁給他！	An Exciting Message
10	correctly	正確地；恰當地	I thought I had correctly answered most of the questions so, when I got my score, it was a real disappointment.	我原本以為我答對了大部分問題，所以在得知分數的時候，我大失所望。	Disappointment or Failure in Your Life
11	deeply	非常；很深地；真誠地	They were deeply in love.	他們當時深愛著對方。	A Story / Book You Read
12	definitely	確切地，肯定地	I thought it was definitely a better choice.	我認為那絕對是更好的選擇。	Something You Bought
13	early	提早，提前	They told me to come early if I wanted to, so I turned up at seven.	他們告訴我，如果我願意，可以早點到。於是我七點就到了。	A Family Event
14	easily	容易地，輕易地	We found the house easily.	我們很輕易就找到了房子。	A Historical Building

	副詞	中文意思	例句	例句翻譯	可以用在這些話題中！
15	extremely	極度，極其	Another thing about her is that she is extremely conscientious.	她的另一個特點就是非常認真負責。	A Friend; A Leader
16	far	遠；久遠；在很大程度上	We had to travel so far to get there but, in the end, it was worth it.	我們走了很遠才到那裡，但終究還是值得一去的。	A Trip / Journey That Took Longer Than Expected
17	fast	快地，快速地；不久，立即	We walked really fast and luckily got there before the ceremony began.	我們走得飛快，所幸在典禮開始前趕到了那裡。	A Family Event
18	forever	永遠；長久地	So she asked him, "Will you love me forever?" He held her gaze and replied, "Forever... and a day."	於是她問他：「你會永遠愛我嗎？」他凝望著她回答說：「永遠……再加一天。」	A Film
19	incredibly	非常地；難以置信地	She was incredibly kind to me when I was in middle school.	上中學的時候，她對我出奇地好。	A Teacher You Remember
20	lately	最近，近來	I haven't seen her lately because she's been busy preparing for her IELTS test.	我最近沒見到她，因為她在準備雅思考試。	A Friend
21	less	較少地，較小程度地	Actually it was less expensive than you might think. And it is so comfortable and elegant. I really like it.	其實它比你想像中要便宜。而且它既舒適又雅致，我很喜歡。	A Piece of Furniture in Your House

	副詞	中文意思	例句	例句翻譯	可以用在這些話題中！
22	more	更，更加，較為	The more he insisted, the more I thought, "No way, it's too expensive."	他越堅持，我的想法就越強烈：「不可能，這太貴了。」	An Expensive Purchase
23	nearly	幾乎，差不多，將近	She called me and said, "Where are you?" And I said, "I'm nearly there, don't go in without me!"	她打電話給我，說：「你在哪？」我說：「我就快到了，等我到了再進去！」	A Film You Saw Recently
24	never	永不，決不，從來沒有	They will never solve the problem if they don't start punishing offenders.	如果他們不開始處罰違規者，他們就永遠不能解決問題。	Law
25	often	經常，時常，多次	He often calls me to chat and talk about his problems with his girlfriend.	他經常打電話給我，跟我聊他和他女朋友之間的問題。	A Friend; A Piece of Advice
26	only	僅僅，才	It sounds weird but I've always wanted to be a botanist, ever since I was a kid. It's the only job I've ever really wanted to do.	我從小就一直想成為一名植物學家。雖然聽起來很奇怪，但這是我唯一真正想做的工作。	A Job You Would Like to Do
27	out	向外，往外，出來	So I grabbed my cellphone and my bag and turned on my heels and walked out of the room.	於是我抓起我的手機和包包，轉身走出了房間。	One Time You Were Angry

	副詞	中文意思	例句	例句翻譯	可以用在這些話題中！
28	really	真正地，確實，實際上	It's a really cool track, one of the best songs on the album.	這首曲子真棒，是這張專輯中最好的歌之一。	Music
29	sometimes	有時，偶爾	I sometimes go to the swimming pool on the weekend.	我有時週末會去游泳。	Staying Healthy
30	usually	通常地	She usually tells me how she's feeling but this time she avoided me for at least a week.	她通常都會把感受告訴我，但這一次她至少躲了我一個星期。	A Family Member

2.7 分副詞

以下 30 個副詞也比較常見，如果能準確應用，得到 7 分就不再是夢喔！

	副詞	中文意思	例句	例句翻譯	可以用在這些話題中！
31	accidentally	意外地，偶然地	It happened accidentally.	事情是意外發生的。	The Memory of An Accident
32	actively	積極地；忙碌地；活躍地	They actively tried to drum up support for the idea but most people weren't interested.	他們積極爭取人們支持這一想法，但大多數人不感興趣。	Law That Would Improve the Place Where You Live
33	actually	實際上，其實	He was actually very concerned.	他其實很擔心。	Something Kind Somebody Did for You

	副詞	中文意思	例句	例句翻譯	可以用在這些話題中！
34	affectionately	深情地，親切地，熱烈地	He spoke to me very affectionately, and I could see he was proud of me.	他親切地跟我說話，看得出他很為我驕傲。	Congratulations from Someone
35	backwards	倒退地，向後地	I took a step backwards and fell over the garden wall.	我倒退一步，從花園的圍牆上摔了下來。	An Accident
36	basically	基本上；基本地，主要地	Basically, it just kept breaking down so we had to take it back to the shop.	它基本上是毛病不斷，所以我們只好將它退回了店裡。	Something You Bought
37	calmly	平靜地；安靜地，鎮靜地	He always acts so calmly on the court, even if the other players are very aggressive.	即使其他選手進攻挑釁，他在球場上也總是沉著冷靜。	A Sporting Event You Would Like to Watch
38	certainly	確實地，實在地	It certainly helps me a lot when I am doing basic research.	這確實大大有助於我的基礎研究。	Websites
39	confidently	自信地；有信心地；有把握地	I felt that I had replied confidently.	我覺得自己回答得很有自信。	A Job Interview
40	consistently	一貫地，一致地；持續地	She consistently gets top marks in her Spanish class.	西班牙語這門課她總是拿最高分。	A Friend or Somebody You Admire
41	conveniently	方便地，便利地	The shop is conveniently located near a coffee bar we often go to.	那家店在我們常去的那家咖啡店附近，很方便。	A Product You Would Like to Buy

	副詞	中文意思	例句	例句翻譯	可以用在這些話題中！
42	deliberately	故意地，有意地	If people do it deliberately, then there has to be some sanction.	如果人們明知故犯，那就需要進行處罰。	Law
43	directly	直接地	I think you should just tell him directly rather than beating around the bush.	我覺得你應該直截了當地告訴他，不要拐彎抹角。	Advice
44	eventually	最終，終於	We eventually got there after spending about two hours in a taxi.	坐了大概兩個小時的計程車，我們終於到了那裡。	Travel
45	financially	金融上，財政上，財務上	That's why my goal is to be financially independent by the time I'm 30.	因此我的目標是到 30 歲時能實現經濟上的獨立。	A Family Member
46	fully	完全地，充分地，徹底地	I made sure the vehicle was fully insured before the test drive.	在試駕前，我確認汽車已經全面投保。	A Vehicle You Would Like to Buy
47	gladly	樂意地，熱切地	I would gladly go to the UK if I got the chance.	如果有去英國的機會，我會欣然前往。	A Place You Would Like to Visit
48	hopefully	有望；抱有希望地	Hopefully, my family will be able to invest some money.	但願我的家人能夠投入一些資金。	A Small Business You Would Like to Start

	副詞	中文意思	例句	例句翻譯	可以用在這些話題中！
49	initially	最初，起初	Initially, my parents were sceptical but in fact it has improved our neighbourhood a lot.	起初，我父母還半信半疑。但實際上，這給社區帶來了很大的轉變。	A Change to a Town or City
50	mainly	主要地，大部分地	It was mainly because it seemed so exciting.	主要是因為它好像很刺激。	A Job You Wanted to Do
51	obviously	明顯地，顯而易見地，明白地	Obviously, at first I made a mess of it but she kept correcting me and now I am really good at it.	顯然，一開始我弄得一團糟。但她不斷地糾正我，現在我已經很在行了。	A Person Who Taught You to Do Something Useful
52	patiently	耐心地	Our maths teacher always spoke very patiently to us.	我們的數學老師總是很耐心地對我們說話。	A Teacher or Leader
53	politely	禮貌地，客氣地	We waited in line for a while and then asked him politely if he had seen the bag.	我們排隊等候了一會，然後很禮貌地問他有沒有看到那個包包。	Something You Lost
54	rarely	很少，難得	Actually, I rarely go to concerts because there aren't many in my hometown — and in Shanghai the tickets are expensive.	其實，我很少去聽音樂會，因為我的家鄉不常舉辦，而在上海票價又很貴。	A Concert; An Artistic Event

	副詞	中文意思	例句	例句翻譯	可以用在這些話題中！
55	seldom	很少，罕見，不常	I seldom get the chance to practise now but, after I graduate, it will be different.	現在我沒有太多練習的機會，但等我畢業以後就會不同了。	Something Interesting You Hope to Do in the Future
56	slowly	慢慢地，緩緩地	I turned round slowly and stared at her.	我慢慢轉過身，注視著她。	Something That made You Angry
57	specially	特地，特意，專門地	They were specially designed for the London Olympics, and they're really cute.	它們是特地為倫敦奧運會設計的，十分可愛。	An Interesting Shop You Have Visited
58	straight	筆直地；立即；連續地	So I said, "Go straight ahead until you see the petrol station, then turn right and it's about halfway down on your left."	於是我說：「一直往前走，到加油站處右轉。大約走半條路就到了，就在左手邊。」	One Time You Helped Somebody
59	undoubtedly	毋庸置疑地，肯定地	It's undoubtedly the most architecturally impressive university in Sichuan.	它無疑是建築風格給人印象最深的四川的大學。	A Building You Like; A college or School Building

	副詞	中文意思	例句	例句翻譯	可以用在這些話題中！
60	widely	廣泛地，普遍地	Oxford and Cambridge are widely considered to be the best unis in the UK, but LSE and UCL are also up there in the top ten.	人們普遍認為，牛津和劍橋是英國最好的大學。但倫敦政治經濟學院和倫敦大學學院同樣是那裡排名前十的名校。	Something Interesting You Hope to Do in the Future

3. 8 分副詞

以下 40 個副詞是有志拿下 8 分的考生需要理解和掌握的！一起來看看它們的使用場景與範例吧。

	副詞	中文意思	例句	例句翻譯	可以用在這些話題中！
61	adroitly	機敏地，靈巧地	He handled the situation very adroitly, and nobody felt uncomfortable.	他駕輕就熟地處理了當時的情況，而且沒有人因此感到不痛快。	Something Embarrassing
62	arrogantly	傲慢地，目中無人地	He spoke arrogantly, as though he was better than everyone else.	他說話的口氣很傲慢，彷彿他比任何人都強。	A Television Program
63	awkwardly	令人尷尬地，使人難堪地	The basketball player fell awkwardly and injured himself.	那個籃球運動員很笨拙地摔倒了，而且受傷了。	A Sporting Event

	副詞	中文意思	例句	例句翻譯	可以用在這些話題中！
64	blatantly	公然地，露骨地	In my opinion, it was blatantly unfair. I mean, he wasn't the only person cheating.	我覺得這件事情顯然不公平。我的意思是説，他不是唯一一個作弊的人。	An Unfortunate Experience
65	casually	漫不經心地；漫無目的地	I was just walking past casually, looking in the window.	當時我碰巧經過，朝窗戶裡看了一眼。	An Interesting Shop
66	continually	持續地，不間斷地	The teachers continually criticized us and, frankly, it affected my confidence.	老師不斷批評我們。事實上，這樣影響了我的自信。	School Memory
67	dangerously	危險地，有危害地	She said that the car had shot past dangerously close to where they had been standing.	她説當時那輛車很危險地從他們站立之處的不遠處飛馳而過。	A Memorable Happening
68	delightfully	令人愉快地，討人喜歡地	She spoke in a delightfully sweet voice.	她用令人愉快地甜的聲音説話。	A Teacher
69	enormously	巨大地，龐大地	It was enormously satisfying for us to win because we had been practising for months.	這次成功讓我們獲得了巨大的滿足感，因為我們勤加練習了好幾個月。	A Sporting Event

	副詞	中文意思	例句	例句翻譯	可以用在這些話題中！
70	endlessly	無止境地；無休止地，永久地	My parents argued endlessly when I was a kid. In the end, they got a divorce.	當我還是個孩子的時候，我的父母總是爭吵不休。最終他們離婚了。	A Family Member
71	falsely	假地，不真實地；不正確地	He was falsely accused of tampering with the medicine.	他被誣陷對藥動了手腳。	A News Story
72	furiously	狂怒地；猛烈地，強烈地	"What do you mean?" I responded furiously, my face flushed with anger.	「你這是什麼意思？」我惱怒地說，氣得滿面通紅。	Something That Made You Angry
73	hugely	巨大地；程度深地	He was hugely impressive in that game.	他在那場比賽中給人留下了深刻印象。	A Sporting Event
74	impatiently	不耐煩地，急躁地	She listened to me impatiently and then, before I had even finished speaking, she stormed off.	她很不耐煩地聽我說話，後來還沒等我說完便氣沖沖地離開了。	An Argument
75	infinitely	極大地；無限地	In my opinion, life experience is infinitely more useful than academic knowledge.	在我看來，生活經驗比學術知識要有用得多。	A Person Who Taught You to Do Something Useful
76	invariably	恆定地；不變地；始終如一地	They invariably ask you some questions about your family and where you are from.	他們總是會問一些有關你家人的問題以及你來自什麼地方。	A Job Interview

	副詞	中文意思	例句	例句翻譯	可以用在這些話題中！
77	listlessly	倦怠地，無精打采地	He sat listlessly on the couch, his shoulders hunched, his eyes half-closed.	他無精打采地坐在沙發上，蜷起身子，眯著眼睛。	A Story; A Film
78	madly	極端地，非常地；瘋狂地	Ophelia was madly in love with Hamlet, but Hamlet thought she was too young.	奧費利婭瘋狂地愛上了哈姆雷特，但哈姆雷特認為她太年輕了。	An Artistic Event; A Film
79	mainly	主要地，大部分地	They mainly sell furniture but they also have some kitchen appliances.	他們主要銷售傢俱，但同時也會賣一些廚房用具。	A Piece of Furniture in Your Home
80	momentarily	片刻地，短暫地	I was momentarily at a loss about what to say, but then I remembered what dad had told me.	我一時啞口無言，但隨後就想起了爸爸告訴過我的話。	Visitors
81	numerically	用數字表示地	The home team are numerically superior.	主場隊在數量上佔優勢。	A Story; A Sports Game
82	outwardly	外表上，表面地	Outwardly he seems confident but, when you get to know him, he is really rather timid.	他表面看起來很自信，但當你瞭解他了就會知道，他其實相當羞澀。	A Friend
83	plainly	清楚地，明白地，顯而易見地	It is plainly the right thing to do, but nobody is prepared to admit it.	顯而易見，這樣做是對的，但沒人準備承認這一點。	Something That Would Improve Your Town

	副詞	中文意思	例句	例句翻譯	可以用在這些話題中！
84	practically	幾乎，差不多	We were practically out of money, and out of petrol too.	我們幾乎用光了所有的錢，汽油也快用完了。	A Journey That Did Not Go As Well As Planned
85	promptly	準時地，守時地；立即，馬上	She returned my call very promptly because she wanted us to book the hotel.	她立即給我回了電話，因為她想叫我們預訂那家酒店。	A Wedding
86	reluctantly	勉強地，不情願地	She reluctantly agreed to let me stay for an extra night.	她勉強同意讓我再留宿一晚。	Something You Learned about Another Culture
87	scathingly	嚴厲地，尖刻地	He responded scathingly, using sarcasm to make me feel small and foolish.	他的回答很尖刻，諷刺的話讓我覺得自己渺小而愚蠢。	A Conversation on the Phone
88	selfishly	自私地	She selfishly kept all the toys for herself and refused to share them with her playmates.	她自私地把所有玩具留給自己，拒絕和夥伴們分享。	A Childhood Memory
89	shrewdly	精明地	She asked me where I had come from and how I had shrewdly managed to survive the storm.	她問我從哪裡來以及如何精明地在暴風雨中倖免於難。	A Bad Weather Experience
90	snobbishly	勢利地	She spoke snobbishly and disdainfully, with her nose in the air.	她說話的語氣傲慢而輕蔑，一副趾高氣揚的樣子。	A TV Program; A Story

	副詞	中文意思	例句	例句翻譯	可以用在這些話題中！
91	steadfastly	堅定地；不動搖地	The police questioned him for hours but he maintained steadfastly that it had nothing to do with him.	員警審訊了他幾個小時，但他一直堅持說那件事和他無關。	Something Interesting or Unusual
92	strikingly	惹人注目地，突出地	She was strikingly good-looking.	她相貌出眾。	Meeting New People
93	substantially	大量地；主要地	The report was substantially true but nobody took much notice of it.	這篇報告基本上是真實的，但沒有人給予足夠的關注。	Law
94	tearfully	淚汪汪地	She tearfully told me that she wished she had had more time to play with me when I was a little girl.	她眼淚汪汪地告訴我，她希望在我還是個小女孩的時候可以有更多的時間陪我玩。	A Reunion; A Family Member
95	tirelessly	不知疲倦地；孜孜不倦地	He worked tirelessly to help students prepare for the test.	他不知疲倦地幫助學生準備考試。	A Teacher; A Person I Admire
96	unemotionally	不流露感情地，不動聲色地	She replied very coldly and unemotionally. I was surprised and hurt.	她冷漠無情地給予了回答。我很吃驚，感覺很受傷。	One Time You Helped Somebody
97	unquestionably	無疑地，無可爭辯地	It was unquestionably one of the best things that has ever happened to me.	這毫無疑問是曾經發生在我身上的最美好的事情之一。	Congratulating Someone

	副詞	中文意思	例句	例句翻譯	可以用在這些話題中！
98	unstintingly	慷慨地，大方地	He gives his time unstintingly, and he is really dedicated to the cause.	他不遺餘力地投入了所有的時間，全身心地奉獻給了這項事業。	A Job That You Think Makes the World A Better Place
99	vigorously	強有力地，積極地	At first, he vigorously denied all the accusations but when people posted photos on the Internet, he had to change his tune.	起初他有力地否認了所有對他的指控，但是當人們把照片傳到網上的時候，他不得不改變說辭。	A News Story; A Crime
100	voraciously	貪吃地；饑渴地	My brother's always hungry. He eats voraciously.	我弟弟時常感到餓，總是狼吞虎嚥地吃東西。	A Family Member

五、錦上添花的俚語
Slang

現在你的基礎詞彙已經掌握得不錯了，還有什麼會為你錦上添花的詞彙呢？那就來學點俚語吧！

「俚語」聽起來很老氣，但實際上它指的是「非正式的常用語言」，所以其實很口語，一點也不老。有一些單字（如 clever）就是俚語出身，最終演變成了標準英語。但也有許多俚語壽命不長，一些七八十年代的俚語現在聽起來已陳舊不已，而一些俚語則只有特定的族群會使用。

在使用俚語時，也應該考慮到說話的對象、場合與時間，有些俚語並不適合在正式的場合使用。所以在學習俚語時，不光要學習俚語的含義，還要瞭解其用法和使用的情境。下頁就列出英式英語和美式英語中經常出現的一些俚語。

	俚語	意思	例句
1	24/7 (twenty-four seven)	24 hours a day, 7 days a week; all the time 時時刻刻都……	• My parents seem to expect me to study 24/7. 我父母希望我日以繼夜地讀書。 • That shop is open 24/7. 那家店 24 小時營業，全年無休。 • After the accident, she looked after me 24/7. 事故發生後，她寸步不離地照顧我。
2	airhead	a stupid person 傻瓜，迷糊的人	Other people think he's an airhead, but to me he's a genius. 別人都認為他是傻瓜，但我覺得他是個天才。
3	awesome	very good 很好的，了不起的	• The concert was really awesome. 音樂會真是棒極了。 • I think he's awesome. 我覺得他可真棒。
4	bored shitless	extremely bored 無聊至極	I was bored shitless in math class at school. 我在學校上數學課時快無聊死了。
5	bust a gut	try extremely hard to do something 竭盡全力	You don't have to bust a gut but come if you can. 你不用勉強，但是能來就來。
6	choice	excellent, very good 優質的，上等的	Hey, this fish is choice, bro. 嘿，這魚真棒，兄弟。
7	heads up	update on a situation 最新情況	Hey, thanks for the heads up! Let me know if there are more developments, OK? See you on Friday! 嘿，謝謝你告訴我最新變化。如果還會有新情況，就再告訴我，好嗎？週五見！

	俚語	意思	例句
8	goof	to make a silly mistake 犯愚蠢的錯誤	I really goofed in the exam and I feel lousy. But my mum talked to me and made me feel better. 我考砸了，感覺很糟糕。但是我媽媽和我談過以後，我的感覺就好些了。
9	hammered	very drunk 醉醺醺的，爛醉的	He was slurring his speech and couldn't walk straight. He was completely hammered. 他說話含糊不清，走路歪歪扭扭，醉得一塌糊塗。
10	hook up	to meet up or to join in 見面，碰頭	She said, "What time do you want to hook up tonight?" 她問：「今晚你想什麼時候出來碰頭？」
11	hot	sexy, very attractive 性感的	Hey, Lily, if you come to the bar on Saturday, I'll introduce you to a hot guy. His name's David. 嘿，莉莉，妳如果週六來酒吧，我就介紹一位帥哥給妳。他叫大衛。
12	no sweat	used to say that you can do something easily 一點也不難，毫不費力	—Can you make it by five? —No sweat. —5 點前來得及嗎？ —沒問題。
13	no worries	no problem 沒問題	He always tells me "No worries, it'll be fine" when I am depressed. 我鬱悶的時候，他總是告訴我：「不用擔心，會好的」。

	俚語	意思	例句
14	out of it	unable to think clearly because you are tired or drunk, or have taken drugs （因太累、酒醉或嗑藥而感到）神智不清	• I hadn't slept all night so when they called, I was totally out of it. 我整夜沒闔眼。所以他們給我打電話的時候，我都迷迷糊糊的。 • He drank too much last night. He was totally out of it when we took him home. 他昨晚喝多了。我們送他回家的時候，他完全不省人事。
15	random	surprising 意外的，隨機的	Hey, check this out! Potato cookies! That's so random! 嘿，快看這個！是馬鈴薯餅乾！太意外了！
16	rip-off	overly expensive 過於昂貴	That outfit cost me 3,000 dollars— it was a bit of a rip-off — and now I hardly ever wear it. What a waste! 那套衣服是我花 3,000 美元買的，真是貴得離譜，而我幾乎從來不穿。真是浪費！
17	Who does that?	used to comment on something surprising, shocking 用以評論某件驚人的、不可思議的事	This woman asked me to give up my seat for her 16 year-old daughter! I mean, who does that? 那個女人竟要我讓座給她 16 歲的女兒。有夠瞎！
18	stoked	very pleased and excited 振奮的，非常興奮的	I was so stoked to receive it. 收到它讓我興奮不已。
19	straight	heterosexual 異性戀的	He is definitely straight, although he doesn't seem so. 雖然他看起來不像，但他絕對是異性戀者。

	俚語	意思	例句
20	suss (out)	to figure out 認識到；明白；發現	You still haven't sussed out why I'm mad at you? No? Well, keep trying. 你還不懂我為什麼對你大動肝火嗎？還不懂喔？那你繼續想吧。
21	sweet as	great 好極了	I told him I had got the tickets and he said, "Sweet as". 我告訴他我拿到票了，他說：「太棒啦。」
22	take the piss (out of)	to make fun of 取笑；嘲弄	We really took the piss out of him. 我們好好嘲笑了他一番。
23	up to speed	having the latest information or knowledge about something 跟上情勢，瞭解最新情況	He asked me if I could bring him up to speed on the situation. 他問我能否為他介紹一下最新的情況。
24	whatever	(something said to ironically indicate disinterest or acceptance) （帶諷刺意味，表示不感興趣或接受）隨你便，無所謂	Ross: Remember, my birthday's in December. Gunther: Yeah, whatever. 羅斯：記得喔，我的生日在 12 月。 岡瑟：喔，隨便啦。
25	yeah right	(something said to ironically indicate disbelief) （帶諷刺意味，表示不相信）是，對	—So, guys, I'm pretty confident China will win the next Football World Cup. —Yeah right. —喂，各位，我有信心，下一屆世足賽中國隊一定能得冠軍。 —是啦，是啦。

六、幫你拿到 7 分的動詞片語
Multi-word Verbs for Level 7

動詞片語在一般英語對話中非常常用，如果你能掌握它們的使用方法，絕對會讓考官留下很好的印象！以下列出身為考官的我們喜歡聽到的 50 個動詞片語，這些都對你衝刺 7 分很有幫助。注意，許多動詞片語都有多重意思喔！

	動詞片語	中文意思	例句	翻譯
1	ask around	到處打聽	I'm not sure if anybody here plays tennis. You need to ask around.	我不確定這裡有沒有人會打網球。你得到處打聽打聽。
2	back down	退讓，認輸	You'd better back down, otherwise he is going to beat you up.	你最好還是認輸吧，不然他會揍你一頓。
3	bottle up	抑制（感情），勉強忍住	There is no point bottling it all up. You need to talk about it with somebody.	沒必要都憋在心裡。你需要找人傾訴一下。
4	cast around for	苦苦思索，拚命尋找	They are casting around for someone who can play the king role in *Richard III*.	他們在四處物色《理查三世》中國王的扮演者。
5	catch up	趕上進度、瞭解近況	Hey, I haven't seen you for ages. Let's get together. It'd be really good to catch up.	嗨，好久沒見到你了。我們聚一聚吧，能敘敘舊最好了。
6	chase up	追查，催促	Hello, I need to chase up an invoice that seems to have got overlooked.	你好，我需要追查一張漏開的發票。
7	chuck away	把……扔掉	That radio has had it. You should just chuck it away.	那台收音機不行了。你該把它扔掉了。

	動詞片語	中文意思	例句	翻譯
8	come down with	得病，病倒	He has come down with a really bad cold so he won't be able to play on Saturday.	他患了重感冒，所以週六無法上場了。
9	die down	減弱，平息	Eventually, the noise started to die down.	終於，噪音開始減弱了。
10	drop out	中途退學，輟學	Steve Jobs dropped out of university when he was about 20.	史蒂夫‧賈伯斯在 20 歲左右時從大學輟學了。
11	end up with	最終處於……的狀態	If you're not careful, you'll end up with nothing.	你要是不小心，就會落得一無所有的下場。
12	fall behind	落後	He is falling behind in his schoolwork because he spends too much time on computer games.	他的學業成績在漸漸下滑，因為他花太多時間玩電腦遊戲。
13	figure out	弄懂，搞清楚	With his help, I was able to figure out the situation and finally came up with a solution.	在他的幫助下，我搞清楚了狀況，並最終想出了一個解決辦法。
14	get behind with	拖欠，進度落後	I have really got behind with my assignments. I'm supposed to hand in the first one next Friday and I haven't even started.	我的作業真是拖欠太久了。下週五就該交第一項作業了，但我根本還沒開始做。
15	give up on	對……不抱希望	I've given up on him. He's hopeless. Every time I try to help him, he just gets worse.	我拿他沒辦法了。他已經無可救藥了。每次我想要幫他，他又會變得更糟。

	動詞片語	中文意思	例句	翻譯
16	grow out of	（因年齡增長而）不再做某事	Don't worry. It's just a passing phase. He'll grow out of it.	別擔心，這是必經的一個階段。他會走出來的。
17	have it out with	講清楚，來個了結	John, you'll have to have it out with him. That kind of behaviour is unacceptable.	約翰，你得跟他講清楚。那種舉動是不能被接受的。
18	heat up	加熱	For dinner, I am just going to heat up something in the microwave.	我打算用微波爐隨便熱點什麼當晚餐。
19	hit it off with	（與某人）一見如故，合得來	They hit it off as soon as they met. They have been friends ever since.	他們一見如故，從那以後就成了朋友。
20	jump at	迫不及待地接受（機會）	I think you should jump at this opportunity, Louise. It's a great company and a great offer.	我想妳應該抓住這次機會，露易絲。這是家好公司，是個好的工作機會。
21	keep up with	跟上，瞭解	I just can't keep up with what's happening in the NBA. I'm so busy studying so I don't have time to watch the games.	我不瞭解美國職籃的最新動向。我忙著讀書，沒有時間看比賽。
22	knuckle down to	（突然）開始努力工作（或讀書）	Listen, Peter, it's about time you knuckled down to some serious work. Your exams are only two months away.	聽著，彼得，你現在到了該認真學習的時候了。你還有兩個月就要考試了。
23	look up to	欽佩，尊敬	I really look up to him. He's successful, and honest.	我的確很敬佩他。他事業有成，為人正直。

	動詞片語	中文意思	例句	翻譯
24	max out	用光，用盡	I have maxed out all my credit cards. Dad is going to be furious.	我刷爆了所有的信用卡。我爸會氣瘋。
25	psych up	使（某人）心理上做好準備	I need to psych myself up for the interview. If I don't act confident, I've got no chance of getting the job.	我得為面試做好準備。要是我表現得沒自信，就沒有機會得到這份工作。
26	put off	拖延	I think you should do it now. Don't put it off till next week.	我認為你現在就應該動手，別拖到下禮拜。
27	put up with	忍受，忍耐	Honestly, I just can't put up with him anymore. He's always moaning and complaining.	說實在的，我再也受不了他了。他總是哀聲歎氣，滿腹牢騷。
28	reel off	一口氣背出	She reeled off an amazing list of accomplishments. I didn't really know what to say.	她一口氣說出一長串驚人的成就，教我無言以對。
29	run away with	輕鬆取勝	This year it looks as though Liverpool will run away with the championship.	今年的比賽中，利物浦隊貌似要輕易奪冠了。
30	run for	參加競選	I think Santorum might run for President again in 2016.	我想桑托勒姆到 2016 年可能還會競選總統。
31	scrape through	勉強通過，勉強應付	It wasn't a very good performance. I scraped through with 60 points.	我的表現不是很好，只得了 60 分，勉強通過。
32	screw up	把（某事）搞砸，弄糟	Be careful, don't screw it up.	小心，別搞砸了。

	動詞片語	中文意思	例句	翻譯
33	send out for	叫外賣	I'm gonna send out for pizza. Anybody want some?	我要叫比薩外賣。有人要嗎？
34	settle down	安頓下來，安定下來	They got married in 2012, went on their honeymoon and then settled down in the UK.	他們 2012 年結婚，度了蜜月，然後在英國定居。
35	shoot for	試圖達到，爭取得到	You should shoot for number one, Cyril. You're capable of it.	你該力爭第一，西瑞爾。你有這能力。
36	step up	站出來，自告奮勇	It's time for you to step up and show what you can do.	該是你自告奮勇出來大顯身手的時候了。
37	stick around	逗留，呆在……附近（等待某事發生）	Listen, if you stick around a while, I'll get that book for you.	聽著，你要是稍等一會，我就幫你把那本書拿來。
38	strike up	建立友誼，建立關係	I struck up an acquaintance with him when we were at college.	我們還在上大學時就認識了。
39	suck up to	奉承，巴結，拍馬屁	He really annoys me. He is always sucking up to the professor, trying to get in his good graces.	他真讓我討厭。他總是討好教授，試圖得到他特殊的關照。
40	suss out	認識到，明白；發現	Julie, if you suss out where Westlife are playing on Saturday, can you text me?	茱莉，妳要是打聽到西城男孩週六的演出地點，傳簡訊告訴我好嗎？
41	swing by	順便拜訪	I'll swing past Saturday about 9 with Alison. If you wanna go, you'd better be ready.	週六 9 點左右我和艾莉森會順便拜訪一下。你要去的話，要先準備好。

	動詞片語	中文意思	例句	翻譯
42	tag along	尾隨，跟隨	Come on, Alison, he just wants to tag along. He's not going to stay for the whole evening.	好啦，艾莉森，他只是想跟著我們一起來，不會待一整晚。
43	take in	領會，理解，記住	He had a Scottish accent and there was just too much information. I couldn't take it all in.	他有蘇格蘭口音，說的話要傳達的資訊又太多，我無法都聽懂。
44	think over	認真考慮	Take your time, think it over. We don't have to decide straight away.	別著急，考慮清楚。我們不必馬上決定。
45	turn down	拒絕（建議、要求或邀請）	It's quite a good offer but I think I am going to turn it down. I just don't want to work for that kind of company.	這是個很好的機會，但我想我會拒絕。我不願意為那種公司工作。
46	turn on	使動心	He really turns me on. It's the way he looks at me, those eyes of his.	他真讓我動心，因為他看我的眼神，他那雙眼睛。
47	turn up	開大，調大（熱度、音量等）	Jamie, can you turn up the sound a bit?	傑米，能把音量調大一點嗎？
48	warm up	做準備活動，做熱身運動	You should warm up before the class. Do some stretching or run on the treadmill.	你應該在課前做熱身運動，伸展一下四肢或在跑步機上跑跑步。
49	watch out for	警惕，注意	You should watch out for that guy, Sara. I really don't trust him.	你得小心那傢伙，莎拉。我真的不信任他。

	動詞片語	中文意思	例句	翻譯
50	wriggle out of	推掉，推辭	I suppose she came up with some excuse, right? She always finds a way to wriggle out of things; she's a smart little minx.	我猜她又想出什麼理由了，對嗎？她總是能找到推脫事情的方法，真是個聰明的小惡魔。

七、 告別老掉牙詞彙：學習近義詞和反義詞
Synonyms and Antonyms

學習近義詞和反義詞是拓展詞彙量的一個好方法。但請注意，要準確使用它們也並不容易。

以形容詞 fresh 為例，fresh 可以用來形容 news（新聞），也可以用來形容 bread（麵包）和 milk（牛奶）。fresh 的反義詞是 old。那麼反過來，可以説 That news is old 或者 That news is ancient（那是舊新聞），但不可以説 That bread is old（那是舊麵包）或者 That milk is old（那是舊牛奶）。也就是説，食物與新聞不是一回事！

形容麵包或牛奶不新鮮了，就應該説 That bread / milk is off 或者 That bread / milk has gone stale。但如果是形容奶油不新鮮，就得説 That butter is / has gone rancid。只要想一想中文中用於形容食物和新聞的詞也會不同，就不難理解了吧！

下面我們選取了 100 個常用單字，並列出了它們的近義詞、反義詞及中文釋義。希望你能好好學習這些詞，並透過這種方法來拓展詞彙量，加深對詞彙的理解！

考官語錄

Only 200 words in your vocabulary? Too puny, too limited! Let's get you some firepower!

考官語錄

Boost your vocabulary by learning synonyms and antonyms.

	單字	同義詞	反義詞	詞性及中文意思
1	absent	away, gone	present	*adj.* 不在的，缺席的；缺乏的
2	absurd	crazy, ridiculous, far-fetched	sensible	*adj.* 荒謬的，愚蠢的
3	abundant	plentiful	scarce	*adj.* 充裕的，豐富的
4	accept	agree, comply with	refuse, resist	*v.* 接受；忍受
5	accidental	by chance	intentional	*adj.* 偶然的，意外的
6	accurate	correct, right, bang on, precise, true	inaccurate, incorrect, wrong, untrue, way off	*adj.* 準確的；精準的
7	accuse	impugn	defend	*v.* 控告；指責
8	admit	confess	deny	*v.* 承認，贊同
9	advance	go forward	retreat	*v.* 前進；（使）進展
10	agony	severe pain	ecstasy	*n.* 極大的痛苦
11	angry	irate, hot under the collar, annoyed	calm, peaceful, kind	*adj.* 生氣的；氣憤的
12	appear	turn up	vanish	*v.*（突然）出現，呈現
13	approve	give the green light	reject	*v.* 批准；贊成
14	arrogant	supercilious, condescending	humble	*adj.* 傲慢的，目中無人的
15	attack	assault, strike	defend	*v.* 襲擊；進攻
16	auspicious	promising	inauspicious, doomed	*adj.* 吉利的；有前途的
17	beautiful	good-looking, attractive, pretty	ugly, horrible-looking	*adj.* 美麗的；美好的，優美的

	單字	同義詞	反義詞	詞性及中文意思
18	bitter	acid, tart, sugarless	sweet	*adj.* 憤憤不平的;苦的
19	boring	tedious, uninteresting	amusing, interesting, fascinating	*adj.* 無聊的,乏味的,令人生厭的
20	brave	courageous, gutsy, valiant	fearful, scared, pusillanimous	*adj.* 勇敢的;無畏的
21	busy	eventful, bustling	free, at leisure, have nothing on	*adj.* 忙碌的;繁忙的;熱鬧的
22	calm	peaceful	nervous, upset, bothered, disturbed	*adj.* 鎮靜的,平靜的;穩定的
23	careful	diligent, thorough, attentive	careless, neglectful, remiss, insouciant	*adj.* 謹慎的;細心的;周密的
24	cheap	inexpensive, lowpriced, affordable, cut-price	expensive, highpriced, overpriced, extravagant	*adj.* 便宜的,廉價的
25	cheerful	smiling, breezy, in a good humour, in good spirits	sad, depressed, glum, gloomy, morose	*adj.* 高興的,興高采烈的;令人愉快的
26	clean	shiny, fresh, laundered, hygienic	dirty, unclean, non-sterile, soiled	*adj.* 清潔的,乾淨的
27	clumsy	uncoordinated, awkward, gauche	well-coordinated, skilled, handy, deft, adroit	*adj.* 笨拙的,不靈活的
28	confident	assured, unhesitating	diffident, insecure, hesitant	*adj.* 確信的,有把握的;有信心的
29	crazy	insane, irrational, mad, deranged, demented	sane, normal, reasonable, rational, clearheaded	*adj.* 瘋狂的;不明智的;精神失常的

	單字	同義詞	反義詞	詞性及中文意思
30	create	make, invent	destroy	*v.* 創造，創建；發明
31	dangerous	perilous, risky, hazardous, dicey, chancy	safe, sure, secure, without risk	*adj.* 危險的，有危害的
32	deep	profound, fathomless	shallow, superficial, skin-deep, ankle-deep	*adj.* 深的；極度的；深奧的，難懂的
33	doubt	uncertainty, doubtfulness, ambiguity	certainty, sureness, inexorability	*n.* 不確定，懷疑
34	dry	arid, unirrigated	wet, moist, soaked	*adj.* 乾的，乾燥的；乾旱的
35	encourage	energize, inspirit, buck up, cheer up	discourage, daunt, dismay	*v.* 鼓勵，激勵；促進
36	enjoy	get pleasure from, like, get a kick out of	dislike, detest, react against, have no stomach for	*v.* 喜歡，享受……的樂趣
37	exciting	stimulating, gripping, heady, intoxicating	dull, boring, lifeless	*adj.* 令人興奮的，使人激動的；刺激的
38	fast	quick, swift, rapid, speedy	slow, dilatory, slow-moving, languid	*adj.* 快的，快速的；立即發生的
39	fat	plump, overweight, chubby, fleshy, pudgy, obese, corpulent	skinny, thin, lean, bony, gaunt, haggard, weedy, scrawny, undersized	*adj.* 肥胖的，肥的
40	find	discover, come across, hit upon, locate	lose, mislay, misplace, lose track of	*v.* 發現，找到
41	forgive	pardon, overlook, disregard, turn a blind eye to	blame, bear a grudge, accuse	*v.* 原諒，寬恕，饒恕

	單字	同義詞	反義詞	詞性及中文意思
42	fragile	delicate, breakable, frail	unbreakable, tough, durable, shockproof	*adj.* 易碎的，易損壞的；脆弱的
43	frequent	regular, recurrent	infrequent, occasional, irregular	*adj.* 經常發生的，頻繁的
44	fresh	like new, juicy, in mint condition	stale, old hat, obsolete	*adj.* 新的，新鮮的；新穎的
45	friend	pal, mate, buddy	enemy, rival	*n.* 朋友，友人
46	funny	amusing, humorous, droll, comic	serious, sober, solemn, stern, unfunny	*adj.* 使人發笑的，有趣的，滑稽的
47	generous	bountiful, giving	stingy, mean, tight-fisted, uncharitable	*adj.* 慷慨的，大方的；豐富的
48	gentle	tender, soft	violent, rough, domineering	*adj.* 和藹友善的；溫和的，溫柔的
49	genuine	authentic, real, reliable, unadulterated	fake, counterfeit, imitation	*adj.* 真正的，真實的
50	good	positive, fine, excellent, virtuous	negative, bad, evil, wicked, diabolical	*adj.* 良好的；令人愉快的，合意的
51	guilty	culpable, reprehensible, blameworthy	innocent, blameless, faultless	*adj.* 有罪的，有過失的；內疚的
52	happy	pleased, glad	sad, miserable, depressed, down in the dumps	*adj.* 高興的，快樂的；令人愉快的
53	hard	difficult, complicated, taxing, draining	easy, undemanding, simple, uncomplicated	*adj.* 困難的，不易的；費力的，費勁的
54	hard	tough, rigid, unbreakable	soft, pliable	*adj.* 硬的，堅固的

	單字	同義詞	反義詞	詞性及中文意思
55	healthy	vigorous, robust, in top form	sick, crook, ailing, unwell	*adj.* 健康的，健壯的
56	hollow	empty	solid	*adj.* 空（心）的，中空的
57	hope	dream of, aspire, promise oneself	despair, lose hope	*v.* 希望，期望
58	include	attach, enclose	exclude, remove	*v.* 包括，包含
59	increase	grow, rise, bump up, augment, amplify	decrease, reduce, diminish, lessen, dwindle, plummet	*v.* 增加，增大；提高
60	infringe	violate	stick to the rules	*v.* 違反，侵犯
61	juvenile	youthful, immature	adult, mature	*adj.* 少年的；幼稚的
62	kind	warm-hearted, benign	cruel, ill-natured, spiteful, bitchy, hurtful	*adj.* 體貼的，親切的，和藹的
63	large	extensive, roomy, ample	small, little, tiny, undersized	*adj.* 巨大的；大量的
64	laughter	humour	tears, pain, sadness	*n.* 笑，笑聲
65	lazy	slack, slothful, indolent, work-shy	active, proactive, hard-working, industrious	*adj.* 懶惰的，不努力的
66	legal	lawful	illegal, prohibited, forbidden	*adj.* 合法的，法定的
67	leisure	free time	work, chores	*n.* 空閒，閒暇
68	luxurious	opulent, superbly-equipped	shabby, threadbare, down at heel, squalid	*adj.* 奢華的，華麗的
69	new	recent, brand-new, novel	old, has-been, lapsed, expired, used	*adj.* 新的，嶄新的；新穎的

	單字	同義詞	反義詞	詞性及中文意思
70	obscure	unclear, confused	clear, transparent, limpid	*adj.* 不分明的，費解的
71	patient	tolerant, stoic, uncomplaining	impatient, irritable, irascible	*adj.* 有耐心的，能忍耐的
72	perfect	flawless, impeccable	imperfect, faulty, defective	*adj.* 完美的；理想的
73	permit	allow, authorise	prohibit, ban, forbid	*v.* 允許，准許，許可
74	praise	compliment, speak highly of, flatter, extol	rebuke, criticize, belittle, disparage, pick holes, run down	*v.* 稱讚，讚揚，表揚
75	precious	valuable, priceless, worth its weight in gold	shoddy, worthless, low-grade	*adj.* 寶貴的，貴重的；珍重的
76	proud	dignified, haughty, overbearing	humble, self-effacing, unpretentious	*adj.* 自豪的；有自尊心的；驕傲的，自大的
77	real	genuine, existing, extant	unreal, false, artificial, imaginary	*adj.* 真的，真正的；確實的，實在的
78	reluctant	reticent, unwilling, dragging one's feet	enthusiastic, willing, raring to go	*adj.* 勉強的，不情願的
79	respect	look up to, esteem	have no respect for, undervalue, despise	*v.* 尊敬，敬重
80	rich	wealthy, affluent, well-off, well-to-do	poor, hard up, badly off, broke, bankrupt, penniless	*adj.* 富有的，富裕的；豐富的
81	rude	insolent, discourteous	polite, courteous	*adj.* 粗魯的，無禮的
82	selfish	egocentric, self-absorbed	unselfish, selfless, self-sacrificing, devoted	*adj.* 自私的，不顧他人的

	單字	同義詞	反義詞	詞性及中文意思
83	sharp	acute, keen, pointed	blunt, unsharpened	*adj.* 鋒利的，尖銳的；劇烈的；刺耳的
84	short	tiny, diminutive	tall, lanky	*adj.* 短的，矮小的
85	shy	timid, retiring, introverted	confident, outgoing, extroverted	*adj.* 羞怯的，靦腆的
86	simple	easy, uncomplicated	complex, difficult, arduous	*adj.* 簡單的，簡便的；簡易的
87	smart	clever, astute, bright	stupid, foolish, unintelligent	*adj.* 聰穎的，機靈的；明智的
88	smooth	streamlined, unencumbered	rough, uneven, pitted, potholed	*adj.* 順利的，無困難的；平穩的
89	sober	clear-headed, unaffected by alcohol	drunk, intoxicated, hammered, blotto	*adj.* 未喝醉的，清醒的
90	spurious	fake, counterfeit	genuine, the real McCoy	*adj.* 虛假的，不誠實的
91	start	begin, initiate, commence	stop, cease, halt, finish	*v.* 開始
92	strong	powerful, influential, muscular	weak, unaided, feeble	*adj.* 強健的，健壯的；強有力的，影響力大的
93	succeed	achieve, accomplish, clear the hurdle	fail, flop, flunk, come up short	*v.* 成功，達成
94	temporary	interim, stopgap	permanent, longstanding	*adj.* 暫時的，臨時的
95	tidy	well-organized, well-kept, well-maintained	untidy, unkempt, messy, cluttered	*adj.* 整潔的，整齊的

	單字	同義詞	反義詞	詞性及中文意思
96	tight	stretched, unyielding	loose, baggy, slack	*adj.* 緊身的，貼身的；緊的，牢的
97	tough	challenging, difficult	easy, a walkover, a cinch	*adj.* 難辦的，費力的
98	victory	triumph	defeat	*n.* 勝利，成功
99	vilify	revile	shower praise on, heap praise on	*v.* 污蔑，中傷，誹謗
100	wealth	opulence, affluence	poverty	*n.* 財富；（某物的）豐富

八、告別老掉牙話題：舊題新說
Cliché Subjects

在雅思口語考試中，有許多男性考生會談論籃球，而許多女性考生會談論購物。這都不是壞事，但可惜的是，考生們重複過來又重複過去的句子早已讓考官厭煩，因為他們已經聽了成百上千遍了⋯⋯

1. 談籃球，你可以換一個方式

在考試時談論籃球會有風險。為什麼呢？因為考官已經聽過上千遍諸如 I like to play basketball with my friends. It helps me to relax myself （我喜歡和朋友們打籃球。這讓我放鬆自己）之類的句子。而且，relax myself 是個常見的基本錯誤，只需要說 It helps me to relax 就行了。

考官語錄

If you like basketball, fine, it's a great sport. The question is, how can you make what you want to say about basketball more interesting?

　　如果你熱愛籃球，當然可以，打籃球是一項很棒的運動。你想說籃球這個話題，也沒有問題。但問題在於，怎樣才能把「籃球」說得精彩？

　　首先，我們可以從各大英語媒體上好好看看每天刊載的籃球相關文章，並搜集這方面的詞彙，而且這些詞要新、奇、巧。看看你都能找到什麼詞彙呢？

　　第二步，把這些詞列在筆記本裡，按照名詞、形容詞、副詞、動詞等詞性進行分類。如果你收集到的詞彙太多，一頁列不完，那就列在另一頁上。這一步完成後，你在手冊中列出的樣子應該和下面的圖類似。

名詞：court, backboard, basket, hoop, stadium, contest, competition, tactics, playoff, timeout, three-pointer, free throw, circle, achievement, center, guard, ...

Basketball

副詞：hugely, awkwardly, ...

形容詞：massive, blatant, fantastic, huge, amazing, ...

動詞：dribble, refocus, shoot, challenge, award, ...

詞語講解：

名詞	court（球場），backboard（籃板），basket（籃框），hoop（籃框），stadium（體育場），contest（比賽），competition（對手），tactics（戰術），playoff（季後賽），timeout（暫停），three-pointer（三分球），free throw（罰球），achievement（成績），centre（中鋒），guard（後衛），...
形容詞	• massive（巨大的，大量的）：Their guard's got massive hands, like a bear. 他們的後衛有一雙熊掌一樣巨大的手。 • blatant（明目張膽的）：The ref was unfair! I mean, it was a blatant foul. Everybody could see that. 裁判不公平！這是公然犯規，每個人都看得出來。 • fantastic（非凡的）：He plays centre and he's got really fantastic vision. He always knows where his teammates are and who he should lay off to. 他打中鋒，有著非凡的眼力。他總是知道隊友在哪裡，應該把球傳給誰。 • huge（巨大的）：In my opinion, even making the playoffs was a huge achievement. 在我看來，即使打進季後賽也是一個巨大的成就。 • amazing（不可思議的）：It was just so amazing to be sitting there in the stand watching these guys in the flesh because up until then I had only ever seen them on TV. 僅僅坐在那裡親眼看到他們就是件不可思議的事，因為之前我只在電視上見過他們。
副詞	• hugely（極大地）：He was hugely influential all the time he was on the court, and he called the shots. 在場上所有的時間，他都發揮著極大的影響力，控制著全場的局勢。 • awkwardly（笨拙地）：And then he fell awkwardly below the basket and injured himself. It was a real shame because he had been playing so well. 然後他笨拙地摔倒在籃框下面，受了傷。他一直打得那麼好，這真是太遺憾了。

動詞	• dribble（運球）: I've never seen anyone dribble like that, the guy is mesmerizing! 我從來沒見過有人像他那樣運球，這傢伙真讓人著迷！ • refocus（改變重點，改變方向）: They called a timeout to give the guys a chance to regroup and refocus. 他們叫了暫停，來重新部署和改變戰術。 • shoot（投籃）: Then they passed to Bird and he shot a fantastic threepointer from way behind the line. 然後他們傳球給博德，而他在遠離三分線處投三分球命中，令人叫絕。 • challenge（挑戰）: Yao Ming challenged him at the basket and got the rebound. 姚明在籃下向他挑戰，搶下了籃板球。 • award（獲得）: They were awarded a free throw and they made no mistake with it. 他們獲得了一次罰球機會，而且沒有將其白白浪費。

2. 談購物，你也可以換一個方式！

我們對於「籃球」這一話題的準備策略同樣也適用於「購物」。如果你想談論購物，可以。但請記住，你需要下很大功夫才能把它說得有新意。如果你還是這樣開頭：I like to go shopping with my friends. It helps me to relax myself（我喜歡和朋友們去購物，這讓我放鬆自己），那麼考官只能在心裡默默感歎：「上帝啊，這樣的話我都聽了多少遍了！再說，relax myself 是不對的，只說 relax 就行了，剛剛不都已經說過了嗎……。」

那麼怎樣才能把購物說得既有趣又有新意？按照上面說「籃球」的方法進行同樣的練習吧！

九、黃金法則
Dos for Vocabulary

▶ **一定要⋯⋯ Do...**

▸ 閱讀、閱讀、再閱讀！讓人遺憾的是，很多華人年輕人讀的書都是課本。學生們常會說：準備考試都沒空了，哪有時間看書？但閱讀是擴大詞彙量的最佳途徑，同時也是開闊視野、觀察和體會生活的不二法門！凡是在雅思口語考試中得了 8 分的考生，毫無例外都是熱愛讀書的人。

Read books, read books, read books. Sadly, virtually the only books that many young Chinese people read are textbooks. This is just as true of university students as it is of the rest of the youth population.

Students say that they have no time to read for pleasure and discovery, that they are too busy studying for their exams. And yet reading has always been the royal road to the acquisition of vocabulary as well as the discovery of other worlds and other ways of viewing and feeling about life. Every single candidate we have worked with who managed to get an 8 in the IELTS test was an avid reader — no exceptions!

第三節 標準三：文法知識的廣度及準確度
Grammar: Range and Accuracy

☞ 一、千萬別犯錯的單字
☞ 二、高分必備的句子
☞ 三、必須掌握的七種動詞時態
☞ 四、如何在第一部分展現文法能力
☞ 五、如何在第二部分展現文法能力
☞ 六、如何在第三部分展現文法能力
☞ 七、黃金法則

考官語錄

Language
needs grammar.
Grammar is the
laws or rules of the
language.

英語中的 grammar （文法）一詞，源於希臘動詞 graphein，意為「寫」。

語言離不開文法。文法是讓我們在表達與交流想法時的規則，因此在雅思考試中考官當然也會使用「文法知識的廣度和準確度」當作評估考生的四大標準之一。不過考生不必太在意句子的「準確度」，在口語考試中尤其如此。口語的文法比書面語的文法自由、流暢，在書面語中會被視為錯誤的文法，在口語中是可以被接受的。

考官語錄

Remember,
grammar is learned
through language,
and not language
through grammar!

如果你能熟練運用各種時態，在說複雜句型時也能保證文法基本上沒問題，還能準確使用冠詞和現在分詞，就算不用什麼超高難度的文法，考官也會給你打高分。別忘了，我們是透過語言得知文法的用法，而不是透過背誦文法來學語言！

一、千萬別犯錯的單字
Words that Need Your Attention

1. 形容詞比較級和最高級

形容詞比較級

❶ 英語中的形容詞比較級很簡單，用來比較兩個事物。如果形容詞為單音節詞，我們只需在形容詞詞尾加上 -er 構成其比較級形式；若以子音字母結尾則需雙寫該子音字母，再加 -er；若以「子音 +y」結尾，則需變 y 為 i，再加 -er。請看以下例子：

■ rich – richer – My dad is a lot richer now, so we have two cars. When he was my age, he had to work in the countryside, picking apples.
我爸爸現在富裕多了，所以我們有兩輛車。他像我這麼大的時候還要在田裡工作，摘蘋果。

■ small – smaller – Actually, Xiamen is smaller than Fuzhou, but it gets a lot more visitors, partly because of the waterfront district and Gulangyu which are really nice to visit.

事實上，廈門比福州要小，但遊客卻比較多，部分原因是因為那裡的濱水區和鼓浪嶼是值得一遊的去處。

■ fat – fatter – Johnny is much fatter than everyone else in the class.

強尼比班上其他人都胖。

■ wet – wetter – Chongqing is much wetter than Beijing. You really need an umbrella if you live there.

重慶比北京要潮濕。如果住在那裡的話，你非常需要一把傘。

■ funny – funnier – This comedy was great, but the one I watched last week was funnier.

這部喜劇很好，但我上禮拜看的那一部比較好笑。

■ happy – happier – I am a lot happier now than I was then, so I don't really miss her any more. I learnt some good lessons from it, and I won't make the same mistakes again.

我現在比那時快樂多了，所以我真的不想她了。從這件事上我吸取了教訓，而且再也不會犯同樣的錯誤了。

■ healthy – healthier – If people make a bit of an effort, they can have a much healthier lifestyle. For example, if they sign up for a yoga class at the gym, that will soon make a difference.

如果稍作努力，人們就能生活得更健康。例如，如果他們報名參加健身房的瑜伽課，很快就能發現生活會發生變化。

❷ 除了以 y 結尾的雙音節詞外，其他多數雙音節詞及多音節詞都以在前面加 more 的方式構成比較級，例如：

■ beautiful – more beautiful – In my opinion, Gong Li has always been more beautiful than Zhang Ziyi. And just look how gracefully she's ageing!

在我看來，鞏俐一直比章子怡更漂亮。你只要看看她多麼優雅地變老就知道了！

■ beneficial – more beneficial – I guess you could stay here to study, but I think going abroad would be more beneficial. I mean, your language skills are going to improve, but also living overseas is just such a great experience.

我覺得你是可以留在這裡讀書，但我認為出國會受益更多。我的意思是你的語言水準就會提高，而且在國外生活也是一種很好的經歷。

■ conducive – more conducive – I like staying at our old house in the countryside. Granted, there's no TV and no internet, but it's quiet and peaceful and more conducive to studying. I can study really well there.

我喜歡待在鄉下的老房子裡。確實，那裡沒有電視和網路，但很安靜祥和，比較有利於讀書。我在那裡可以讀得很好。

■ courageous – more courageous – I think it is a more courageous choice, Sharon. You like him a lot, and you like being with him, so why not say yes? You're just scared something will go wrong. You have to be brave.

莎倫，我認為這是一個比較勇敢的選擇。妳那麼愛他，也喜歡和他在一起，那為什麼不同意呢？妳只是害怕可能會出問題。妳應該勇敢一點。

■ disappointing – more disappointing – It was so disappointing when they cancelled the trip. It was even more disappointing for us, because we had been planning the trip for months, and Peter's parents were really looking forward to seeing us.

他們取消旅程的事讓人沮喪。對我們來說則更失望，我們已經計畫這次旅程好幾個月了，而且彼得的父母也很期望見到我們。

■ ferocious – more ferocious – Tigers are more ferocious than lions. A lion wouldn't have a prayer in hell if it had to go up against a tiger in a fight.

老虎比獅子更兇猛。如果獅子與老虎打起來，獅子是贏不了的。

■ important – more important – I know it's a real shame if we can't stay at the beach, but I think it's more important that we see your family. They've been looking forward to this reunion all year.

我知道如果不能留在海邊是非常遺憾的事。但我認為見你的家人更重要。他們整年都在期盼這次團聚。

■ interesting – more interesting – Hey, Tony, get a load of this! This game is much more interesting!

嘿，東尼，來看這個！這個遊戲比較有趣啦！

■ promising – more promising – My current job is more attractive and more promising than my previous one.

與我之前的工作相比，我現在的工作比較有趣，且比較有前途。

■ uncomfortable – more uncomfortable – When he asked me if I wanted to go to Australia, I felt even more uncomfortable. I mean, I wanted to go, but I just didn't feel ready to get into a relationship. You know what I mean?

當他問我想不想去澳洲時，我就更不安了。我的意思是，我的確想去，但我還沒有準備好確立戀愛關係，你懂我的意思嗎？

❸ 有些形容詞有不規則的比較級：

■ good – better – I think you can have a better lifestyle in the countryside. OK, the shopping isn't great, but the food is better and there's a lot less pollution.

我覺得你在鄉村會過得更好。的確，是沒什麼好買的，但食物比較好，污染比較少。

■ bad – worse – I thought the first film was pretty bad but the second was even worse. In the end we gave up and watched TV instead.

我覺得第一部電影很糟糕，但第二部更差。最後我們乾脆不看了，轉而看電視。

■ far – further – You're joking! Wuhan is a lot further from here than Xi'an. Look on a map!

你開玩笑吧！去武漢比去西安還遠，看看地圖吧！

形容詞最高級

❶ 形容詞最高級也很簡單，用來比較三個或三個以上的事物。如果形容詞為單音節詞，我們只需在形容詞詞尾加上 -est 構成其最高級形式；若以子音字母結尾則需雙寫該子音字母，再加 -est；若以「子音 +y」結尾，則需變 y 為 i，再加 -est。如果形容詞為雙音節詞或多音節詞，我們都以在前面加 most 的方式構成最高級。有些形容詞有不規則的最高級形式。請看右頁例子：

■ quick – quickest– It was the quickest way to get from Rome to Milan.
這是從羅馬到米蘭最快捷的路線。

■ tall – tallest–Jim is the tallest of the three.
吉姆是三人中最高的。

■ fat – fattest – Joey is the fattest guy in the class.
喬伊是班上最胖的人。

■ tidy – tidiest – He is the tidiest person I have ever lived with.
在與我同住過的人中，他是最愛乾淨的一個。

■ wealthy – wealthiest – If you go by the GNP per head figures, then Qatar is one of the wealthiest countries in the world.
如果按照人均國民生產總值計算，卡達是世界上最富裕的國家之一。

■ good – best – Kirsten Dunst got the prize for Best Actress.
克斯汀·鄧斯特獲得最佳女主角獎。

■ bad – worst – It was China's worst-ever performance in a World Cup.
那是中國在世界盃表現最差的一次。

■ far – furthest – The furthest west I've ever been in China is Xining. I've never been to Xinjiang.
我去過的中國最西部的地方是西寧，沒去過新疆。

■ annoying – most annoying – He is one of the most annoying guys I know. He just won't leave me alone.
他是我認識的人當中最討厭的傢伙之一，老是來煩我。

■ arrogant – most arrogant – He is one of the most arrogant people I have ever met. He thinks he's so great.
他是我見過的最傲慢的人之一。他認為自己非常棒。

■ fascinating – most fascinating – As far as I am concerned, space travel is the most fascinating topic anyone can imagine.
就我個人而言，太空旅行是任何人可以想像到的最有趣的話題。

■ impressive – most impressive – In my opinion, *To Live* is Zhang Yimou's most impressive film. You know, the one where Ge You plays the landowner who loses all his money.

在我看來，《活著》是張藝謀拍過的最令人印象深刻的電影。在那部電影中，葛優扮演一個傾家蕩產的地主。

2. 不可數名詞

❶ 可數名詞與不可數名詞的區分是英語中的一個重要問題，因為它牽涉到一個名詞的形式和它前面加不加冠詞以及加哪個冠詞的問題。可數名詞使用起來比較簡單，但有不少名詞在英語中是不可數的，而在中文中卻是可數的，不能直接用 a 或 an 來修飾。下面列出的這些都是不可數名詞，在使用時要注意。

不可數名詞	中文意思	正確用法	錯誤用法
advice	建議	☑He always gives me good advice. ☑She gave me a piece of advice that I have never forgotten.	☒She gave me an advice. ☒He gave me some advices.
information	資訊	☑She gave me a lot of information.	☒That book contains a lot of informations.
water	水	☑Can I have a glass of water?	☒Please give me some waters.
furniture	傢俱	☑We have a lot of furniture in our home.	☒We have a lot of furnitures in our home.
luggage	行李	☑I had to carry all my luggage along the street.	☒I had to carry all my luggages along the street.
milk	牛奶	☑She drank so many glasses of milk I thought she would burst.	☒She drank so many milks I thought she would burst.

knowledge	知識	☑I like doing the experiments because I can learn a lot of knowledge about chemical reactions.	☒You can learn many knowledges.
blood	血液	☑She lost a lot of blood.	☒She lost many bloods.
progress	進步	☑He has made so much progress since he started working with me.	☒He has made so many progresses since he started working with me.
homework	家庭作業	☑I did all my homework before seven o'clock.	☒I did all my homeworks before seven o'clock.

❷ 有些名詞可以兼作可數名詞和不可數名詞，比如我們説 coffee 時意為「咖啡」這種物品，是不可數的。但要「一杯咖啡」時，卻又可以説 a coffee：

• Let's get a coffee.
我們喝杯咖啡吧。

• Coffee is one of Sierra Leone's main exports.
咖啡是塞拉里昂主要的出口產品之一。

除 coffee 之外，還有許多這種名詞：

不可數名詞	可數名詞
glass 玻璃	a glass 玻璃杯
copper 銅	a copper 銅幣
tin 錫	a tin 罐頭
wood 木頭	a wood 樹林
youth 青春	a youth 青年
relation 關係	a relation 親屬
necessity 必要性	a necessity 必需品
pleasure 高興，愉快	a pleasure 使人感到愉快的事

3. 冠詞：用 the ？ a ？ an ？或什麼都不用？

❶ 我們在談論具體或特定的事物時用 the 來修飾。換句話說，這時我們認為與我們談話的人知道我們在討論什麼。a 或 an 則一般用來泛指。試比較以下幾組句子：

Let's watch the movie (*we are referring to a specific movie*).
我們去看那部電影吧（我們都知道具體是哪部電影）。
Let's watch a movie (*we mean any movie rather than a specific movie*).
我們去看一部電影吧（指任何一部電影而不是具體的某部電影）。

Hey, give me the pen (*we are referring to a specific pen which you can probably see*).
喂，把那支筆給我（指特定的一支筆，可能在你的視線內）。
Hey, give me a pen (*we mean any pen, not a particular one*).
喂，給我一支筆（指任何一支筆，而不是某支特定的筆）。

I have to go to the meeting this afternoon (*the speaker assumes that the listener knows about the meeting*).
我下午要去開那個會議（說話者認為聽者知道是哪個會議）。
I have to go to a meeting this afternoon (*the speaker assumes the listener does not know about the meeting*).
我下午要去開個會（說話者認為聽者不需要知道是哪個會）。

❷ 在特定狀況下，例如在物質名詞和抽象名詞前，可以省略冠詞：

* Tea grows in India and China（不是 The tea）.
  茶產自印度和中國。

* Oil and gas are Saudi Arabia's chief exports（不是 The oil and the gas）.
  石油和天然氣是沙烏地阿拉伯主要的出口產品。

* Japanese cars are extremely reliable（不是 The Japanese cars）.
  日本汽車非常可靠。

* I like dogs（不是 the dogs）.
  我喜歡狗。

* Happiness is contagious（不是 The happiness）.
  快樂是可以感染他人的。

練習 EXERCISE

用 a、an、the 填空，或什麼都不填。

1. Do you remember _____ opening scene from *Saving Private Ryan*?

2. I've just seen _____ latest movie by Zhang Yimou.

3. _____ freedom is the greatest treasure in this world.

4. _____ girl standing at the bus stop is called Lulu.

5. Hey, have you got _____ pen?

6. Giovanni had _____ pizza for lunch.

7. I really like _____ Kuala Lumpur, because the food there is totally amazing.

8. On _____ Sundays, I sleep until lunchtime, then I get up and do some housework.

9. _____ movie we saw last week was really stupid, but Carrie liked it.

10. What did you think of _____ love scenes in the movie?

11. I am not very fond of _____ vegetables but my mum insists I eat them.

12. _____ T-shirt I bought on the weekend has got something written on it in Spanish.

13. Judy has found _____ earrings she lost.

14. Have you cleaned _____ car?

15. I would like to have _____ good explanation of what _____ Qing Ming stands for.

16. We want to buy _____ Easter egg.

17. Most foreigners like _____ Chinese dumplings.

18. Most boys enjoy playing _____ football and basketball.

19. _____ boys in my class also like playing badminton.

20. Are you interested in _____ team sports?

答案：

1. the   2. the   3. 不加   4. The   5. a   6. a   7. 不加   8. 不加   9. The   10. the
11. 不加   12. The   13. the   14. the   15. a, 不加   16. an   17. 不加   18. 不加   19. The   20. 不加

4. 介系詞：小詞有大用處

下面列出的介系詞是英語中最常用的一些介系詞，例句則表達了它們最常用的意思。英語中的介系詞非常靈活，可以在許多不同的地方使用。介系詞與形容詞動詞、名詞之間有著廣泛的搭配關係，因此要掌握介系詞的用法也要特別注意這些搭配。

to

- The teacher has returned to Chengdu.
  那個老師已經回成都了。
- She is moving to Hong Kong in September.
  她九月要搬去香港。
- Thanks to you, I am going to get a good score on this test.
  多虧了你，我會在這次考試中取得好成績。
- I did it to earn money.
  我這樣做是為了賺錢。

at

- I'll see you at nine o'clock.
  我們九點鐘見。
- The petrol station is at the crossroads.
  加油站位於十字路口處。
- It's the best option at the moment.
  這是目前最好的選擇。
- The cat's at the top of the stairs.
  那隻貓在樓梯頂端。

in

- The cat's in the attic. I can hear it.
  那隻貓在閣樓上。我能聽到牠的叫聲。
- I think she's in her dormitory, probably studying.
  我想她應該在宿舍裡，可能正在唸書。
- Beijing is in China.
  北京在中國。
- Those shoes are really in.
  這些鞋真的很時尚。

on

- Do you know the song *You Can Leave Your Hat On* by Joe Cocker? It's superb.
  你知道喬‧科克爾唱的那首《你可以繼續戴著你的帽子》嗎？那首歌太棒了。

- I left my wallet on my desk. Has anyone seen it?
  我把錢包放在桌上了，有人有看到嗎？

- Stop worrying. Life will go on even if you don't see her for a month.
  別擔心。即使你一個月沒見她了，生活還是得繼續下去。

with

- I went to the movies with Susan.
  我和蘇珊一起去看電影了。

- The warrior strode up to the throne with a sword in his hand.
  武士手裡握著劍，大步走上王位。

- Come with me, please. I need you.
  請和我一起去吧，我需要你。

- With some help from my parents, I managed to get a job in Shanghai.
  在我父母的幫助下，我終於在上海找到一份工作。

through

- The water trickled slowly through the pipe.
  水緩緩地流過管子。

- The cat crouched down, hesitated for a second and then jumped through the window into the kitchen.
  那隻貓彎下身子，猶豫了一秒鐘，然後穿過窗戶跳入廚房。

- I have been going through these old photos, and there are some really funny ones.
  我翻看了這些老照片，有些真有趣。

of

- Who's the owner of that motorbike?
  那輛摩托車是誰的？
- The capital of Mali is Bamako.
  馬利的首都是巴馬科。
- It's at the top of the stairs.
  它在樓梯的頂端。
- One of my favourite novels is *Of Mice and Men* by John Steinbeck.
  我最喜歡的一部小說是約翰·史坦貝克的《人與鼠》。

off

- The paper fell off the table onto the floor.
  報紙從桌上掉到了地板上。
- Turn off the TV, please. I want to talk to you.
  請把電視關掉，我想和你談談。
- Let's get off the bus right this minute and go back and look for that poor little cat!
  我們現在就下車，回去找那隻可憐的小貓。
- His attitude really turned me off.
  他的態度真得讓我興味索然。

before

- You should do it before we go.
  你應該在我們走之前做。
- Make sure you arrive before ten.
  你一定要在十點前到。
- Always check the tire pressure before you set off on a long car journey.
  在駕車進行長途旅行前，一定要檢查一下輪胎氣壓。

behind

- The cat is behind the sofa.
  那隻貓在沙發後面。
- Don't talk about him behind his back.
  不要在他背後議論他。
- I am falling behind with my studies. I have to focus.
  我學業退步了，應該專心唸書才行。

beside

- The cat is beside the fridge.
  那隻貓在冰箱旁邊。
- We live beside the park.
  我們住在公園附近。
- There is a 7/11 just outside the building, beside the Post Office.
  大樓外面就有 7-11 便利店，就在郵局旁邊。

up

- She walked up the stairs two at a time.
  她上樓時一次跨兩個臺階。
- The sales figures went up in November.
  十一月的銷售額猛升。
- Inflation has gone up this year — everything seems to be more expensive.
  今年通貨膨脹更嚴重了，似乎所有東西都漲價了。
- It's up to you, Jamie. You have to make the decision.
  這取決於你，傑米。你應該做決定。

under

- The cat is under the bed.
  那隻貓在床底下。
- The road goes under the overpass.
  那條路從高架橋下穿過。

around

- Let's walk around the park.
  我們在公園裡到處走走吧。
- I cycled slowly around the building.
  我繞著大樓慢慢地騎車。

after

- After you, Susan.
  妳先請，蘇珊。
- After she went into the room, I picked up my briefcase and followed her.
  她走進房間後，我拿起公事包跟著她進去。
- I hope to go to the UK after I finish my degree at Beijing University.
  我希望從北大畢業後可以去英國。

during

- It was during my time at Wuhan University that I got interested in microbiology.
  我在武漢大學時開始對微生物學感興趣。
- During the lecture, a lot of students fell asleep.
  講座期間，很多學生睡著了。
- Sometime during the afternoon, he returned to the scene of the crime.
  下午的某個時候，他返回過案發現場。

二、高分必備的句子
Sentences that You Need to Use

1. 簡單句和複合句

❶ 簡單句中只包括最基本的句子成分：一個主謂結構。句子成分都由單字或片語擔任，且要能表達一個完整的意思，例如：

- Remy waited patiently for his girlfriend.
  雷米耐心地等待他的女朋友。
- The plane was late.
  班機延誤了。
- Samantha and Gloria took Line 4 to Nanpu Bridge.
  薩曼莎和葛洛麗亞坐四號線去南浦大橋。
- George chatted with them in the bar.
  喬治和他們在酒吧聊天。
- Anna arrived at the party early and left before I arrived.
  安娜很早就來參加了聚會，而且在我到之前就離開了。

❷ 複合句由一個主句和一個或多個子句組成，子句由連接詞 after、although、because、since、when、while 等來引導。

- Because I arrived late, I didn't see Anna.
  由於我到得比較晚，沒有看到安娜。

- When she got to the airport, Vivien realized that she had left her camera in the apartment.
  薇薇恩到機場後才發現她把相機留在公寓了。
- After she got on the plane, Samantha realized that she had forgotten Alan's gift.
  薩曼莎上飛機後才想到她忘記了艾倫的禮物。

2. 條件句

　　條件句是由「條件狀語子句 + 主句」構成的複合句。如果你想得 7 分，就必須學會使用條件句。考試時準確使用條件句能讓你脫穎而出。英語的條件句很讓人頭痛，因為其中可能會出現各種時態的不同組合。請看下列表格中的句子以及條件句要表達的意思。注意其中的動詞時態組合：

考官語錄

Using the conditionals effectively will really make you stand out.

❶ （子句）一般現在式 +（主句）一般現在式→表達：事實／習慣

一般現在式 SIMPLE PRESENT	一般現在式 SIMPLE PRESENT	表達的是…… EXPRESSING
If you heat water to 100 degrees Celsius,	it boils.	事實 fact
If you don't eat for a long time,	you get hungry.	
Whenever we go shopping,	we always stop at Starbucks for coffee.	習慣 habit
Every time Sally comes,	we drink wine.	

❷ （子句）一般現在式 +（主句）一般未來式→表達：威脅／承諾／預測

一般現在式 SIMPLE PRESENT	一般未來式 SIMPLE FUTURE	表達的是…… EXPRESSING
If you're late one more time,	I'll sack you.	威脅 threat

（續上頁）

If you think aspirin will cure it,	I'll take a couple tonight.	承諾 promise
If she becomes CEO,	she will invest in innovation.	預測 prediction
If it rains this afternoon,	everybody will stay home.	
If we go to the party,	we'll see Susan.	
If she never works overtime,	she won't get promoted.	
If she takes that flight,	she will arrive at about 6.	
If you decide to act in that play,	you'll get some great experience.	
If you keep all the windows shut,	of course you'll get a headache.	

❸ （子句）一般過去式 +（主句）一般未來式→表達：不確定的期待

一般過去式 SIMPLE PAST	一般未來式 SIMPLE FUTURE	表達的是…… EXPRESSING
If she took that flight yesterday,	we will see her tomorrow.	不確定的期待（説話者不確定她是否乘坐了那個航班） "uneasy" hope (*the speaker is not sure whether she took the flight or not*)

❹ （子句）一般過去式 +（主句）would + 動詞不定式→表達：預測／願望／威脅

一般過去式 SIMPLE PAST	would+ 動詞不定式 WOULD+INF	表達的是…… EXPRESSING
If I won the lottery,	I would buy a car.	預測／願望 prediction/wish
If he said something like that to me,	I'd hit him.	預測／威脅 prediction/threat

❺ （子句）would + 動詞不定式 +（主句）would + 動詞不定式→表達：意願

would+ 動詞不定式 WOULD+INF	would+ 動詞不定式 WOULD+INF	表達的是…… EXPRESSING
If it would make Vivien happy,	I'd give her the money.	意願 offer

❻ （子句）一般過去式 +（主句）would + 現在完成式→表達：與事實相反的情況

一般過去式 SIMPLE PAST	would+ 現在完成式 WOULD+PRESENT PERFECT	表達的是…… EXPRESSING
If she took that flight yesterday,	she would have arrived at 6.	與事實相反的情況 situation that is now unlikely

❼ （子句）虛擬語氣 +（主句）would + 現在完成式→表達：與事實相反或不可能發生的情況

虛擬語氣 SUBJUNCTIVE	would+ 現在完成式 WOULD+PRESENT PERFECT	表達的是…… EXPRESSING
If I were him,	I would have grabbed that chance with both hands.	與事實相反或不可能發生的情況 situation that is unlikely or impossible

❽ （子句）過去完成式 +（主句）would + 動詞不定式→表達：與事實相反或不可能發生的情況

過去完成式 PAST PERFECT	would+ 動詞不定式 WOULD+INF	表達的是…… EXPRESSING
If you had done your job properly,	we wouldn't be in this mess now.	與事實相反或不可能發生的情況 situation that is unlikely or impossible

❾ （子句）過去完成式 +（主句）would + 現在完成式→表達：與事實相反或不可能
發生的情況

過去完成式 PAST PERFECT	would+ 現在完成式 WOULD+PRESENT PERFECT	表達的是…… EXPRESSING
If she had taken that flight yesterday,	she would have arrived at about 6.	與事實相反或不可能發生的情況 situation that is unlikely or impossible
If you had called me,	I would've come.	
If I had known about it last month,	I would have already submitted my application by now, and maybe already have received the confirmation letter.	

三、必須掌握的七種動詞時態
Seven Verb Tenses You Need to Be Able to Use

文法的重點有很多，但其中動詞絕對是最重要的。如果你還沒有掌握一般現在式和一般過去式，那老實告訴你，你最好就不要參加考試了，因為這兩種時態在口語表達中幾乎佔了一半。但只掌握這兩種時態又是遠遠不夠的！下面我們大致按照重要性列出了考生必須掌握的七種動詞時態。

你現在能掌握幾種動詞時態？想知道你能得幾分嗎？讓考官現在就告訴你！根據考官們的經驗總結，依據動詞時態打分數的標準大致如下：

- 只能正確使用兩種動詞時態的話，最多能得 5 分
- 最多可正確使用四種動詞時態，能得 6 分或 6 分以上
- 能夠十分準確地使用六種以上動詞時態，就能得 7 分或 7 分以上。考生，你太棒了！

看看下面列出的這些動詞時態。你可能在學習英語的過程中都已經遇到過，但你能在口試時正確使用它們嗎？你必須向考官展現出廣泛的文法知識。

1. 一般現在式（The Simple Present Tense）

　　一般現在式是口語中最常用的兩種時態之一，主要用於描述人物、情境和狀態，以及我們經常做的事情。用於第三人稱時，動詞後的 -s（或 -es）是必不可少的，如：

* he like**s**
* he doesn't like
* Does he like?

　　這是華人考生經常會犯的基本錯誤。考生一般都懂這個時態，也瞭解這一文法規則，但在開口說的時候還是會犯錯誤，比如 He like rugby，應該是 He likes rugby。

　　下面這些句子都是正確的：

* My parents and I live in an apartment.
* I sometimes feel lonely there because there are no Chinese people in my class.
* She really doesn't like rugby. She says it's too brutal.
* My parents really don't like Lady Gaga. They think her music is terrible.
* Tom gets up every day at seven and takes the subway to work. He changes at Taipei Main Station. That station is always very busy.
* My boyfriend is tall and kind of cute, and he likes bungee jumping – he's crazy.
* Which brand do you like best – Burberry or D&G?

　　如果考官問考生下面這類問題，考生就應該用一般現在式來回答：

* Do you like flowers?（你喜歡花嗎？）
* How do you manage your time?（你是怎麼安排時間的？）
* Do you think...?（你認為……嗎？）

2. 一般過去式（The Simple Past Tense）

　　一般過去式是英語口語中用得最多的動詞時態，用來描述過去發生的事情。令人驚訝的是，雖然這是考生應該掌握的最基本的時態，但仍然有很多人會用錯。下頁這些句子都是正確的：

- Last year I went to Qingdao.

- I spent almost three thousand yuan on that phone. It was really expensive.

- When I was a kid, I played basketball every day after school.

- She asked me if I wanted to go with her and I said yes.

- I didn't take enough clothes with me and so I felt cold all the time.

- During the interview, they didn't test my Japanese at all. They didn't even ask me about my level. I was surprised. I got the impression that English was much more important for them.

　　如果考官問考生上一個假期做了什麼，他們回答：「Last summer I go to Qingdao...」，這很明顯有問題。用錯動詞時態是文法準確度的問題，但這個基本錯誤也會表示考生的文法知識不夠廣泛。換句話說，考官認為該考生只會使用最基本的動詞時態。這表示該考生在文法方面最多只能得 5 分。

3. 一般未來式及 BE GOING TO 結構 （The Simple Future Tense and BE GOING TO + INFINITIVE）

　　一般未來式是英語中用起來很簡單的時態。你要做的就是記住「will + 動詞原形」或「縮略形式 'll + 動詞原形」結構，例如：I will try 或 I'll try。

　　用 be going to 結構也可以達到同樣的效果。will 和 be going to 有些細微的差別：will 表示將來要發生的事情，而 be going to 表示計畫和打算幹某事或即將發生某事，例如：

- I will go to the UK next year.

  I am going to go to the UK next year.

- I'll study engineering in Australia, in Brisbane.

  I am going to study engineering in Australia, in Brisbane.

- I think the economic situation will get better next year because China is still growing strongly.

  I think the economic situation is going to get better next year because China is still growing strongly.

　　所有參加考試的考生都會對將來有所打算，所以找機會用一個未來式的結構並不難。請主動一點說說看吧！

4. 現在進行式（The Present Continuous Tense）

現在進行式用來描述現在或將要發生的動作或情況，或表示暫時的情況。

- — Hi Samantha! Are you at home? What are you doing?
  — I'm just sitting here reading a book and feeling lonely. How about you?
- Right now our class is studying fashion marketing. It's really interesting.
- I am living in Guangzhou at the moment, but next month I will move to Fuzhou.
- Actually, I have never had any driving lessons but my mum is learning to drive at the moment.
- I'm living in a dormitory on campus – but only until June. In July I will move back to my home town.

對考生來説，在考試時用到這一時態並不難吧！

5. 過去進行式（The Past Continuous Tense）

過去進行式用來描述過去某個時候一個正在進行的動作。

- When I was walking along the street, I bumped into her.
- When I was studying in the UK, I met a guy called Pete who was very interested in photography.
- She told me she was talking to a friend on the phone and suddenly she felt this weird pain in her stomach.
- I was just sitting there, not doing anything special, and then suddenly I had a brainwave.
- I wasn't really paying attention in class. I was trying to send a text to a friend without anyone noticing me, and then suddenly I looked up and the teacher was right beside me.
- She wasn't really listening to me so I decided to do something to surprise her.

考生在考試的第二部分，可能會找到機會用這個時態。

6. 現在完成式（The Present Perfect Tense）

在中文和其他很多種語言中，都沒有與英語中的現在完成時等同的時態。我們將其用來描述過去發生並持續到現在的動作，或雖然發生在過去，但對現在還存在影響的事情，比如在新聞報導中就經常用到。請看下頁例句：

- I have been living in Beijing for five years.
- I have never been to Thailand.
- My sister has been working for a company in Hong Kong for the last two years. She started as a Marketing Assistant but now she works in Sales.
- I haven't seen *Kung Fu Panda 2* yet.
- The Minister of Defence has announced that the country will build three new aircraft carriers over the next ten years.
- Sina have announced several new features for the Weibo platform.
- Oh look! Somebody has broken the window.

> **考官語錄**
>
> To be considered a competent user of English, you need to be able to use the present perfect correctly.

只有能正確運用現在完成式，你的英語水準才能稱得上良好。至於現在完成式與一般過去式的區別，請參見下面第 8. 項的內容。

7. 過去完成式（The Past Perfect Tense）

過去完成式表示某事發生在過去某個時間之前。在下面的例子中，忘記手機的行為發生在傑利（Jerry）離家前。

- Jerry got up at 7 o'clock. He had a shower and then got dressed and made some breakfast. He left the house and walked to the station. When he got to the station, he realized that he had forgotten his cell phone at home.

下面是其他例子。通過過去完成式，我們可以瞭解到哪件事情是先發生的。

- Mrs Robinson told the doctor that she had taken the medicine before she ate the sandwich.
- If I had got a good score in the IELTS test last summer, I am sure they would have accepted me.

8. 用現在完成式還是一般過去式

這是英語文法中很難的一點。為了能將二者區別開來，我們可以這樣理解：一般過去式描述的是已經完成的動作，而現在完成式一般指動作或時間段持續到現在。請看右頁的例子。

- I worked in Beijing for five years. (Action completed, so I no longer work there.)
  我在北京工作了五年。（動作完成了，我不在那裡工作了。）

- I have worked in Beijing for five years. (Action not completed, I am still working there.)
  我在北京工作五年了。（動作沒有完成，我還在那裡工作。）

- I have been working in Beijing for five years. (Action not completed, I am still working there.)
  我在北京工作五年了。（動作沒有完成，我還在那裡工作。）

另外，我們還會用現在完成式來描述我們的經歷，因為經歷就是我們的生活，而我們的生活自然還沒有結束！

- Have you been to Guilin? (in your life)
  你去過桂林嗎？（你的一生中）

- Have you seen *Kung Fu Panda 2*? (in your life)
  你看過《功夫熊貓 2》了嗎？（你的一生中）

現在完成式也可以表示動作已經完成，但對現在造成了影響。請看以下對話：

丹尼爾： Look, somebody has broken the window!
看，有人把窗戶打破了！

（使用了現在完成式，因為儘管事情發生在過去，但丹尼爾現在才注意到。）

陳老師： No, that happened a couple of weeks ago, when you were in Hong Kong.
不，幾週前就破了。那時候你在香港。

（使用了一般過去式，因為對陳老師來說，這件事情發生很久了，而之後又發生了很多其他事情。）

丹尼爾： So why haven't you fixed it?
那你為什麼還沒有修好呢？

（用現在完成式表示從事情發生到現在這段時間。）

陳老師： A guy is going to come and fix it tomorrow.
明天會有人來修的。

（使用一般未來式表示將來要發生的事情。）

基於同樣的原因，我們在新聞報導中也使用現在完成式，表示事情才剛剛發生：

- The Minister of Railways has announced that a new high-speed rail link will come into service between Xi'an and Wuhan.

  鐵道部宣佈，將開通一條西安至武漢的新高鐵線路。

- After twenty years of success on stage, she has finally decided to retire.

  經歷過二十年輝煌的舞臺生涯後，她終於決定要退休了。

四、如何在第一部分展現文法能力
Displaying Grammatical Range in Part One

下面請看一位考生如何在第一部分回答考官提出的有關購物的問題，要注意看考官的點評喔！

話題：購物（Shopping）

1. I'd like to move on to talk about shopping. How often do you go shopping?
   我想談一談購物。你多久去購物一次？

考生回答：Mmm, about once a week or once every two weeks, usually in one of the big shopping centres in the city centre.

考官點評 文法準確，無錯誤。回答流利，但尚無文法變化。

2. What kind of things do you generally buy?
   你一般會買些什麼呢？

考生回答：I guess clothes, mainly, and make-up, but you know I often go shopping with my girlfriends and it's not just buying things. It's fun to hang out together. I mean, whenever we go shopping, we always stop for a coffee somewhere and chat.

考官點評 文法仍然很準確，在以下方面表現出了廣泛的文法知識：
   （1）在 buying things 中使用了動名詞形式。
   （2）whenever we go shopping, we always stop for a coffee... 這句話使用了簡單的條件子句。
   （3）能熟練使用話語標記，如 you know、I mean。

3. **Do you prefer shopping in small shops or big shopping centres?**
   你比較喜歡在小商店還是大型的購物中心購物呢？

考生回答：Actually, I usually prefer big shopping centres because there is so much to see... but, you know, sometimes that's a problem. I mean, we wander around chatting and looking at everything and don't buy anything and then, when I get home, I say to myself, oh my God, if I had bought that green skirt, I could have worn it to the party tomorrow!

考官點評 　沒出現文法錯誤。令人印象深刻的是該考生使用了虛擬語氣（if I had bought that green skirt, I could have worn it... ），這表明她的文法知識很廣泛，在文法方面可能得 7 分或 8 分。

考官總評：

　　請注意該考生在最後怎樣用一個虛擬情境進行了回答，以及如何使用了一個虛擬子句，所以給考官留下了深刻的印象。

五、如何在第二部分展現文法能力
Displaying Grammatical Range in Part Two

　　下面請看一位考生如何在第二部分回答考官提出的有關旅行的問題，要注意看考官的點評喔！

話題：旅行（Journey）

1. **I'd like you to talk about a journey that took more time than you expected. You should say where you were going, what the reason was for the delay, and how you reacted to the situation...**
   我想請你談一談自己一次比預期花費時間要長的旅行，內容應該包括你去的地點、耽擱的原因以及你如何應對了這種情況……

考生回答：Well, actually, it happened just a couple of weeks ago. I was at Hongqiao Airport and I was going back to Guangzhou but the plane is delayed. Actually, you never really know why the plane is late. They always say something like air traffic conditions or something like that. Actually, I think there was bad weather in Guangdong and that was why the plane hadn't arrived in Shanghai. Anyway, I tried to phone my boyfriend but I didn't get through to him and I was a bit worried about it because we had had a really big argument the day before, probably the worse one we ever had, and I knew he was still mad about it... and then I realized that my phone was out of battery and I thought, oh no, I've already checked in my battery charger. It's with my shoes in my luggage, so what do I do? So I am sitting there thinking about it for a moment, and I noticed this guy sitting opposite me, so I smiled and asked him if I could use his phone, and then I called my boyfriend again, and he still didn't answer, and then about ten minutes later he rang back to the guy's phone, and I could tell he was wondering who this guy was and what was going on. Anyway, finally we got our call on board and we got on the plane, and took off, and the flight was fine, and we landed in Guangzhou and then I realized that we were at the wrong terminal. So I had to go and get my luggage, and get my charger out of the suitcase, and then I found a powerpoint

考官評價

該考生能夠在說一大段話時保持文法的準確性。

動詞時態：運用了多種時態，讓人印象深刻，包括一般現在式（they say）、一般過去式（tried、didn't get through、realized、sat、noticed、called...）、過去進行式（I was going、he was wondering）、現在完成式（I've already checked in）和過去完成式（hadn't arrived）。

形容詞：根據上下文判斷，the worse one we ever had 中的 worse 應用其最高級 worst。

文法準確性：出現了三個時態方面的錯誤，其中 is delayed 應為 was delayed，the worse one we ever had 應改為 the worst one we've ever had，以及 am sitting there thinking 應改為 sat there thinking。

介系詞及代名詞：使用準確且適當。只有一個介系詞用錯了：rang back to the guy's phone 應改為 rang back on the guy's phone。

句型：考生能夠使用複合句，比如 Anyway, I tried to phone my boyfriend but I didn't get through to him and I was a bit worried about it because we had had a really big argument a couple of days before, probably the worst one we've ever had, and I knew he was still mad about it...

and I was charging my phone when my boyfriend showed up, and then we both just kind of burst out laughing, cos the whole situation was kind of ridiculous, and then we took the train into the city together and it felt so good to be home and to get everything sorted out at last.

總體錯誤率：低。

評分：該考生在文法方面可得 7 分。

2. Do you travel often?
   你經常旅行嗎？

考生回答：Not that often.

考官點評 在回答這種表示就要接近結尾的「過渡性問題」時，這樣的簡短回答很不錯。

考　官：Thank you. Can I have the topic card and the paper and pencil back please? Thank you. Well, we've been talking about a plane journey you made that took more time than you expected and now I'd like to go on and ask you some more general questions about this...
謝謝。把話題卡、紙和鉛筆還給我好嗎？謝謝。嗯，我們剛才討論了一次比預期時間要長的飛機旅行。現在我們繼續，我想大致問幾個這方面的問題……

六、如何在第三部分展現文法能力
Displaying Grammatical Range in Part Three

下面請看一位考生如何在第三部分回答考官提出的有關成功的問題，注意看看考官的點評喔！

話題：成功（Success）

1. 考官：Well, we've been talking about a successful person you know — your aunt — and I'd like to go on to ask you some more general questions about this. Let's consider first of all

success in business. What kind of qualities do you think a person needs to have in order to succeed in business?

嗯，我們討論了一位你認識的成功人士：你的姑姑，我想再問一些關於這方面的問題。我們先談談商業上的成功。你認為要想在商業上取得成功，應該具備哪些素質？

考生回答：To succeed in business... Well, I think they have to be... mmm, ummm, how I can say? I think a businessman or businesswoman have to have a clear idea about what he want to sell people, and... then they have to know to make that idea become a reality. You know, if you have an idea, that's good, that's the beginning, but to organize a company, that's something... different. You have to have organize skills. For example, look at Ma Yun, he's the guy who started Taobao and Alibaba, he is that...

考官點評 文法水準有限。

動詞時態：能夠運用的時態有限，基本上都是一般現在式和一般過去式（he started）。

文法準確性：錯誤很多，如 how I can say 為語序錯誤，應為 how can I say 或更好一點的 how can I express it。一般現在式的第三人稱運用上有兩個錯誤：a businessman or businesswoman have to 應為 a businessman or businesswoman has to... 以及 he want 應為 he wants。

形容詞和副詞：詞彙量非常有限。

介系詞和代名詞：還可以。

句型：目前來看，考生主要就是將簡單的句子和片語堆砌在一起。雖然考生試圖用複合句，但沒有用好。

總體錯誤率：高。

2. 考官：He's got what, exactly?

具體說來，他有什麼特質？（考官認為該考生的回答含糊不清，所以開始引導考生。）

> **考生回答：**I mean, he got his idea about the Internet — you know his first job is do an English teacher — but he still have his idea about the Internet. And then he make some websites and some more websites and then he created his company, called Alibaba, and he has grown up the company to make it bigger. That's what I mean, he has the ability to organize a company and make the people work for him.

考官點評

動詞時態：試圖使用現在完成式，但詞語用法不對（正確的應為 he has grown the company），其他都是一般現在式和一般過去式。

文法準確性：he got 應該是 he has，is 後不應該有 do。還犯了一個一般現在式第三人稱的基本錯誤：he still have 應為 he still has。另外，he has grown the company to make it bigger 中的片語 to make it bigger 是多餘的，因為 grow 本身就有「發展壯大」的意思。再就是 the people 應改為 people。

介系詞和代名詞：介系詞使用準確（idea about the Internet、work for him）。

總體錯誤率：太高。

3. 考官：Do you think people are born leaders, or can they learn to be leaders?

你認為領導者是天生的還是後天培養的？（考官轉到這個問題的一個新角度來提問。）

> **考 生：**Mmm, I think people which are leaders are something different than other people... They have to be good at the communication, so they can... communicate, so they can make the people to follow them. And organization.

考官點評

句型：表達含糊不清，沒有真正掌握各種句型的用法。最後兩個詞也不能算是個完整的句子。考生不會運用複合句。

文法準確性：

（1）good at the communication 中 communication 前不必加 the。

（2）different than 用法不正確，應為 different from。

（3）make the people to follow them 應為 make people follow them。

介系詞和代名詞：修飾 people 的定語子句的引導詞應為 who，故 which 應改為 who。

總體錯誤率：太高。

4. 考官：OK, but those skills of organization, and communication, and vision. Can they be learnt? Or are people born with those capacities?

好的，但像組織能力、溝通能力以及有遠見之類的素質是能夠學到的嗎？還是人們天生就有這些能力呢？（考生並沒有直接回答問題，所以考官再次有力重申了這一點。）

考生：Mmm, well I think...maybe, maybe they born with them because, well, take Ma Yun. I don't think he can learn that when he is an English teacher so he must already get that inside him.

考官點評

文法準確性：主要是動詞的用法錯誤：they born 應為 they are born；can learn 應改為 could learn；is 應為 was；he must already get 應為 he must already have had。

5. 考官：In your opinion, is it more important to succeed in professional life or in personal life?

在你看來，是事業成功更重要還是個人生活成功更重要？（談話並不流暢，所以考官從另一個角度提出了一個新問題。）

考生：Well, take me for example. Like I said before, I want to study finance in Australia so I can have a good job but for me family is also very important, and to have time to do things I like to do, like dancing...

考官點評

文法準確性：這次稍好一點。I like to do 也不算錯，但在表示愛好時，用 I like doing 更好一點。

6. 考官：Do you think parents in China put too much pressure on their children to succeed?

你認為中國家長在成功方面給孩子的壓力太大了嗎？

> **考 生：**In China, that's for sure, that's for sure. We have so much pressure on us, on us shoulders. I mean, if I get one bad mark on a test, then my parents complain me and blame me, so I always feel the pressure to be the success. Sometimes it is driving me crazy.

考官點評

文法準確性：

（1）us shoulders 應改為 our shoulders；

（2）complain 不是及物動詞，所以 complain me 是不對的，用 complain about me 或 criticize me 都可以；

（3）the pressure to be the success 應改為 the pressure to succeed；

（4）Sometimes it is driving me crazy 應該用一般現在式，即 Sometimes it drives me crazy。

7. 考官：Do you think money is important to success?

你認為錢對於成功來說重要嗎？（考官發現考生無法回答複雜的問題，轉而問了個簡單的問題。）

> **考 生：**Yes, I think it is. I mean, money is not everything, but if you don't have the money, what can you do? You can do nothing. You need money, just to live, to buy food, or to take care your family.

考官點評

文法準確性：在自然的談話中，應該用 it 來代替 the money；you can do nothing 比較道地的表達是 you can't do anything；take care your family 的用法也錯了，應該是 take care of your family。

考官：Thank you very much. That is the end of the speaking test.

非常感謝。口語考試結束了。

考官總評：

　　錯誤率太高。考生不能運用複合句，經常出現停頓，語速太慢，有一些語句的重複。總之，在文法和語言流暢度方面的得分都為 5 分。

七、黃金法則
Dos and Don'ts

▶一定要⋯⋯ Do...

▸▸ 練習使用各種動詞時態和條件句，這樣考試時就能用上。相信我們，為了給考官留下「你的文法知識很豐富」的印象，你肯定需要它們！

Practise with the verb tenses, including the conditionals, so that you can use several. Believe us, you need them in order to give an impression of grammatical range.

▸▸ 注意 the 和 a 的區別。如果你遇到一些複雜的問題，不確定哪個是正確答案，就去詢問老師或通過 ieltsyes.net 網站聯繫我們。

Work on the difference between "the" and "a". If you come across a tricky sentence and are not sure of the right answer, talk to your teacher or contact us at ieltsyes.net.

▸▸ 練習使用複合句。

Practise using complex sentences.

▸▸ 透過做文法習題和到網站上寫信給我們來練習文法。

Practise your grammar by doing grammar exercises and by writing to us at www.ieltsyes.net.

▶千萬別⋯⋯ Don't...

▸▸ 不要認為你憑藉一般現在式就能順利通過考試。

Don't think you can get through the test successfully with just the simple present.

第四節 標準四：發音
Pronunciation

☞ 一、讓考官告訴你：如何評價你的發音

☞ 二、華人學生「總是發不標準的九個音」

☞ 三、教你改善英語發音

☞ 四、五大發音要素，如何各個擊破

☞ 五、同形不同音，意義有不同

☞ 六、考官不會介意你的口音

☞ 七、來自世界各地的聲音

華人在學英語時，會感覺有些音特別難發，比如會經常念錯 clothes（衣服）、development（發展）和 usually（通常）。事實上，如果你能清楚地說出 I usually wear formal clothes to talk about criteria to measure international trade in Vienna，你就可以跳過這一章。

不過，多數情況下，考生身上真正的問題並不是個別單字的發音，而是說話的節奏。英語的節奏與其他語言不同，這是英語學習者需要掌握的。

這一節主要談華人學習者在學習英語過程中碰到的發音、節奏和重讀音節等問題，還會介紹考生改善發音的幾種切實可行的方法。

一、讓考官告訴你：如何評價你的發音
How to Evaluate Your Pronunciation Level

大家一定想知道，在發音方面雅思口語考官真正看重的是什麼？第一點不用說，考官首先要看自己是否能聽懂考生說的話。如果考生在說的時候，他們感覺聽得很費勁，那麼考生的得分很可能超不過 4 分。如果考生的發音不好，到考官聽不懂的程度，多少會給考

官留下不太好的印象喔！不過，考官的任務是要按四個標準全面考查考生，因此即使考生的發音不好，但在詞彙和文法方面的表現還不錯，考官也會注意到。例如，考生在流暢度、詞彙和文法方面得 6 分，而發音只有 4 分，這種情形也是有可能發生的。

考官都是經過訓練的，很快就能判斷出考生的發音能力如何，通常講不到一分鐘就能知道得很清楚。只要考生一開口，考官就會感覺到他的發音能力、母音的發音情況等。考官會注意考生的發音是否清晰、是否能按照意思斷句、重音是否準確等問題。這裡特別提到一個「母音的發音」，是因為和中文相比，英語中母音的發音更多樣，所以華人考生比較難掌握。別忘了，英語只有 26 個字母，但卻有 44 種發音，需要認真去學才能搞懂。

如果考生的發音很難聽懂，那不用説，在發音方面肯定是打 4 分以下的分數。但假如考生的得分在 4 分以上，考官怎樣區分他們之間細微的不同之處呢？其實看一下雅思公布的評分標準就知道，要想得 6 分，考生的發音要能展現出英語的許多發音特點，包括能夠在合適的地方斷句、重音要落在正確的音節上等等。不用每個字都要發得很精準，但發不清楚的音最好不要太多。考官評分時會有詳細的標準做參考，而且在確定最終分數時還會再參照這些標準，所以少錯一個音，搞不好就會讓得分再高一點喔！

那麼，發音能得 7 分或 8 分的人，會是什麼情況呢？這些考生的發音已經接近母語人士了，發音清晰、重音位置準確、節奏自然。什麼叫「節奏自然」？這是指考生已經掌握了英語發音的特點：即英語的節奏是根據「強調的重點」而定的。語句讀起來需按照意思進行停頓，不重要的詞可以輕輕帶過，但重要的詞要發重音。所以，有些人會説：學音樂的考生發音也會比較好，我們認為這可能真的有關係！聽力靈敏在學語言上本來就是一種優勢，可以幫助你抓住發音的重音與節奏，彷彿在演奏樂器一般。

二、華人學生「總是發不標準的九個音」
Difficult English Sounds for Chinese Learners

根據許多華人考生在口語考場的表現，我們為你總結出了華人最難發的 9 個音，在這裡一起練習念念看吧！

1. 在發 /ʒ/ 音時，例如讀 usually /ˈjuʒuəli/、measure /ˈmeʒə/、casual /ˈkæʒuəl/ 時，常會讀不標準。華人通常會把 usually 讀成 /juzrəli/。

2. 在發 clothes /kləuðz/ 中的 /ðz/ 時，華人常讀成 /ziz/，這樣 clothes 聽起來就像 closes。

3. 中文中沒有 /v/ 這個音，因此考生常把 /v/ 和 /w/ 弄混，例如會把 invite /ɪnˋvaɪt/ 讀成 /ɪnˋwaɪt/，把 development /dɪˋvɛləpmənt/ 讀成 /dɪˋwɛləpmənt/。

4. 在讀 train 或 trade 中的母音 /e/ 時，華人很容易把它和 bed、thread、head 或 tread 中的母音 /ɛ/ 讀得一樣。

5. 讀 kind 或 mind 時要特別注意母音 /aɪ/ 的讀法。

6. school 或 movie 裡的母音 /u/ 和 full 裡的母音 /ʊ/ 容易混淆，必須區別開。請通過下面這個句子來體會二者的區別：
   His wallet may be full /fʊl/, but he is still a fool /ful/.

7. lot、cotton 或 shot 裡的母音 /ɑ/ 在中文中沒有對等的音節，因此考生容易混淆 shot /ʃɑt/ 和 short /ʃɔrt/ 的讀音。

8. 有些華人會容易混淆 /l/ 和 /r/ 的發音，會把 fried rice 說成 flied lice。

9. 華人英語學習者有時會誤讀詞尾的子音連綴音節，因為在中文中很少發這種音。有一些考生會在子音後面額外加一個母音，如把 basketball 發成 /ˋbɑskɪtbɔlə/。同樣地，如果一個單字出現子音連綴，例如讀 asks，有些學習者會添加音節，發成 /ɑskəz/。還有一些人會把子音去掉，發成 /ɑsk/。

　　如果你把以上提到的錯誤發音糾正後再去考試，那麼你一開口就會留給考官一個良好的印象。這樣你的分數可能就會在 6 ～ 8 分之間，而不是 4 ～ 6 分之間囉！

三、教你改善英語發音
Methods for Dealing with Pronunciation Problems

① 找出你有哪些發音讓別人難以聽懂，然後看看這些發音是母音還是子音。

② 聽聽英語為母語的人如何發這些音。

③ 把你的發音錄下來。錄音時，不要單獨發孤立的音，而是要放在句子中去讀。

④ 找出自己的發音與母語人士發音的區別。

⑤ 找出正確的發音方法，即應該以什麼樣的口形發、如何運用發音部位。如果身邊有母語是英語的人，你可以密切觀察他們發音時的口形。

⑥ 在不同情境中進行練習。例如，這個音在句子的開頭怎麼發，在句子中間又如何發。把自己的發音錄下來並仔細辨聽。

❼ 請母語人士聽一段你連續說話的發音，並給出評價。你也可以把錄音上傳到 www.ieltsyes.net，我們來幫你評分！

❽ 如果要使用 KK 音標練習發音，要確認你知道每一個音標怎麼發音，尤其是母音。

❾ 練習放慢速度讀句子。如果你說的語速太快，就無法知道自己哪個發音有問題。

❿ 聽發音標準的人說話（可使用影片或音檔），模仿、反覆傾聽並進行比較。

四、五大發音要素，如何各個擊破
Five Key Success Factors for Pronunciation

1. 節奏和重音

Track 005

語言學家把英語稱作「有重音節奏的語言」，意思是說英語的節奏是按照強調的重點來劃分的。

所謂的「重點詞彙」，就是具有實際意義、需要強調的詞，而其他的詞就不必強調，因此通常你聽不到這些詞的讀音，但是可以猜出來它們的存在。這種形式被稱為「弱讀」。看看下面這句話：

I went to New York for three weeks.

哪一個詞需要發重音？答案是：具有重要資訊的詞。那麼這個句子中到底哪些詞重要？會不會是 I？很顯然，I 是重要的，但事實上 I 不需要重讀，因為通常情況下聽者都知道是誰在陳述。

那麼 went 是重點詞嗎？ went 的確是重要的，但如果說話者是在回答「Where did you go?」這個問題，那麼 went 就不需要發重音。重點詞應該是 New York 和 three weeks，這些詞才具有實際含義，因為它們告訴我們說話者去了什麼地方，去了多久。看看下面的變化形式你就明白了：

I went to	/tə/	Tokyo	for /fə/	five days.
I went to	/tə/	London	for /fə/	a week.
I went to	/tə/	Mogadiscio	for /fə/	a month.
I went to	/tə/	Perth	for /fə/	two weeks.
I went to	/tə/	Kunming	for /fə/	the weekend.

與原句相比，句子結構沒有改變，改變了的是：地點（目標城市）和持續時間（five days、a week、a month、two weeks、the weekend）。因此，說話者要強調這兩個部分，讓自己表達的意思更清楚。請注意，單字 to 和 for 在這裡被弱讀成了 /tə/ 和 /fə/。這些詞的音發得非常輕，可能會聽不到。為什麼會有這種情況呢？因為我們認為這些詞是理所當然會有的：介系詞 to 表示活動的目標，介系詞 for 表示持續的時間。無論你是去雪梨還是莫斯科，永遠是 to 加地點；同樣地，無論是去五天還是一年，始終用 for 來表示。這些介系詞是必需的，所以無需強調。

2. 弱讀音節

在以上例句中，to 和 for 都被弱讀了，沒有重音。與中文不同，英語中有大量的弱讀音節。因此，華人在讀英語句子時就習慣於把每個音節都讀出來，不會弱讀。還是以句子 I went to New York for three weeks 為例，如果把 to 和 for 的音全發出來，而不弱讀，那麼整個句子就失去了節奏。

3. 語調和態度

 Track 006

英語中會用很多種不同的語調來表達驚奇、嘲弄、懷疑、諷刺或質問。語調不同，要傳達的態度也不同。

surprise = 驚奇

"John! Amazing! Wow, what are you doing here? I thought you were still in Vietnam! That's incredible! When did you get back?"

teasing = 戲弄

"So that means you don't want to go to the movies, right? You prefer to hang out at home and just revise your IELTS stuff, right, and leave me here all lonely and sad? Oh, so you do want to go? I mean, you're sure you can spare the time? Hey, I don't want to take you away from something important now..."

disbelief = 懷疑

"Now, hang on, let me get this right. You're telling me that the reason you couldn't come to school yesterday is because your poor old uncle — who's too sick to answer the phone, right? — he wanted you to read stories to him? Ah-huh. And is this poor uncle feeling better now? Could I speak to him and wish him well for the New Year?"

sarcasm = 諷刺；挖苦

"Let me get this right... You've been here all day and you haven't had time to do the dishes. Oh, I understand, sitting in front of the computer must have been so tiring, right? Yeah, the concentration. Oh yeah, of course. And I guess you had to haul your ass into the kitchen to get a beer! How exhausting for you. Yeah, yeah, I understand. No problem, no, no, no problem. I really wouldn't want you to strain yourself, you know. Please, take it easy. Don't exert yourself too much."

question = 質問

"Mr. Li, I'm asking you if you've seen this man? When? Thursday? Friday? Which? How do you know it was Friday? OK, so was he alone? Was he alone when you saw him? I'm asking you. Was he with anybody? What did he look like? Tall, short, well-built, fat, skinny? Hair colour? What was he wearing? C'mon, Mr. Li, what else did you notice about this guy? It's important. We need to find him. OK, now Mr. Li, would you recognize him again? If we showed you a photo?"

4. 連讀和停頓

 Track 007

由於中文詞語基本上都是單音節詞，所以華人在讀英語句子時，總是習慣一個詞一個詞地分開讀，而不是將它們順暢地連成一體。要想流利地説英語，就必須把詞彙流暢、自然地連在一起讀出來。換句話説，你必須學會把詞彙連續地説出來，該停頓的地方停頓，該連讀的地方要連讀。

那什麼地方該連讀呢？以子音結尾的單字，後面跟著一個首字母發母音的單字時，就應該連讀，如 cup of tea。如果我們説：Would you like a cup of tea?，單字 cup 與 of 就要連讀為 /kʌpəv/。

再舉一個雅思考試中會出現的例子。當考官介紹第二部分的考試要求時，注意他是如何使用語調和重音的，以及為了突出以下重點詞和片語是如何停頓的：topic、 one to two minutes、one minute、notes、paper、pencil、notes、topic、television program that you dislike。

Now, I'm going to give you a topic and I'd like you to talk about it for one to two minutes. Before you talk, you'll have one minute to think about what you are going to say. You can make some notes if you wish — do you understand? Good, now here's some paper and a pencil for making notes, and here's your topic. I'd like you to talk about a television program that you dislike.

5. 體會抑揚頓挫

有些學生在學習英語的過程中可能會聽說過一本由卡洛琳‧格雷厄姆（Carolyn Graham）寫的書《爵士韻律》（*Jazz Chants*）。書中介紹了諸如擊掌之類的加強節奏感的技巧，幫助學生體會英語中的抑揚頓挫。

下面請透過經典英文名著中的兩個片段來練習英語的節奏。第一段節選自 1601 年莎士比亞所著的《哈姆雷特》；第二段節選自狄更斯於 1852 年至 1853 年間出版的小說《荒涼山莊》。

 Track 008

❶ To be, or not to be, that is the question:
Whether 'tis nobler in the mind to suffer
The slings and arrows of outrageous fortune,
Or to take arms against a sea of troubles,
And by opposing end them? To die, to sleep
No more, and by a sleep to say we end
The heartache, and the thousand natural shocks
That flesh is heir to, 'tis a consummation
Devoutly to be wished. To die, to sleep
To sleep: perchance to dream, ay, there's the rub
For in that sleep of death what dreams may come
When we have shuffled off this mortal coil
Must give us pause: there's the respect
That makes calamity of so long life
For who would bear the whips and scorns of time
The oppressor's wrong, the proud man's contumely
The pangs of despised love, the law's delay
The insolence of office, and the spurns
That patient merit of the unworthy takes
When he himself might his quietus make
With a bare bodkin? Who would fardels bear
To grunt and sweat under a weary life
But that the dread of something after death
The undiscovered country from whose bourn
No traveller returns, puzzles the will
And makes us rather bear those ills we have
Than fly to others that we know not of?

Thus conscience does make cowards of us all,
And thus the native hue of resolution
Is sicklied o'er with the pale cast of thought
And enterprises of great pitch and moment
With this regard their currents turn awry
And lose the name of action. Soft you now!
The fair Ophelia!

❷ In Chancery

 Track 009

《荒涼山莊》（Bleak House）是查理斯·狄更斯所著的一部極其偉大的小説。小説諷刺了 19 世紀英國法律制度和司法機構的黑暗和殘酷。下文中提到的一些地點：倫敦法學會（Temple Bar）、橫平法院（Chancery）等都與倫敦法律界相關。在小説的開頭，狄更斯描述了 11 月份雨霧籠罩下的寒冷的倫敦。

LONDON. Michaelmas Term lately over, and the Lord Chancellor sitting in Lincoln's Inn Hall. Implacable November weather. As much mud in the streets as if the waters had but newly retired from the face of the earth, and it would not be wonderful to meet a Megalosaurus, forty feet long or so, waddling like an elephantine lizard up Holborn Hill. Smoke lowering down from chimney-pots, making a soft black drizzle, with flakes of soot in it as big as full-grown snowflakes—gone into mourning, one might imagine, for the death of the sun. Dogs, undistinguishable in mire. Horses, scarcely better; splashed to their very blinkers. Foot passengers, jostling one another's umbrellas in a general infection of ill-temper, and losing their foothold at streetcorners, where tens of thousands of other foot passengers have been slipping and sliding since the day broke (if this day ever broke), adding new deposits to the crust upon crust of mud, sticking at those points tenaciously to the pavement, and accumulating at compound interest. Fog everywhere. Fog up the river, where it flows among green aits and meadows; fog down the river, where it rolls defiled among the tiers of shipping and the waterside pollutions of a great (and dirty) city. Fog on the Essex marshes, fog on the Kentish heights. Fog creeping into the cabooses of collier-brigs; fog lying out on the yards, and hovering in the rigging of great ships; fog drooping on the gunwales of barges and small boats. Fog in the eyes and throats of ancient Greenwich pensioners, wheezing by the firesides of their wards; fog in the stem and bowl of the afternoon pipe of the wrathful skipper, down in his close cabin; fog cruelly pinching the toes and fingers of his shivering little 'prentice boy on deck. Chance people on the bridges peeping over the parapets into a nether sky of fog, with fog all round them, as if they were up in a balloon, and hanging in the misty clouds. Gas looming through the fog in divers places in the streets, much as the sun may, from the spongy fields, be seen to loom by husbandman and ploughboy. Most of the shops lighted two hours before their time—as the gas seems to know, for it has a haggard and unwilling look. The raw afternoon is rawest, and the dense fog is densest, and the muddy streets are muddiest near that leaden-headed old obstruction, appropriate ornament for the threshold of a leaden-headed old corporation, Temple Bar. And hard by Temple Bar, in Lincoln's Inn Hall, at the very heart of the fog, sits the Lord High Chancellor in his High Court of Chancery.

練習 EXERCISE

練習朗讀下面的句子，並用錄音機錄下來。然後將其與本書的 MP3 進行比較，模仿看看！

1. I invited Aunt Antonia for dinner but she didn't arrive until ten. I really didn't mind because she's so kind. While I was heating up the pasta, she switched off the telly and surfed the Internet.

2. Aunt Antonia usually has a whisky when she gets home from work—she works hard, you know, and needs to relax.

3. Some of the videos on the Internet are really very violent. Personally I try to avoid them.

4. Lily, can you please check the chicken in the kitchen, put the rice on to "cook", and turn down the heat under the veggies while I take a shower? And can you pour me a fruit juice?

5. Living in a wonderful villa on a hilltop in Venezuela, Olivia loves to dive in the deep blue sea. In the evening, she dances with her friends for hours.

6. When visitors arrive, Olivia serves them fried egg and seafood with ice cream and white wine, and dreams about Willy Wakefield, the wily property developer who makes her heart go wild.

7. What I think we need to do, guys, over the next few months, is to develop a vast communication program to validate some of the very vital advantages highlighted by your research.

8. On weekends I usually wear casual clothes but if I have to attend a job interview, I put on formal clothes — you know, jacket, tie, business shirt.

9. Sometimes when I get home from school I download a movie from the Internet and watch it. Sometimes I sit up in bed really late studying my books on international trade. But, eventually, sleep overtakes me and my attention begins to fade.

10. Do you have any advice for Vincent about the vicious attacks on his colleagues? They're very worried, you know.

11. I usually practise my saxophone in the evenings. But sometimes the neighbours get irate and bang on the walls.

12. All through that first semester, Christine went away twice a week and nobody knew exactly what she was up to. But, as far as I know, there was no one in her room on the ninth of June.

13. I sometimes travel by plane but it makes my head ache. I hardly ever travel by car. Personally, I love travelling by train. Trains are much better than planes—more comfortable, faster, and safer.

14. Tomorrow is the third Thursday of this month and I'm really hoping that some of our listeners who have sent in lovely, long letters will be the winners when we do the lucky draw!

五、同形不同音，意義有不同
Heteronyms

同形異音異義詞是指拼寫相同，但發音與含義不同的詞。英語中大概有 80 多個此類單字，現在在這裡列舉最常見的十幾個。在學習和運用這些詞時，一定要注意：不同的發音對應的是不同的含義。如果你只是讀錯了重音，也許意思就相差了十萬八千里！

1. content

Track 011

- *n.* /ˈkɑntɛnt/ 內容

  重音：在第一個音節

  例句：I find the content of this book very interesting, particularly the chapter on pronunciation.

- *adj.* / kən`tɛnt/ 滿意的，滿足的

  重音：在第二個音節

  例句：Ever since his daughter returned home, he's been happy and content.

2. desert

- *n.* /`dɛzət/ 沙漠

  重音：在第一個音節

  例句：The pilot feared that his plane would crash in the desert, miles from help.

- *v.* /dɪ`zɝt/ 遺棄，拋棄

  重音：在第二個音節

  例句：One of the worst things a soldier can do is to desert his comrades.

- 還有一個字：dessert /dɪ`zɝt/ *n.* 餐後甜點，甜品

  當然，這個詞不是 desert 的同形異音異義詞，因為拼寫中多了一個 s，但實在是長得很像所以還是列出來說明。這個字的重音在第二個音節上。

  例句：I really like their chocolate cake dessert. It's delicious.

3. excuse

- *n.* /ɪkskjus/ 藉口；理由

  重音：在第二個音節

  例句：If I don't go to class today, I have to think of a good excuse.

- *v.* /ɪk`skjuz/ 原諒；給……找理由

  重音：在第二個音節

  例句：I'm so sorry I'm late, Mr Chen. Please excuse me.

4. live

- *adj.* /laɪv/ 活的；精力充沛的；現場直播的

  例句：I really like listening to live music. I often go to a bar in Sanlitun where they have a good jazz band.

- *v.* /lɪv/ 居住；生長；活著

  例句：One day, I want to live in France. It's such a romantic place.

5. minute

Track 015

- *n.* /`mɪnɪt/ 分鐘

  重音：在第一個音節

  例句：It will only take you about five minutes to get there. It's very close.

- *adj.* /maɪˋnjut/ 極小的；極詳細的
  重音：在第二個音節
  例句：The crystal contains minute traces of sulphur.

6. present

- *n. & adj.* /ˋprɛznt/ *n.* 禮物 *adj.* 到場的；現在的
  重音：在第一個音節
  例句：Are you going to buy a Christmas present for Alison?
  It's easy to use the present tense in English.
- *v.* /prɪˋzɛnt/ 頒發；展現；上映
  重音：在第二個音節
  例句：Our Committee would like to present Mr. Lee with a gold watch in recognition of everything he has done for us over the past three years.

7. polish

- *v.* /ˋpɑlɪʃ/ 擦亮；修改
  重音：在第一個音節
  例句：If you are going to an interview, then you should polish your shoes.
- *adj.* /ˋpolɪʃ/ 波蘭的，波蘭人的
  重音：在第一個音節
  例句：The film *Danton*, about the French Revolution, was made by the Polish film director Andrzej Wajda.

8. project

- *n.* /ˋprɑdʒɛkt/ 項目；工程
  重音：在第一個音節
  例句：The boss has asked me to work on a new project.
- *v.* /prəˋdʒɛkt/ 預計；放映；傳播
  重音：在第二個音節
  例句：Try to project your voice so that the people in the back row can hear you.

9. record

- *v.* /rɪˋkɔrd/ 記錄；錄製
  重音：在第二個音節
  例句：Grab your recording device and record yourself saying the following sentences.

- *n.* /ˈrɛkəd/ 紀錄，檔案；履歷；唱片

  重音：在第一個音節

  例句：In August 2008, at the Beijing Olympic Games, the Jamaican team featuring Usain Bolt set a world record for the 4x100 relay.

10. row

- *n. & v.* /ro/ *n.* 行，排，列 *v.* 劃（船）

  例句：Please ask the children to line up in rows.

  He has been around boats all his life. He can row really well.

- *n. & v.* /raʊ/ 爭吵，吵架

  例句：Last night the couple that lives next door to me had a huge row. They were shouting at each other. I could hear almost every word they said. It was awful.

11. use

- *n.* /jus/ 使用；用途

  例句：This mobile phone has a lot of different uses: camera, calendar, street finder etc.

- *v.* /juz/ 使用；耗費

  例句：Which website do you use for your travel bookings?

12. wind

- *n.* /wɪnd/ 風

  例句：The wind blew my hat off.

- *v.* /waɪnd/ 纏繞；轉動；蜿蜒

  例句：The fishing rod bent violently. I tried to wind in the line but it was impossible.

六、考官不會介意你的口音
How Important Is Accent?

　　據估計，世界上說英語的人有 15 億，說中文的人有 11 億。這兩個資料背後隱藏的最大區別是以其為母語的人數：在 15 億說英語的人中，英語是母語的僅佔25%，而中文是母語的人高達 11 億人的 83%。這表示有很多母語不是英語的人都會說英語。在工作中，你可能會和美國人、英國人或澳洲人等母語人士用英語進行交談，也可能會和巴基斯坦人、德國人等非母語人士進行交談。你的目的不是為了模仿他們說話，而是要達到真正的溝通和理解。

主考雅思的考官也一樣，來自於世界各地說英語的國家，不只是美國、英國、加拿大和澳洲，也有一些來自愛爾蘭、尚比亞、紐西蘭、印度和奈吉利亞。因此，他們的口音也各有差異。

當你進入考場時，請記住，坐在你對面的雅思考官不會介意你的口音聽起來比較像美國英語、英國英語還是格拉斯哥英語。也就是說，你的口音並不重要；重要的是，你要讓他們知道你在說什麼。

七、來自世界各地的聲音
Pronunciation Samples

請聽聽看以下發音範例，他們的口音來自世界各地。他們所說的內容是第二部分可能會考到的話題。其中有一些是華人，還有一些是母語為英語的人。仔細聆聽，用心體會不同口音之間的差異，感受語言的多樣魅力吧！

1. Feeling Angry (US Pronunciation)
Speaker: Stan Seiden (US)
Researcher & Improviser

 Track 023

I grew up in a suburban town called Wayland, Massachusetts, and my sister and I shared a bathroom as we grew up. This was fine. In the mornings we would go and I would perhaps take my shower first, or maybe she would take her shower first, but we had very different habits when it came to showering. I would carry my clothes into the bathroom, shower, dry off and then put them on. My sister would go take a shower, then take the towel with her back to her bedroom where she would then change her clothes. To each his own, that's fine, but my sister had this other habit of, after drying off, leaving her towel in her bedroom. This is fine as well. We both had our own towels. However, the next day my sister would go back to the bathroom, take a shower and discover that her towel was not there because it was sitting, damp, on the floor of her bedroom. So, being resourceful, she would simply take my towel which was sitting on the rack and use that as well. I am happy to share my belongings with my sister but, almost without fail, my sister would then take my towel into her bedroom as well and leave that towel lying on the floor of her bedroom. Not to fear, we had a linen closet in the bathroom with backup towels, so I would simply grab one of those towels, use it and hang it on the rack to dry, and sure enough, come the next day, that towel too would be missing from the bathroom, lying on the floor of my sister's bedroom. After a few days of this had gone by, and I had already spoken to my sister several times — which is an important step in conflict resolution, you must first initiate contact with the conflictee and discuss the problem with them — I would get fed up and need a way of getting revenge. So I would travel to her bedroom, collect all the towels, return them to the bathroom, and then go back to her bedroom, remove all the sheets from her bed, and then find a place in the house to hide them. This seemed like a good idea but the kink in the plan was that I had a bunk bed in my bedroom and my sister would simply spend the next night sleeping on my top bunk, thwarting all of my plans and meaning that I now had to share both my towels and my bedroom with my sister.

2. A Business I Would Like to Start
   (UK Pronunciation)
Speaker: Chris Defty (UK)
Businesswoman & Writer

 Track 024

What I would like to do is set up my own furniture business, importing furniture from Europe into China. I think there's a lot of interest amongst people here in China in things from Europe, historical things, so there's a lot of good quality furniture that was produced over the last 400 years that could be brought here to China and I think would be greatly appreciated. So what I would like to do is to set up a link with an antique centre in the UK which already sells furniture to other parts of the world, then I'll go over there and find the kind of furniture that I think would do really well here in China and arrange for it to come over here and try to sell it through established shops, antique furniture shops here, that are already based here. I think there are probably going to be some problems with doing this. I think perhaps one of the biggest problems is importing older things into China because with older wood you're not really sure whether there are some insects inside it, or there are some problems, so you'd have to make sure that the wood was properly treated in order to bring it through Customs, to make sure it was safe to actually bring it into China. So I can see that that might be a problem but I don't think that there would be any big problems in selling it because I think people are very interested in this sort of thing.

3. Book (UK Pronunciation)
Speaker: Chris Defty (UK)
Businesswoman & Writer

 Track 025

There are loads of books that have made an impression on me. I could go through lots of works of literature and talk about how I enjoyed the characters and so on. But, there's another kind of book, a book that's made a very big impression on me for a long time. It's a book called *Mrs Beeton's Book of Household Management*. Now, when I first moved away from home, had my own place to live in, my mum bought me this book. It's a huge book, very very heavy, and half of it is a cookery book with recipes to show you how to cook lots of traditional British food. But the other half of it is about how to run your home. It tells you, for example, that if you live in a cold place, where the water freezes in the winter, you need to put salt in the toilet to stop it freezing in the winter time. It will tell you how to write letters to different people. It will tell you how to find somebody to help you clean your house. It will tell you, if you've got something wrong with the roof of your house, and you need someone to come and fix it, it will explain how you can give instructions to people, how you can check that they've done a good job, and how you can pay them. So it will explain all the things that you need to know when you start to live in your own home. So anytime I had a problem I could go to this book, I could look up any of the problems that I had and then I could deal with them without having to pay somebody to tell me what I should do, or without me having to ring somebody up and ask them what to do. So I suppose it gave me a bit more independence and it's been a very useful book and I still have it on my shelf. Actually, I still have it in my iPad.

4. Another Culture (UK Pronunciation)
Speaker: Paul Creasy (UK)
Teacher & Comedian

I used to live in the Czech Republic, in Prague, and I learned several things about Czech people while I was there. One of the things I learned was that people like it when you take off your shoes before you go into their houses. But they don't just like it; it's considered something that is incredibly impolite not to do. The only problem is that, in Czech they say, when you go into their houses, to be polite they say, you don't have to take off your shoes, which can be a problem for foreigners who've just arrived in the Czech Republic, because it leads to a lot of foreigners embarrassing themselves in front of their Czech girlfriend or boyfriend's family by walking dirt all over their houses because the people have just told them that they don't have to take off their shoes. Another thing is that there's a famous Czech dumpling that they serve that looks like a, a sort of a handkerchief, a napkin, that you would get in a restaurant. One businessman once embarrassed himself by being served one of these, thinking that it was actually a napkin and kind of unfolding it, and wiping his face with it... um, which kind of embarrassed him in front of his new Czech business partners as it was the first time that he had met them in the Czech Republic. Another thing is that there's a famous Czech author called Milan Kundera who is very very popular abroad but he's not popular at all in the Czech Republic because of the fact that he has kind of renounced his Czech citizenship and decided that he is more French than he is Czech. So, being in a conversation with a Czech person, obviously you are going to try to bring up Czech people that you like and admire. Um, if you bring up Milan Kundera, then the Czech person you are talking to will probably think that you are being incredibly rude and spiteful about Czech people.

5. Furniture (Canadian Pronunciation)

Speaker: Penny Colville (Canada)

Editor & Educational Technologist

 Track 027

Well, I wish I could talk about the kind of furniture that I really like and where I bought it and how much I'm enjoying it, but the fact is I rent a furnished apartment and therefore all of the furniture, or almost all of it, belongs to the landlord. I thought I had the jump on getting some control on that when I realized that the flat had no furniture in it at the time of rental and my landlord assured me that I would get to select the furniture, or have some say in the furniture that he was going to put in the apartment. And I gave him some basic requirements and one of these was a couch. So he went off to shop for the couch by himself, communicating with his wife by cellphone picture and with me by cellphone picture, and he sent this horrible, this picture of this horrible, you know, puffy, floral, chintz couch and not just one but two couches and a huge armchair to match, and I'm in this diminutive space and my apartment can only really take so much. I texted him immediately and said "No no no, this is overstuffed. I want something clean and modern and low, and can't you just get me something like that?" "Nope, no". The three items of furniture were delivered. They barely fit inside the living room. I had to move the armchair to another room. I got used to it eventually, but for the first couple of weeks, honestly, I felt like I was in my grandmother's house with all of these large and threatening-looking flowers beaming up at me from every, every seat in the room.

6. Game (US Pronunciation)
Speaker: Sara Burt (US)
Teacher & Actress

 Track 028

A game that I remember playing in my childhood was playing House. We would just say "Let's play House", and someone would pretend to be the Mum or the Dad, and then someone would be the baby, or the child. I guess I would say that this wasn't necessarily my favourite game, because it got old really fast, because kids aren't always that creative, and they're always falling into the same, like whiney-baby role, or scolding mother. But what I really enjoyed about playing House was when we had special materials to play with, so for example outside, in the playground, when there was a sandbox, we would play with sand and make mud pies, or actual mud, and then sometimes we'd also play in the playground structures themselves, so there'd be metal structures and they looked more like a house, or something, and then it became a little more physical as well. Then we got more away from the play-acting and the typical roles that were not so creative, I thought, and we actually made something with the mud pies. What I really would have liked was a tree house. I always dreamed of having a tree house but there weren't so many trees around where I grew up so I guess it would have been hard to make a tree house. And the best House experience I had, I guess, playing House, was when we had a big box, especially refrigerator boxes, those were the best. So of course they didn't come around very often, but when we had a very big nice refrigerator box, we would be able to make it into a clubhouse. It could be just a house, but sometimes we'd make it into a clubhouse and we'd cut windows, and use markers and decorate on the outside, and it would be a totally kids-only world, a place where adults wouldn't go, and where we could let our imaginations run wild and create a fantasy. And we'd have rules, like rules about only having fun, and of course no adults. And we practiced roles of leadership and everything would be fun. So it would've been nice if it were a tree house, I always liked that the best, but the best place was the clubhouse where I had the most fun.

7. Law (US Pronunciation)

Speaker: Stan Seiden (US)

Researcher & Improviser

 Track 029

I want to talk about making a law in my apartment building. My apartment building has two elevators. Technically, it has three elevators but no one has ever seen the third elevator work and, to be honest, we're not even sure there's an elevator behind those doors. It might be just a cave. However, the problem with these two elevators is that they're not on the same system, meaning that if you push one button in the lobby calling for the elevator, it will only call one elevator. If you want to call both elevators, you have to push both buttons. The problem is, almost everyone in our apartment building thinks that they should push both buttons, no matter where they're going or which floor they're on. This is usually fine but it means that, if I am standing in the lobby and both elevators are on floor 10, and someone on floor 20 is in a hurry and pushes both buttons, I have to sit and watch as both elevators go all the way up to floor 20 so that one person can get into one elevator and then wait for both elevators to come back down because, chances are, I got tired of waiting and pushed both buttons myself. Therefore, I think my apartment building desperately needs a rule where you are only allowed to push one elevator button. It's up to you which button you push. Hopefully you'll make the right choice and you won't have to wait too long, but it's also possible you'll push the button just to discover that even though the elevator was just one floor below you, someone in the lobby pushed it first and now you have to wait for it to go all the way down and come all the way back up. Yes, that may be frustrating, but it's far less frustration than everyone down in the lobby is feeling as they watch both elevators go all the way up to the top of the building and come all the way back down again. I'm not entirely sure what the punishment should be for violating this law. Maybe it should be that you don't get to ride the elevator for a week. Maybe it should be that you have to share your apartment with everyone who you made wait for an extra couple of minutes or for, I don't know, a day or two. Whatever the punishment, it should be very strict because I think it is very important that this law can be enforced effectively, improving the lives of everyone in my apartment building.

8. My Personality (Canadian Pronunciation)

Speaker: Penny Colville (Canada)

Editor & Educational Technologist

 Track 030

I suppose I'd like to think that one good part of my personality is optimism, that I tend to have an optimistic character. But I wrestle with this, because on other occasions I think that it's not really optimism; it's recklessness or it's blindness, or it's not tempered with enough realism, and in that case I call it my fatal optimism. The worst parts of being too optimistic are of course that you don't give up on things when really you should give up on things, and redirect your energy along a much more fruitful path, and then what you're dealing with is not just optimism but a kind of stubbornness, a determination to make things work that really you have no business wasting your time on. You should draw the line sooner and, what do they call it? "cut your losses", and remain optimistic, but by moving on to another and better objective. I don't know where I get the optimism from, but I know that it has contributed to other good things like endurance. I'm not a fast swimmer; I'm not a fancy swimmer, but I can swim long distances; I'm an endurance swimmer. And endurance is — particularly when you're in difficult modern times like we are now, or when you're in a new culture, or when things aren't going well — endurance is always a good quality and I think optimism is a good part of that, and it might be, maybe, part of a British streak in my character. My father was always very positive and expected the best and generally got it.

9. A Practical Skill (US Pronunciation)

Speaker: Sara Burt (US)

Teacher & Actress

 Track 031

Baking is something that I learned when I was pretty young. And I was probably younger than most kids when I learned how to bake and cook because my mum was special. Most mums are very cautious with their kids in the kitchen and would never let them independently experiment with baking and cooking due to all the dangerous things like the heat source, like the stove top and the actual oven where you could burn yourself. And I did burn myself several times, although I think everybody does in the process of learning how to cook and stuff. And another thing is, you know, knives that are sharp. And the last thing is the mess that you can make. So most mums wouldn't necessarily be patient about their kids making a big mess in the kitchen, or else they would hover over their kids, and make sure that they were cleaning up after each little step. Well, my mum was special in both regards, in two regards at least, because she let me cook basically whenever I wanted to, and she didn't hover over me, she just kind of let me make my big mess, and I think she had to nag me probably to clean up, and then she probably had to finish helping me clean up afterwards. I probably didn't do a good job, but I'm very grateful to this day to the opportunity that she gave me because it's become a hobby for me my whole entire life and I enjoy cooking to this day. And what attracted me to cooking was partly because I just love creating things and I like making things for other people, but more than that was probably that I just love to eat and I especially love to eat sweet things. And, you know, mothers wanna feed their kids green vegetables and healthy stuff, and cookies are not healthy, especially the favourite cookie, the chocolate chip cookie which is probably what I made the most and what people rave over the most and loved the most in America. So I was indulgent and I wanted to eat my sweet food and I didn't mind making a mess and I was very lucky to have a mum that allowed me to do this and my friends today are lucky that they can come to my house and enjoy my good baking and cookies.

10. Restaurant (French Pronunciation)
Speaker: Norah Cotterall-Debay (France)
University Student in the UK

 *Track 032*

I like going to the restaurant beside my high school and not just because it's so close. Actually, there are a bunch of reasons why I like it. Well, first off, the food is really not expensive, which is a pretty important consideration when you're a student, right? Well, and even if the food isn't always the best quality, or made from the best nutrients, there's nevertheless a huge choice of dishes. There are so many different things on the menu. Um, I reckon I could go there for a year and I still would not get to the end of it! Because it's like a popular restaurant, you never feel uncomfortable there. They have small tables but they are not too close together. Um, I think they redid the decoration about a year ago and now everything is red, and there's a kind of glitter substance on the table tops which looks really cool and they also made a bigger window so you can see out into the street better. I go there two or three times a week with my friends. It's noisy too, but in a nice friendly sort of a way, like you tuck yourselves around the table and you can eat great food and you can chat and have fun and feel very relaxed. And the staff are super nice as well, they're always smiling and easy-going, and they always greet us when we go in. Um, for example , I remember once the waitress advised me to order a particular dish. It was *Disanxian*, because I really did not know what to have and I thought it was delicious. So I guess they really know how to treat their customers and make you feel welcome, and that's another reason why I really like it.

11. Sporting Event (UK Pronunciation)

Speaker: Paul Creasy (UK)

Comedian

 Track 033

A sporting event that I haven't attended that I think is the most important sporting event in the world, and the one that I would like to go and see the most, is definitely the World Cup final. By the World Cup final I mean the football World Cup final. By the football World Cup final I mean the soccer World Cup final, as Americans would say. I feel like it's the best sporting event in the world, still. Now, in football, there's the European Champions League, which has kind of overtaken the World Cup as the competition that perhaps people and the players consider the most important, um, probably because of money, they get paid so much nowadays. But I feel like the World Cup is still the most important in terms of prestige, because it's playing for your country; it's playing in front of millions of people worldwide, and it's playing for the hopes and dreams of an entire nation which I still think is the ultimate accolade in football. And I'd love to go there and know that the events that were happening before me were something that was going to be kind of written into folklore for years to come. People still talk about World Cup finals of the past, as if they were family events that happened to them during their childhood. Many of my strongest memories from when I was younger are of football matches and the effect that they had on me. Watching the England team over the years has been often a painful experience, occasionally glorious but mostly disappointing, something that has kind of had a massive effect on the way that I see the world. So I feel like if I was going to go to the World Cup final and England were involved in it, number one they would probably lose but I'm used to that happening anyway. But, number two, it would be something that I would never forget because the idea of the entire hopes and dreams of a country being played out before the world is an amazing thing.

12. Wild Animal (New Zealand Speaker)

Speaker: Daniel Cotterall-Debay (New Zealand)
IELTS Examiner, Consultant, Trainer & Actor

 Track 034

The wild animal I like best is the tiger because I think they're just magnificent animals. They look superb. I think they look incredibly beautiful, the beautiful coat they have on them. They have superb muscle tone, and like all felines they move with such grace, and of course there's that sense of incredible power, because they have such strong legs with great big paws on the end. Um, I think big tigers weigh up to about 200kg, or maybe more. They're a huge animal, much bigger than a lion, incredible looking. They're so graceful. They have that aerodynamic look, and that sense of silent power because tigers don't make much noise when they move through the jungle, you know. They don't lie sprawled in the sun like a lion in Africa. They're much more elegant-looking animals. I've visited the park in Harbin where they have a lot of Siberian tigers, and you can actually feed them which is pretty incredible. I forget how many they have there, about 200 I think, and they really are amazing. I mean, they're big, but so graceful in the way they move, and they sit there so, or lie there, or stand there so still and self-contained, except if there's food of course. Yeah, in Harbin, you can actually feed them. You go in a kind of little bus with bars on the sides and you can put, for example, chickens down a shoot and the tigers grab them and eat them. It's pretty scary, actually. They've got some white tigers there as well but my favourite is the Siberian tiger...

"第6章"

高分考生面面觀

第一節 高分考生應知識全面
The "I"DEAL Candidate Is "I"nformed

表現優秀的考生都會時時刻刻關注世界各地的時事，所以考試時才總是有話可說。

▶一、讓考官告訴你：要關心世界新聞
Know What's Happening in the World

發生在世界各地的事非常容易出現在考試當中。想要得到高分，考生不但要英文好，更要關注世界各地的新聞，而不是只注意自己國家發生了什麼事。別忘了，考官大多來自英語系國家，閱讀的是外國報紙和網站，所以雖然他們對發生在你的國家的事有點興趣，但也一定會對歐洲與其他英語系國家發生的事情感興趣。他們會看許多國外的電影、發生在中東的消息、發生在各地的天災人禍等等。也就是說，如果你的話題要和考官搭上線，那這些世界各地的新聞你就非知道不可啦。

從我們這些考官的角度來看，瞭解時事新聞對雅思考生很重要。要了解這些新聞，對話的內容才會新鮮、生動。遺憾的是，現在有很多考生忙著增進英文能力，根本沒空去管時事新聞，也不太知道周遭世界發生的一切。這樣對考雅思是非常不利的！考官希望可以看到你侃侃而談各地的災難事件、體育新聞或娛樂新聞，最好可以從比較特別的角度切入，例如大家談起周杰倫時，常會說很喜歡他的音樂，但這樣的內容考官都已經聽過幾百次，已經不太感興趣了，所以如果你在談周杰倫時，說到他的表演、父母的離異、小時候得過的疾病等等，考官就能感受到你真心地對這個話題感興趣，而在心裡給你大加分。

還要注意：考官大部分是英語系國家的人士，不見得會說中文，而且大多數人到 65 歲之間，所以你可以想像他們感興趣的話題大概會屬於哪個方面。例說你喜歡五月天、陳綺貞，就得先跟他們解釋一下五月天是什麼，而不是歡他們，否則考官可能會聽得霧煞煞，不知道你到底在講一個樂團、一個名叫五月天的人。

▶二、在第三部分展現全面的知識
Informed in Part Three

　　現在來說說看如何在第三部分展現全面的知識吧！我們來看看一個範例。下面這個例子中的考生在第二部分的討論中已經展示了語言的流暢度、詞彙和文法，除此外還傳達了大量的資訊（見本書 p.060）。在第三部分，考官想延續考生在第二部分留給他的好印象，看看考生在問答一些更寬泛、更抽象的問題時的表現。

考官： Well, we've been talking about a news story that interested you, concerning Fukushima, and now I'd like to ask you some more general questions in relation to this. Let's consider first of all access to the news. Do you think it's easy to access news these days?

嗯，我們已經討論了你感興趣的有關福島的新聞。現在我想問幾個與這方面相關的問題。首先，我們來談談獲得新聞的途徑。你覺得現在瞭解新聞容易嗎？

考生： Definitely. We all have mobile phones. People are constantly online. There's a whole bunch of news websites that you can click on at any time of the day or night. So we can access the news really really easily and I think that's, um, that's a big change from when I was a kid.

考官點評　由於很多能給人們帶來影響的事物也會給人們的生活和生活態度帶來改變，所以當遇到這樣的問題時，就從我們周圍的生活說起，一定就會有話可說。bunch、news websites 和 click 這些詞彙都用得很好。

考官：What was the situation like back then, when you were a kid?
那你小時候的情形是怎樣的？

考生：Well, I remember when I was just about maybe ten years old, my dad would come home with the newspaper and sit down in a chair with a cup of tea, and read the news and make comments to my mum and, you know, take his time over it, think about it, whereas nowadays we do everything much faster... we get news from Weibo, maybe just a flash or an image or even a video clip, and then we maybe tweet that to someone else to test it and find out what's going on. We just don't have enough time to sit back and digest the news the way my dad did.

考官點評　tweet 和 digest 都是讓人印象深刻的詞彙。語意連貫，複合句把握得非常好。在回答童年的問題時，考生勾勒出了一幅場景，但並沒有回答那時的消息是不是靈通。

考官：Why is that? Is it because the pace of life is too fast these days? Or because the news is too complicated?
為什麼會這樣呢？是因為當今的生活節奏太快了嗎？還是因為新聞太複雜了？

考生：Mmm, maybe both, actually. I think that the pace of life is very fast in China. There's a lot of pressure on people to make money or succeed in their studies or whatever. So they have a lot on their plate. And a lot of the news, yeah, it's complicated, but it also seems to be very distant from our lives, you know. There's no real connection. I mean, if the news is about the elections in Russia, frankly I don't know anything about the factions or the parties there, and also it doesn't really have any impact on my life so I'm basically going to tune it out. And, anyway, maybe some of the information is wrong, or inaccurate.

考官點評　語言通順連貫，文法準確，have a lot on their plate 和 tune it out 用得很好。由於該考生的知識面非常廣，所以能夠提到俄羅斯選舉。這些例子能證實他的觀點，也有助於他流利地説下去，並用了專業的詞彙，如 factions。

考官：**You mentioned news being inaccurate. Do you think that, in general, the news media are objective?**

你提到了新聞的不準確性。總體來說，你認為新聞媒體客觀嗎？

考生：Actually, no. I think that there's always — aaagh, what's the word? Bias! Yeah, bias, bias in the news. I mean, if it's the Japanese media writing about China, for example about the South China Sea and the Diaoyu Islands, then the way they write and what they say is going to be influenced by historical events that occurred for one hundred years. But not just in Asia. I mean, when the US and the American press reports on China, then there are a lot of beliefs about China, or even fears about China, that influence the way they report things. So they're not objective. They have their own agenda. And so, you have to be aware of that, I think, you have to be aware that the news is inevitably biased. It's never objective.

考官點評 該考生的知識面很廣。他能談古論今，如目前的釣魚島問題，從而論證了自己覺得新聞報導難免偏頗的觀點。在文法方面，考生對於長句子的運用很準確。在詞彙方面，使用了 bias、objective 和副詞 inevitably 等讓人印象深刻的詞彙。但是，for one hundred years 這一說法有問題，應該用 over the last one hundred years。

考官：**So you don't think the American media report accurately on China?**

所以你認為美國媒體對於中國的報導並不準確？

考生：No, like I said, they have their own agenda. I mean, whether it's the new aircraft carrier last year, or articles about the Chinese yuan, they are always trying to present their view. It's not objective at all.

考官點評 該考生在時事方面掌握的大量資訊（無論是航空母艦還是人民幣的新聞）都可以有力地證明自己的觀點。該考生可得 8 分。

考官：**Thank you very much. That is the end of the speaking test.**

非常感謝。口語考試到此結束。

第二節 高分考生應與眾不同
The I"D"EAL Candidate Is "D"istinctive

考官每個週末要考 30 位考生，其中 85%～ 90% 的考生年齡都在 18 ～ 25 歲之間。這表示考官會不斷見到生活和學習經歷類似的考生。也就是說，你必須要更加努力才能脫穎而出，才能與眾不同。

你在很多方面都可以與眾不同，你的穿著打扮、心情和態度等都行。但請記住，這是場語言考試。所以最重要的是你要在語言能力和想法上表現得與眾不同，甚至是你對話題的解讀要與眾不同。

下面我們來看一個第二部分的考生範例，該話題的題目是：A Friend of Yours，話題卡上的描述是：You should say who this friend is, how you met, what you do together and why this friend is important to you.

該考生在卡片上寫下了下面三個詞。

Macy
----
not aggressive
----
trust

Actually, the friend I want to talk about is a sheep, called Macy. Not a real sheep, she's a toy, a fluffy toy, you know, about this big. Macy and I met about two years ago, in a shop, the day I broke up with my boyfriend. So I bought her... She was so cute, and I needed somebody to talk to, somebody soft, somebody I could

考官點評

考官聽到這樣的回答可能會驚訝，但更多的是驚喜。該考生擁有描述幻想的語言。

trust. So Macy entered my life... yay! Actually, I call her Macy. It's her English name, cos at that time I had just started studying fashion and I really admired a designer from South China called Ma Ke. It sounds a bit like Macy.

What do we do together? We just hang out, especially in the evening. We listen to music together. I tell her about what happened to me during the day. I tell her my secrets, and she listens. She's a great listener, you know, and sometimes I put my head on her, like a pillow, and she's very soft and warm and she never complains. Not like my ex-boyfriend! Macy is much more patient and mature!

Yeah, Macy is really important to me... I remember one time, when I was visiting my aunt in Wuxi, I left her behind when I took the train back to Shanghai. I really missed her! I had to call my aunt, and wait a week before my uncle came to Shanghai and gave her back. Ummm, also Macy is very fashionable. You know, she's a Yang, like people born in the Year of the Sheep, so that means she's quiet, and elegant, and also Yang people try very hard not to hurt your feelings. Just like me, they need to feel loved and protected! They're maybe not very good about big decisions—not about love anyway—but actually deep down they are very passionate!

文法：不僅用了一般現在式和一般過去式，也用了過去完成式（I had just started）、過去進行式（I was visiting）。另外，還用了情態動詞（somebody I could trust）和動名詞（studying fashion）。

文法準確性：很準確。兩分鐘內沒有出現一個文法錯誤。

詞彙：用詞豐富、準確，用了很多形容詞，如 fluffy、mature、patient、elegant、fashionable 和 passionate，還用了一些動詞片語，如 I broke up with my boyfriend 和 leave something behind。介系詞和名詞的用法也都正確。該考生的得分在 7 分至 8 分之間。

第三節 高分考生應融入對話
The ID"E"AL Candidate Is "E"ngaged

　　能夠融入對話的考生不僅僅只是願意表達或者能夠表達自己的想法，而是更甚於此。即使他們意識到考官可能會不同意自己的觀點，他們依然會堅持。這樣的考生喜歡認識不同的人，並樂於與他們交談。當自己的想法受到質疑時，他們能夠想到其他辦法為自己的觀點找到充分的理由，並用例子來證明。

　　融入與考官的討論表示要準備好表達自己的觀點，並為自己的觀點辯護。記住，雙方的交流永遠沒有正確答案。如果你覺得考官並不同意你的看法，不要擔心，也不要退縮。如果你能夠從容地為自己的觀點辯護，考官會更加尊重和讚賞你，而你的分數自然也會提高。

　　下面我們就來看一個這樣的成功案例，該名考生正是由於在第三部分表現突出而提高了自己的分數。第二部分的話題是「可以使世界更美好的職業」，而他的回答是想成為銀行家。由於他在這一部分犯了許多詞彙和文法錯誤，所以考官將其分數基本定為 5 分。到了第三部分，考官問了一個似乎與考生觀點不一致的問題，考生堅持了自己的觀點，並給出了很好的回答。這樣就有助於考官提高他的分數。

考官：**Well, we've been talking about a job that you think makes the world a better place, being a banker, and now I'd like to ask you some more general questions related to this. Let's consider first of all the role of banks. What do you think is the role of banks?**

嗯，我們剛討論了什麼工作能讓世界變得更加美好，你的回答是銀行家。現在我想問一些與這個話題相關的問題。首先，我們來談談銀行的功能。你認為銀行的功能是什麼？

考生：I think banks are very important. They have a key role to us. All of us need banks. I mean, for common people, you receive your salary and you don't want to keep it in your safe. You can access the money easily, because banks have machines everywhere for cash. Also they can give you a credit card to make your life more convenient.

考官點評　語言很流利，但有一些文法錯誤：第一句中的 to us 多餘。另外，在英語中，我們形容「普通人」時一般用 ordinary people，而不用 common people。So you put... 一句中的 put 後少了代名詞。is safe 前應加 it。

考官：What about companies? What kind of services do banks provide to companies?

那麼公司呢？銀行為公司提供什麼樣的服務？

考生：Companies have money going out all the time. For example, to buy raw materials and to pay their staff. At the same time they are asking money to their customers. So, to make everything smooth... and keep a balance, the bank gives the money so the company can operate easily — what it wants to pay and what it wants to receive. So, for companies, credit from banks is very important.

考官點評　此處的回答比剛才好。考生很篤定地談到了購買原材料和給員工發薪水的問題。雖然文法和詞彙方面還是有些錯誤（比如 gives 應是 provides；asking money to their customers 應該是 requesting payment from their customers），但考生融入了討論之中。

考官：You've been talking about the positive role that banks play. But don't banks also have a negative side? For example, weren't banks largely responsible for the financial crisis in 2008?

你剛才談到了銀行起到的正面作用。但銀行也有負面的一面吧？例如，銀行對 2008 年的金融危機不就應該負主要責任嗎？

考生：Well, I know that in the US and the UK, some banks bankrupted themselves during that crisis. My professor told us about a bank in the UK called RBS. They made so many mistake. It was a big problem for the UK Government.

考官點評　除了 mistake 應該用複數形式外，沒有其他文法錯誤。動詞時態也很準確。用詞準確，只有一處不恰當，bankrupted themselves 應該是 went bankrupt。

考官：**OK, take the case of RBS. Weren't the managers of that bank paid massive salaries? Isn't that part of the problem?**
好的，以蘇格蘭皇家銀行為例。銀行的經理不是拿很高的薪水嗎？難道這不是部分原因嗎？

考生：Maybe, but in China, the bankers are not paid that much. In China the regulations are more strict. There is not the same difference in the amount of salaries.

考官點評　考官似乎還想繼續追問 2008 年金融危機中銀行應承擔的責任。但考生並沒有緊張，平靜地應對了挑戰，有力地維護了自己的觀點。more strict 應改為 stricter。

考官：**A lot of people in the West say that the financial crisis was largely due to the greed of bankers and the finance industry as a whole. What do you think about that?**
很多西方人說金融危機的主要原因是銀行家及金融業的貪婪。你怎麼看？

考生：I don't agree with that. It's true that traders who play on the money markets can get big bonus. But in fact that bonus that you get is justified because you have to be able to make the money first; you have to find the good deals. If you find the good deals, you can get the bonus. So it's fair.

考官點評 文法準確，除了第一處的 bonus 應改用複數形式 bonuses。為了給自己的觀點辯護，考生甚至還使用了條件句，回答得非常連貫。不管考官是否認同他的觀點，也必須承認他回答得很好。

考官：**Yes, but those traders... I read that in the US the finance industry accounted for something like 40% of all corporate profits in 2008. Is that normal?**

是的，但這些經紀人……我有讀到，在 2008 年的美國，金融行業的利潤佔所有企業利潤總額的 40%。你覺得這正常嗎？

考生：It's not like this in China. Here we are a manufacturing country. We make so many things for export and also for our domestic needs. Take the car industry for example. Maybe the car industry makes pollution in the cities but at the same time the car industry is very important for the economy in China. For common people, it is a big day when they buy a car. For me, too, because my girlfriend will be happy. If people buy a car, money will circulate through the national economy, and that is good because it is activity, and activity is going better. These days, people don't buy a car with cash money. They pay with their bank card. So that shows how important the banks are to, to make money flow through.

考官點評 考官的話：Is that normal ？顯然表示他持有不同的看法。但從他的角度來看，考生並沒有退縮。即使他是間接地進行了回答，但他自信地表達了自己的看法，並舉例說明。文法和詞彙方面還是有些錯誤（比如用 progress 比 going better 要好一點），但回答流利、投入。正因為如此，他才能夠用上這些詞：manufacturing、domestic needs、car industry、pollution、national economy、flow、economic activity。

　　由於該考生在前一部分的回答中出現了多處錯誤，有可能只能得 5 分。但他在第三部分的良好發揮使他最終拿到了 6 分。

考官：**Thank you very much. That is the end of the speaking test.**

非常感謝。口語考試到此結束。

第四節 高分考生應思路流暢
The IDE"A"L Candidate Is "A"ble to Run with an Idea

　　思路要流暢的意思就是說：可以用生活中的例子或新聞中看到的事件來證實和闡述自己的觀點，而不是只是簡單背誦陳詞濫調和老生常談的內容。討論時，你需要在對話中注入一些活力、色彩和例子。

一、在第三部分無法展現流暢思路的案例分析
Not Able to Run with an Idea in Part Three

　　下面來看看一個考生的例子。這個考生沒有充分利用好第三部分的討論機會。注意看評論部分。

考官：**Well, we have been talking about a book you enjoyed reading, *Gossip Girl*, and I'd like now to discuss with you one or two more general questions related to this. Let's consider first of all owning books. Why do you think people like to own books?**

嗯，我們剛談論了你喜歡讀的一本書：《花邊教主》。我想問你一兩個關於這方面的問題。首先來談一下藏書。你認為人們為什麼喜歡藏書？

> **考生：**Well, I think that maybe they like to reread them, so it's convenient to have them right there in their house. They can put them on the shelf and look at them. And maybe it gives them a sense of fulfillment. But personally I prefer e-books.

考官點評　用到了 reread、shelf、e-book 和 sense of fulfillment 等很好的表達。回答流利、連貫。目前來看，該考生 7 分有望。

考官：**OK, let's talk about e-books. What are the advantages of e-books?**

好的，那我們來談談電子書吧。電子書的優點是什麼？

考生：They are very convenient. I can read them on my phone when I am in the subway. You can download them very easy. You know, that is a big advantage for us nowadays.

考官點評　有一處小的文法錯誤（easy 應改為副詞 easily）。其他方面還可以，只是回答太短了。如果考生能再舉個例子會好得多。

考官：**Do you think that e-books will replace traditional books, that traditional books will eventually disappear?**

你認為電子書會取代傳統書籍嗎？傳統書籍最終會消失嗎？

考生：Maybe. I think that can happen. But some people like old books. Especially old people, they are not very modern. And maybe those old people are not so familiar to technology so it is more difficult to them to use it.

考官點評　回答內容過於平淡。文法錯誤率不高，familiar to 應改為 familiar with。考生回答的邏輯性強，但詞彙沒什麼變化，沒有例證，觀點未能展開深入闡述。old people are not very modern 的表達是種贅述，觀點也不夠新穎。這種陳述只會減弱討論效果。

考官：**Let's talk about the benefits of reading. What are the benefits of reading?**

我們來談談閱讀的好處吧。閱讀有哪些好處？

考生：Well, I think that when you read, you can relax yourself and also you can expand your horizons and learn more knowledge. You can expand your knowledge of different aspects of your life and you can study more. That will help you in your life.

考官點評 考生的回答依然連貫、流利，用到了詞彙 aspects。文法方面犯了一個基本錯誤（relax yourself 應為 relax）。最主要的問題是，她還是不能舉例來深入討論自己的觀點，多數陳述是陳詞濫調（expand your horizons），使用的句子也都是簡單句，不能充分展示詞彙和文法水準。7 分已經岌岌可危。

考官：**Do you think it's important to encourage children to read?**
你認為鼓勵兒童閱讀很重要嗎？

考生：Yes, I think children should read books because they can learn a lot from them. And if they want, they can read it out, and so they get used to the sounds. I mean, I think reading is good for developing language ability of the children.

考官點評 考生的回答還是很有邏輯性，但詞彙量有限，還出現了幾處文法錯誤：Read it out 應該是 read the story aloud；developing language ability 應是 developing the language ability。而且，她的觀點很標準化，無個人特色。其實她舉點例子並不難，比如「我的侄女她……」。換句話說，她應該從自己的生活中給考官舉出一個例證，這會讓她的回答更富有原創性，同時也讓自己有機會用上更豐富的詞彙和文法。

考官：**You read *Gossip Girl* and you have also seen the TV series. In general, do you think it is a good idea to read a book before you see a film or a tv show made from the book?**
你讀過《花邊教主》，你也看過它的電視劇。一般來說，你認為閱讀某本書前先看翻拍的電影或電視劇好嗎？

考生：I don't think it is necessary for everybody. I think it depends on the person. People are different from each other. Some people like to read books but other people just like to watch TV, because it is more convenient. It helps them to relax themselves. In my opinion, I think both ways can be OK. It depends on your preference, and maybe the time you have, which one you will choose.

考官點評 考生反覆用一些基礎詞彙。觀點也毫無新穎之處。文法知識把握得很好，但廣度不夠，依然未能深入對觀點展開論證，這表示該考生的語言資源不夠豐富。考生的分數只能為 6 分。

考官：Do you think books make good gifts?
你認為書是很好的禮物嗎？

> **考生：** I think so. But I think it depends on the person. Some people don't really like reading. Maybe they prefer to watch some TV programs, or maybe they just like to be with their family, or hang out with their friends. But other people like me like to read books because they are interested to know more about a subject. So, if somebody gives them a book, and it is a book they like, they will be happy.

考官點評 考官從一個新的角度進行提問，因為之前的討論沒有達到預期的效果。但考生還是反覆使用基礎詞彙（depends on the person）。文法沒有出現錯誤，還使用了條件子句（if somebody gives them a book...）。然而，考生仍然未能舉證來深入說明自己的觀點。

考官：Have you ever given someone a book as a gift?
你送過書給別人作禮物嗎？

> **考生：** Actually, yes. I gave my boyfriend a book about music because he really likes music, especially the blues. It is his favourite.

考官點評 考官看了看計時器，問了一個私人問題。這可能是因為考官覺得即便再問具體的問題，也不會有其他收穫。

考官：Thank you very much. That is the end of the speaking test.
非常感謝。口語考試到此結束。

二、假如能在第三部分展現流暢思路
Able to Run with an Idea in Part Three

看看下面的正面例子吧！這個考生在第三部分能與考官進行深入生動的探討，他們的討論非常精彩，可以學習看看喔！

考官：Well, we have been talking about a book you enjoyed reading, *Gossip Girl*, and I'd like now to discuss with you one or two more general questions related to this. Let's consider first of all owning books. Why do you think people like to own books?

嗯，我們剛討論了你喜歡讀的一本書：《花邊教主》，我想和你談一兩個關於這方面的問題。首先來談一下藏書。你覺得人們為什麼喜歡藏書？

考生：Well, I think that maybe they like to reread them, so it's convenient to have them right there in their house, you know, close by. They can put them on the shelf and look at them, And maybe it gives them a sense of fulfillment too. But personally I prefer e-books.

考官點評 用到了 reread、shelf、e-book 和 sense of fulfillment 等很好的表達。回答流利、連貫。目前來看，該考生有望得 7 分。

考官：OK, let's talk about e-books. What are the advantages of e-books?

好的，那我們來談談電子書吧。電子書的優點是什麼？

考生： Well, first of all, they are very convenient. I can read them on my phone when I am in the subway. You can download them very easy. For example, recently I downloaded a book by Lao She—in English. In Chinese the book's called *Luotuo Xiangzi*, it's about a young guy called Xiangzi who works in Beijing, trying to make a living, struggling a lot. In English it's called *Rickshaw Boy*. It's set in old China, before 1949. I've already read it in Chinese but now I want to read it in English.

考官點評　有一處小的文法錯誤（easy 應改為副詞 easily）。考生舉了老舍作品的例子，這讓她有機會用上 make a living，struggle 和 rickshaw 等詞彙，也能展現文法知識，如一般過去式（I downloaded）、現在完成式（I've already read it in Chinese）、-ing 形式（trying 和 struggling）及介系詞（by、about 和 before）。

考官： **Do you think that e-books will replace traditional books, that traditional books will eventually disappear?**
你認為電子書會取代傳統書籍嗎？傳統書籍最後會消失嗎？

考生： Maybe. I think that could happen eventually. It's a kind of evolution. But old people still prefer traditional books. Like I said before, they can own them and enjoy having them on the shelf in their house. And usually old people are not so familiar with modern technology so it's not easy for them to change their habits and get accustomed to e-books. But, I guess, in fifty years or so, the old people will be the ones who grew up with e-books so things will be different then!

考官點評　考生回答得很好，並用上了一些好詞（evolution、get accustomed、change their habits）。文法準確，邏輯合理、連貫，與考生之前的回答也能夠銜接得上。

考官：**Let's talk about the benefits of reading. What are the benefits of reading?**

我們來談談閱讀的好處。你認為閱讀有哪些益處？

考生：Well, I think that when you read, you can relax and also you can expand your horizons and discover new things, discover the lives of people in other countries for example. I have a foreign friend from Canada who has read *Luotuo Xiangzi*, and Lu Xun. Those books are fascinating and he said they help him understand China better. And, likewise, a lot of my friends and classmates like reading stuff from overseas. Actually, my cousin is reading a book by an Australian author. I forget his name, but she really likes it — it's about teenagers in Australia during an invasion of their country. It's a whole series. She's reading in English too, so she can expand her vocabulary. And, actually, she wants to go to Australia for study, so I guess it's a good introduction to Australia for her...

考官點評　考生一開始便用了經典的陳詞濫調：expand your horizons，但接下來沒有出現類似的情況。她透過列舉自己國外朋友閱讀的書籍和自己表姐的事例來證明自己的觀點，展開回答。在介紹表姐時，她用上了 teenagers、invasion 和 series 等較好的說法，回答得很生動也很連貫。最後，考生又重申了讀書的好處。注意，因為考生有很多話要說，所以考官問的問題比較少。如果能夠這樣回答，考生的分數可為 7 分。

考官：**Thank you very much. That is the end of the speaking test.**

非常感謝。口語考試到此結束。

第五節 高分考生應充滿活力
The IDEA"L" Candidate Is "L"ively

優秀的考生應該精力充沛、充滿活力，就像在舞臺上表演一樣。記住我們前面說過的話，考官每週要考 30 位考生。這表示這份工作是重複性的。所以只有透過生動和外向的表達，並表現出你的活力，你才能讓考官覺得時間過得快一點。

那怎樣才叫做充滿活力呢？接下來，我們會討論什麼樣的肢體語言、眼神接觸、姿勢和語言會讓你顯得活力四射。

考生該怎麼在考試過程中顯得精力充沛、充滿活力？有很多方面都可以注意。首先，手勢和面部表情很重要。考生坐在座位上，所以無法四處走動，但他們依然可以充滿活力地和考官交流。我們發現，很多考生會面無表情，精力全部集中在要說的話上面，所以表情跟動作幾乎和靜止的雕像沒兩樣。

建議這樣的考生，要用手或胳膊做出一些姿勢，表達才能顯得更生動，這些姿勢也會讓思考的過程更順暢，因為姿勢和生動的面部表情都是日常英語談話的一部分，講話的時候作動作，會對表達自己的意思沒有很有幫助。

另外還有一個重點是眼神接觸。在口語考試中，考官會發現靠死記硬背作答的考生會經常看天花板或空中，試圖回憶背過的內容。這樣馬上就穿幫啦！那如果並不是死背答案，只是害羞、緊張而不敢看考官呢？我建議可以盡量與考官進行 3 ～ 5 秒鐘的眼神接觸，然後稍稍將眼神右移或左移，但不要看天花板或地面。很多西方人會將不敢進行眼神接觸的人視為不自信甚至不誠實的人，所以要盡量看著考官喔！

考生還需要注意的另一方面，就是語言要生動。很多緊張的考生不僅沒有肢體語言和活力，還總是說一些陳腔濫調。例如，如果考生談論交通，可能會說：「台北經常出現交通問題。這對我們來說是個問題。」考官就不會對他使用的詞彙或文法有印象，因為實在太普通了。如果考生改說：「在台北，每天都會塞車，這是令政府非常頭痛的問題，因為他們也不想讓憤怒的司機不耐煩地坐在汽車裡，感覺既沮喪又惱火。」這樣考官就會比較有印象了。如果在說的同時再加上一些手勢或模仿憤怒的司機，這樣的交流就更有效啦！

第六節 黃金法則
Dos and Don'ts

▶ **一定要……** Do...

▸▸ 享受使用英語的樂趣。樂趣＝生動！
Have fun with English. Fun = lively!

▸▸ 積極地應對考試。積極產生自信，而自信的人交流起來也更有效。
Think positively about the exam. Optimism breeds confidence, and confident people are more effective communicators.

▸▸ 說話時練習使用手勢。
Practise using gesture when you speak.

▸▸ 以演戲劇的方式來練習說話，要有重音、語調和感情。和你的朋友或同學一起朗讀英語劇本。
Practise saying things in a dramatic way, with stress, intonation and feeling. Read a play script in English with your friends or classmates.

▸▸ 你可以從網上下載電視劇的劇本。這樣你可以訓練自己的表現力。
You can download scripts of tv dramas, for example, from the Internet. By doing this, you will train yourself to sound more expressive.

▸▸ 關注時事，這也是培養生動性的管道之一。
Notice what is on in the news. Liveliness is partly a question of being up with what's happening.

▸▸ 生動性是個性、活力、肢體語言、語調和話題的結合，也是語言的問題。請不斷豐富自己的語言資源。
Liveliness is a question of personality, energy, body language, intonation and choice of subject. It is also a question of language. Keep developing your language resource.

▶ **千萬別……** But don't...

▸▸ 不要背誦所謂的「正確答案」，因為這些回答並不能展現你的想法或感受，而且聽起來毫無新意，讓考官厭倦。
Don't learn off a set of "right answers" to the test because those answers do not represent your thoughts or feelings and will sound stale and tiring to the examiner.

NOTE

第7章

考場外的準備

第一節 考前倒數計時
Countdown

▶一、考前一週
The Week Before the Test

雖然你一直忙著準備考試，但是也不要忘記鍛鍊身體。要確保自己補充了足夠的蛋白質和足夠的睡眠，熬夜唸書到凌晨三點是毫無意義的！只有這樣，你才能保證自己有精力和精神來應對一週後的考試，否則只會導致考試當天狀態不佳。

Don't forget to do some exercise. Be sure to eat plenty of protein and get some sleep.

考前一週，會收到考試單位寄來的 e-mail，通知你考試流程。一定要盡快弄清楚考試地點的確切位置以及到達那裡的最佳交通方式。最好對當天的交通狀況做好最差的心理準備，以決定乘坐哪種交通工具最合適：計程車、腳踏車、公車、捷運還是自己開車或走路？

Check that you know how to get to the test centre.

▶二、考前一天
The Day Before the Test

把書扔到一邊吧！現在再背也來不及了。去健身房練練瑜伽，吃頓好吃的，定好鬧鐘，早點上床睡覺。

再確定一遍考試時間以及應該到達考試地點的時間。需要帶的東西也要檢查一遍：考試報名表、身分證或護照、眼鏡、紙巾、鉛筆與橡皮擦、手機等。買塊巧克力或者其他什麼零食，放在包包裡，為明天做準備。

▶三、考試當日的早晨
The Morning of the Test

早晨醒來後，就開始用英語和自己對話。可以說說天氣，說說你的感受，還可以對自己的分數進行預測，或回憶之前的三四週裡你看過的新聞。要用英語對自己說，而不是中文喔！

好好吃早餐，吃完了接著繼續說英語給自己聽。把準備好的零食放到包包裡，確認該帶的考試用品和證件都已經帶齊。

早點出門，如果遲到了，你是進不了考場的。所以請準備好足夠的時間趕到考場，並留足時間進行拍照和辦理其他考前手續。

如果你到太早了，可以到周圍走走，繼續進行口語練習。如果口渴的話，可以買杯咖啡或其他飲料。

▶四、考試當日
Test Day

整個上午，你都坐在考場中努力奮戰，拼命理解聽力段落的細節，盡力在寫作時想出點新花樣，並幾度為閱讀文章裡的詞彙迷惑不解。等這幾部分結束後，你就終於熬過了考試的大部分，可以暫時喘口氣了！

下面馬上就要面臨口語考試了，很多考生尤其害怕這一部分。但如果你之前已經做好了準備，並積極應對，這會是一個展示你聰明才智的機會呢！

如果你的口語考試被安排在寫作考試完成後的當天，你至少會有兩個小時或更多時間為考試做準備。如果考試在週末，而你的口語考試被安排在週日的話，你就會有大量的準備時間。

相信之前你已經為這次考試準備了數月的時間，那麼在最後的這幾個小時裡應該做些什麼呢？首先有一件事是肯定的，那就是你絕對不要再埋頭苦讀任何一本口語書了！就連這一本也不行！在這最後關頭，千萬不要再去試圖記憶任何語句和表達方式。你真正需要做的是讓你的頭腦進行熱身運動，激發積極性，培養注意力。所以最好的方法就是自己説英語給自己聽，緩慢、平靜地説出腦海中出現的任何想法！不要擔心會出現停頓或重複，這在講話時都是正常現象。但這種自我表述的方式能有效地幫助你緩解緊張情緒，同時讓你的聲音、頭腦都能提前進行熱身，為考試做好準備。

請看下面這位考生在口語考試前如何和自己説話：

Track 035

> **考官語錄**
>
> **If you are prepared, and lively, this is an opportunity to show your talent!**

> **考官語錄**
>
> **In the final hours, don't bury your head in a speaking book. Don't try to memorize sentences. What you need to do is to warm up your mind, warm up your personality, warm up your attention. So talk to yourself! Slowly, peacefully, say whatever comes into your mind!**

Well, it's the 11th of March, and it's Sunday and I've just got up and it is speaking interview day for the IELTS and, uh, I'm a little bit nervous but, uh, I know I shouldn't be. I know it's not a good idea to look in my book now. I just need to think about some of the topics I've just been working on for the last few months and maybe also I can talk about Women's Day, because that was this week, and maybe I can say something about my mum getting a nice present at work. What was it again? Oh yeah, a cosmetics set from the... cosmetics set, cosmetics set. I better make sure I get the pronunciation right if I mention it. Anyway, she got it from her boss. All the women in the office got one, so I don't know, maybe that could come up in one of the topics or... if they ask me about gifts or something, it sounds fresh. But I've done so much work on different topics. I've done stuff on animals. I've done stuff on what you can learn in a new culture. I've done stuff on, you know, pollution and travel. There are so many things, and also I've been reading news online, so I guess I need to... There's been some good vocab there, about conflict, for example, or elections, or troops... like American troops that were in Afghanistan before they got... what's the word, not retreated, before they got withdraw, withdrawn, yeah. Today I'm gonna have some breakfast. I told mum that I would do it myself. I am just going to make a couple of eggs this morning and have some zhou, zhou... porridge, porridge, yeah. This word, porridge. And I guess I'll... I think my interview is at 11:35, so I'm going to leave here about, I think, I think about 9:30, so pretty soon, and just head over there and... maybe even take this little digital recorder with me and just keep talking a bit to myself in the street even if people think I'm crazy, um, just so my voice is warm, and um, I'm used to pronouncing things, saying things, and I'm not — you know — thinking in Chinese when I go into the room, so if I get there early I'm going to sit in the waiting room and maybe just keep running through a few topics and stuff in my mind. Well, I went to the gym last night so I feel pretty bouncy. I think, I think that's good because they told me that when you go into the testing room you need to feel lively, you know, maybe not be too much, be excessive, but be able to show the examiner that you're lively, you know, that you're listening and also you move your upper body a little bit, and have a little bit of hand gesture, so I think all the work I've done over the last six months must be useful. I don't think I'm going to be too nervous. I'm not going to take any books with me. I'm just going to head out there and hope for the best, and hope I get a good start and if I get a good start, I'm sure it is going to go well, oh yeah!

考官語錄

Remember, you have paid for this test and you have no reason to be afraid of the examiner.

考官語錄

If you are a well-prepared, well-informed candidate willing to express your own ideas, then the examiner will warm to you.

　　透過以上這種自我表述的方式，你就可以讓自己的頭腦進行充分熱身，減少緊張感，並準備好將自己的想法用語言表達出來。下面就要進入考場了！先進行一次深呼吸！記住，你已經為考試付了費用，所以沒有必要懼怕考官。也許考官當天會心情不好，但如果你已做好了充足的準備，並願意積極表達自己的想法，考官就會以熱情的態度對待你。所以抓住這次機會，盡情談論你的生活、夢想和抱負，向考官展示你的聰明才智吧！

▶五、考試過程中
During the Test

很多學生在考試前都會感緊張，這很正常。其實緊張也可以激發你的潛力！如果你一點都不緊張，那反而才不好，因為你很容易就鬆懈、分心，反而拿不出最好的實力。很多知名演員都說過，無論他們排練過多少次，在登台前還是一樣會緊張。所以，緊張不見得是壞事，反而可以幫助你集中精神和注意力，發揮出最佳水準。

第二節 提前瞭解國外文化
Culture in Study, in Family, at Work, in Life

你很快就要參加雅思考試了，而且希望順利通過後，就能開始在國外唸書。那麼，與國內相比，英語系國家：美國、英國、澳洲、加拿大、紐西蘭等國的文化到底有什麼不同呢？如果先知道一些重點，不但對出國生活與上學有助益，甚至在口語考試中也能幫上忙，因為你知道你的考官很可能會比較習慣哪些想法、哪些生活模式，也知道你的考官對怎樣的概念不容易理解，需要你多做說明。因此，先瞭解英語系國家的文化，不是要你捨棄自己的文化而去配合英語母語人士的喜好，而是一種幫你在考試時佔一點優勢的策略。

常有人說，文化之於人如同「水之於魚」。換句話說，我們每天都像魚一樣暢遊在自己國家的文化源泉中，對於我們來說，身邊的一切都是如此熟悉與自然，以至於我們幾乎沒有感覺到它的存在，更沒有意識到文化其實是詮釋世界的一種具體方式。只要比較一下華人、法國人、美國人的問候方式就明白了。對於華人來說，他們認為自己的問候方式很正常，而法國人和美國人也覺得他們的問候方式再自然不過。但到底什麼是正常而自然的，這在不同的文化中就會有不同的含義。

當然了，文化也是會改變的，但沒有你想像中那麼快！跨文化研究領域的一位先驅海爾特‧霍夫斯泰德曾在他的書中寫道：「文化在改變……速度如同冰山融化一樣快！」儘管事實的確如此，但在如今全球變暖的大環境下，冰山融化的速度比以往要快多了，而現在我們面臨的多元文化影響也比任何時候都更廣泛和強烈。

下面讓我們透過一項一項分析，一起來瞭解一下英語國家的文化吧！看完這一節，你也會對自己將來在國外的生活充滿信心的。

考官語錄

It has been said that culture is "water for fish". In other words, we swim in our own culture all day long.

▶一、我在教室裡應該怎麼做？
How Should I Behave in the Classroom?

在我們習慣的課堂上，一般都是老師們佔據主動權；而在英語系國家的課堂上，老師則期望學生們可以掌握主動權。

台灣學生在課堂上大部分還是會遵循傳統的中式教學方式，聽講往往多於思考。很多孩子小時候聽到的最多的話就是「要聽老師的話」，意思是只要照老師的話去做，就是好學生。老師們也比較喜歡聽話的孩子，如果學生聽話，就算是一個班上很多學生的大課堂也可以進展得很順利。

英語系國家的學生則被要求要有自己的理解和觀點，而非從別人那裡獲得資訊，這就是主要的區別。因此要去考雅思的你就必須明白：雅思考官來自英語系國家，以前他也是個英語系國家的學生，所以也會期待你可以像英語系國家的學生一樣，表現得很主動。

現在其實台灣的教學方式已經有慢慢在改變了，學生在課堂上也會與老師有很多的互動，但和英語系國家比起來，台灣的老師還是比較處於主導地位，而有些學生很可能一整堂課都一言不發，這種現象在中國的文化和教育體系中已經根深蒂固了！安靜地坐著聽老師講課，不提任何問題，是許多華人學生在課堂上常見的表現，但在英語系國家，尤其是在人數比較少的課堂中，要是你一直不說話，老師不會覺得你是「乖孩子」，說不定下課後還會找你過來談談，看你是不是學習上碰到問題。

▶二、我在工作或唸書時，能直言不諱嗎？
Can I Be Outspoken at Work and at University?

在華人的傳統觀念中，人們應該一直維護和諧，儘量避免正面衝突。然而，在英語國家中，真實表達自己的想法是一個人誠實的標誌。

如果你是一個在英語系大學求學的學生，在課堂上從不發言，你就會給別人留下一種消極的印象。英語系國家學校的老師會希望每個學生都能通過口頭表達的方式參與任何活動。同樣地，如果你在英語系國家的公司中工作，你也應該盡量在會議上表達自己的看法。

華人學生大多數時間都在聽老師講，養成了一種惰性。到了英語系國家的教育環境中以後，起初很多人可能會覺得奇怪：老師講課的時間不夠多，反而常常都是學生在講，這樣真的能學到東西嗎？隨後，他們意識到老師是在努力調動他們的思維，並鼓勵他們更積極地思考和學習。

▶三、在英語系國家的大學裡，我需要主動學習嗎？
Do I Have to Be Active at a Western University?

華人學生習慣從老師那裡得到事先已經整理好的資料；但英語國家會強調學生自己開展研究的能力。

在英語系國家的課堂上，小組討論和互動是很常見的活動。老師也會經常要求學生做報告，以加強自學能力和自覺意識。但是在台灣，很多時候學生們只需要坐著等從老師那裡拿到已經準備好的資料。有時候他們甚至還會根據老師發放的資料有多少，來判斷這個老師有多好。所以，看在英語系國家人士的眼中，會覺得華人學生不夠有創造力，總是等著老師提供正確答案，自己不會去找資料。

積極主動是西方文化極為重視的行為準則之一。在史蒂芬‧柯維所著的暢銷書《高效率人士的七個習慣》中，他提到的第一個習慣就是要積極主動，而且這種人的特點是：

• 覺得主動創造是自己的責任。
• 覺得找到幸福生活，是自己的責任。

• 掌握主動權。

• 從不為自己的行為抱怨周圍環境或條件因素。

在英語系國家的課堂上也是這樣，老師會期望學生能掌握主動性，可以提出問題、自己搜索資訊、並對於想要達到的學習目標具有責任心。

▶四、我什麼時候能夠獨立？
When Can I Start Being Independent?

華人重視服從家庭的觀念，而英語系國家更加注重個人的獨立性。

所有英語系國家都十分重視個性化，尤其是個人的獨立性。他們鼓勵孩子在很小的時候就要獨立。以在澳洲長大的考官我本人來說，我的小兒子 6 歲時就開始自己去上學，不用家長送。我的大兒子高中畢業後沒有直接去讀大學，而是到南美洲的幾個不同國家生活了三年，在那裡學習語言、打工、交朋友並培養獨立能力。這在台灣現在還是比較難達到的，因為多數家長怎麼可能會願意讓小孩不去讀大學，先去玩三年呢？

在台灣的家長眼中看來，英語系國家的家長太放縱了，而在英語系國家的家長眼中看來，台灣的父母給予了孩子過多的關愛。年輕人中有很多想變獨立，但卻無法逃脫父母的保護罩。在我看來，出國唸書對於這些孩子來說不但是學習，更是可以獲得獨立的機會。

▶五、在西方國家找工作……
Getting a Job in the West...

在台灣的一些公司裡，受雇和升職與員工的家庭背景和人際關係有一定的關連。但在英語系國家裡，員工的受雇與晉升只會考慮公司制度和個人能力。

在我們英語系國家的人看來，台灣雖然已經很少有這種「家庭背景」影響的事情發生，但還是偶爾會有這種有欠公平的事情出現，也偶爾還是可以聽到有人憑藉著「我爸是誰誰誰」就受到和別人不同的待遇，「靠關係」之類的事也還是時有所聞。建議考生可以從腦中摒除「關係」的概念，最好能通過自己的奮鬥去獲得自己想要的，而不是依賴高層人士給你幫助。正如古人所說，旅程遠比目的地本身更加重要！而且當你靠自己的力量做事時，你可以從中獲得更多的樂趣，學到更多的東西。

對許多英語系國家的人來說，動用家庭關係獲得工作是一種會受到指責的行為。整體來說，人們不太喜歡和家人一起工作，因為他們認為雇用家庭成員，很容易會被說是偏袒或優待親屬，受到多方指責，而且家庭關係也很容易影響到處理工作事務的客觀性。

▶六、關係和工作，哪個更重要？
Relationship or Task: Which Comes First?

在台灣，關係比工作更重要；在英語國家，工作要比關係更重要。

在台灣，如果你正在會見一位供應商或客戶，卻突然接到老闆的電話，你一定會立即接電話。在台灣，一定要維持好與老闆的關係，再來考慮辦好眼前的任務。但在英語系國家，情形卻不相同。人們會想先「做好正事」，完成任務後再去考慮發展關係。在台灣人的眼中看來，這些西方人處理關係的方式可能顯得有點冷漠，甚至比較天真吧！但入境隨俗，如果真的到英語系國家工作，也要試著以理性的方式處理手頭上的工作。如果個人的事情總是影響到工作，工作就作不完了。

▶七、如何與老闆互動？
How Should I Behave with the Boss?

在很多台灣的公司裡，員工最好不要經常給老闆提出負面的或者不同的意見，而多數西方公司則鼓勵下屬提出有建設性的不同意見和回饋。

傳統的中國是個重視等級體系的社會，所以受儒家教育的我們，也從小被教育要尊重權威。在學校，我們安靜地點頭，很少反駁老師。等到工作後，我們也用同樣的方式對待老闆。開會時，我們不說出自己的想法，而是等著聽到老闆的意見，然後表示附和。英語系國家的員工在開會時則會直接表達出自己的想法，但台灣人多半會表現得很低調。其實你們沒發現的是，在西方的公司裡，你必須積極表現出自己的才華並贏得認可，才能獲得升職的機會。

西方公司普遍採用一種被稱為「360 度回饋」的諮詢體系。經理採用這種體系可以收到很多人的回饋意見，包括自己的下屬在內。根據我們的瞭解，台灣的公司並沒有採用這樣的體系，而且在這些公司中，下屬提意見會顯得既不合適也不合乎情理。

▶八、人與人如何交流？
How Do People Communicate?

華人的交流方式比較間接，而西方人的交流方式比較直接。

在英語國家，人們的表達方式比較直率一點，換句話說，就是說話更加明確。他們經常重複關鍵資訊，以確定表達得夠清晰。但是台灣人和日本人、法國人一樣，對很多事情並不會說很明白，會有所保留，因為在他們看來，有些事情不需要說很清楚就可以理解。

如果你是個好的聽眾或者善於觀察的人，你就應該開始調整自己與他人的交流方式，以適應新的文化，因為台灣人的交流方式容易引起英語系國家的人誤解。台灣人自己可能覺得已經解釋得很清楚了，但英語系國家的人會覺得還有很多內容不夠明確，所以台灣人不得不學著要更明確地表達自己的想法。一開始可能會覺得講這麼直不太舒服，但逐漸可以適應的。

▶九、什麼方式的身體接觸才合適？
How Much Physical Contact Is Normal?

華人通常在見面的時候避免身體接觸，而大多數西方人喜歡擁抱或者親吻，不過具體上要選哪種方式，還是要看當下的氛圍與文化的不同。

並非所有的西方人都用同樣的方式來問候彼此。在法國和義大利，人們用親吻的方式來打招呼。美國人喜歡擁抱，而英國人則相對比較保守。問候時的身體接觸方式在不同的文化環境中也會不同。到底什麼方式合適，取決於身處於哪種文化。西方人到台灣後，在問候台灣朋友時也會學著保持適當距離，減少身體接觸。他們也會發現身體接觸的問候方式在台灣並非常態。

在台灣文化中，我們並不習慣用身體接觸來表達情感。在古代裡，人們打招呼的方式甚至只是拱手作揖，完全沒有身體接觸，現在則開始會握手了。不過既然要去其他的國家，就入境隨俗吧！如果有人試圖以親吻的方式和你告別，別嚇一跳、往後退，因為這樣的反應在對方看來不是很禮貌。

▶十、如何表達謝意？
How Do I Show Thanks?

在英語國家，口頭表達感謝是非常重要的。但在台灣，有時如果向朋友道謝太多次，只會讓對方很困惑。

我來跟大家說說我剛從澳洲搬到亞洲來時的故事。有一次，有個當地的朋友陪我去看房子。她很厲害，問了房東很多實際的問題，都是我根本沒考慮到的。我們離開房子後，我謝了她，一起吃了飯，然後就告別了。在回家的路上，我發了簡訊給她，再次表示了感謝。對方回覆我說：「丹尼爾，你幹嘛又要謝我？我們不是朋友嗎？」我當時覺得很疑惑，因為在西方，特別是在英語國家，我們總是會為對方的幫助表示感謝，所以我以為我這樣道謝是很正常的。

我問了一些其他當地朋友後，才知道在中式文化中，會對不太熟悉的人非常有禮貌。和他們在一起的時候，經常表達自己的感激之情，這也是一種有教養的表現。但當和對方熟悉了之後，就不會再總是說「請」或者「謝謝」之類的話，因為這樣會讓對方覺得你們之間有距離，或者是你的感謝是一種禮節，而禮節就等於距離！所以，和朋友在一起的時候，東方人比較不常說謝謝，但都心存謝意。台灣學生到國外後，可以試著多對你的朋友說謝謝，對他們為你做的事表達你的感激之情。感謝的話永遠不會嫌多！

NOTE

附錄

特別收錄 ❶ 瞭解考官的想法：雅思考官的一天
A Day in the Life of an IELTS Examiner

6:10 瀋陽，飯店房間

Track 036

6:10 a.m. Sunday. The phone rings in my hotel room in Shenyang but I'm already up. Luckily for me, this hotel is one in which you can open the windows... The weather is getting chilly at this time of the year in Liaoning, but personally I still like to have a finger of air coming into the room rather than depending on the hotel air conditioning.

今天是星期天。飯店的晨喚電話響起，但我已經起床了。幸好這是一家可以打開窗戶的酒店。這個季節的遼寧，天氣已經開始轉冷。但我個人還是更喜歡讓一絲新鮮空氣進入房間，而非總是開著空調。

6:35 酒店餐廳

Track 037

6:35 a.m. Hotel restaurant. Breakfasts are something these 5-star hotels really do well—dumplings, vegetables, zhou, eggs, sushi, fish, cheese, pastries, yoghurt, muesli, bread, five different types of fruit juice, coffee and tea... It's all there. Not much time to enjoy it though, because the bus is leaving for the test centre at 7 a.m. Because of security procedures and photo requirements, the supervisor has to be on site early, and so the examiners have to leave early too.

這些五星級酒店的早餐做得的確很好，有餃子、蔬菜、粥、雞蛋、壽司、魚、乳酪、糕點、優酪乳、乾果全麥片、麵包、五種果汁、咖啡還有茶……真是應有盡有。但我卻沒有多少時間去享受，因為大巴士 7 點鐘就要出發去考試中心了。有鑒於考前要進行安檢和照片認證等程序，考試人員需要很早到達考場，所以考官也不得不早點動身。

7:10 大巴士上

 Track 038

7:10 a.m. The atmosphere in the bus is pretty upbeat for this time of day! The people who tried out the hotel buffet last night are happy. It seems like the fish was particularly delicious! Some people went to the spa and some to the swimming pool.

在一天當中這麼早的時間，車上的氣氛已經算相當活躍了！昨晚嚐過酒店自助餐的人都很開心，大概是因為昨天的魚特別鮮美！有些人去做了水療，還有一些人去游了泳。

8:01 考試中心

 Track 039

8:01 a.m. At the test centre, there is a gaggle of candidates standing around the entrance, many of them clutching revision notes. I always want to tell them, "Hey, throw away those notes. They won't help you now. It's much better to forget the notes, think about something positive and then go into the test room with energy, enthusiasm and presence of mind." Sometimes, even in the corridor, the candidates are still huddled over their cram sheets. How can they expect to be spontaneous and engaging when they are poring over things they have learnt by heart?

在考試中心門口，已有一群考生在等候，其中有不少人還緊握著複習筆記。每當看到這樣的情景，我總想告訴他們：「嘿！把筆記扔一邊去吧，現在看也沒什麼用了。最好忘記筆記上的東西，想些積極的事情，然後精力充沛、氣定神閑地走進考場。」有時，就連站在走廊裡的時候，考生仍然不捨得和複習資料分開。他們若是一心忙著死記硬背，又怎能指望自己在考試中表現得積極主動呢？

8:05 工作人員休息室

 Track 040

8:05 a.m. We say hello to the test centre staff and collect our materials from the supervisor's room. The supervisor gives us a quick briefing for the day and then examiners grab a coffee from the machine and head off to their test rooms to prepare.

跟考試中心的工作人員打過招呼後，我們就去工作人員休息室拿考試材料。考試負責人員對當天工作進行了簡要說明後，考官們從咖啡機接了一杯咖啡就直奔考場去做準備。

8:15 考場

8:15 a.m. My test room is spacious and full of light with a nice comfortable chair for the examiner — after all, I'm going to be sitting in the room all day — and a more basic one for the candidate. I look through the photo sheet. As usual, the vast majority of the candidates are around 20 years old, though a couple are as young as 16. It is rarer and rarer for examiners to get candidates who are over 30 but it's always interesting to listen to those candidates' life experience.

我監考的考場寬敞明亮，為考官配有一把舒適的椅子。畢竟我要在這裡坐一整天啊！還有一把比較普通的椅子給考生。我翻看了考生的照片冊。如往常一樣，絕大多數考生都在 20 歲左右，除了兩個只有 16 歲。考官遇見 30 歲以上考生的機會越來越少，但聽這些人說說人生經歷挺有趣的。

8:30 考場

8:30 a.m. After scanning through the topics for the day and setting out the clock and the notepad, I am ready to begin. The first candidate is a guy about 20 who seems confident when he walks in. His responses are pretty quick and natural in Part 1 but in Part 2 and 3 he does not have a lot to say and starts to repeat himself. His vocabulary is fairly limited and there are frequent grammatical mistakes.

瀏覽了當天的話題，調好鐘錶，擺好記事本後，我就準備開始了。第一個考生是個大概 20 歲的男孩，走進考場時顯得信心十足。他在回答第一部分的問題時，反應迅速，回答自然。但在第二部分和第三部分中，他卻沒有什麼可說的，並不斷重複自己的話。他的詞彙量非常有限，而且時常犯文法錯誤。

8:50 考場

8:50 a.m. The next candidate is very nervous. When I ask him the standard question, "Do you have a mobile phone?", he shows me his ID card! I'm sure it's just nerves that is making him momentarily deaf! I ask him the question again and he says, "No, I don't take it today." Ouch! The test hasn't begun yet, but already he is making basic grammatical mistakes. I smile and try to calm him down a bit, and the test begins...

第二位考生非常緊張。我先按照慣例問他：「Do you have a mobile phone?（你有手機嗎？）」他卻向我出示了他的身分證！一定是他過於緊張而暫時失聰了！我又重複了一遍問題，他說：「No, I don't take it today.（沒有，我今天沒帶手機）」唉！考試還沒有開始，他就開始犯基本的文法錯誤了。我對他微笑，試著讓他平靜下來，然後開始考試……

9:00 考場

9:00 a.m. Loud construction noises suddenly start up outside! A few minutes later the noise stops. Thank you, supervisor!

外面突然響起了刺耳的施工噪音！幾分鐘後噪音停止了。謝謝你，監考人員！

11:30 考場

11:30 a.m. Just before lunch, a very extroverted young lady comes in. She is funny and forthright, not the kind of candidate who simply recites memorized responses! I find myself laughing with her because she is so spontaneous and full of life. Her exuberance is backed up by some good vocabulary and good control of grammar. She gets the highest score of the morning session.

午飯前，進來一位非常外向的年輕女孩。她風趣又直率，不是那種只機械背誦應試段落的考生！我發現自己情不自禁地和她一起笑，因為她的回答都是積極主動的，充滿了活力。她的活力源自於良好的詞彙基礎和文法駕馭能力。在上午的考生中，她的得分是最高的。

12:14 餐廳

12:14 p.m. Lunch consists of a lunchbox—vegetables and rice for me—and the examiners chat. Some people talk about what's happening back in the US, then the conversation turns to funny or surprising things that happened with the morning candidates. The reality is that examiners like it when candidates do well.

今天的午餐是便當，我吃蔬菜和米飯，考官們都在聊天。有人談論美國發生的時事，後來話題轉向了上午考試中發生的趣事或出人意料的事。實際上，考官們還是喜歡考生有好的表現。

14:30 考場

2:30 p.m. One of the afternoon candidates is very shy and diffident. His English appears to be quite reasonable but he is so shy and lacking in confidence that he pulls his score down with hesitations and silences. It is very tempting in these cases for the examiner to say something to the candidate afterwards to try and encourage them, but the rules prevent it.

下午的考生中有一位非常靦腆膽怯。他的英語還算不錯，但他過於靦腆和缺乏自信，所以他的猶豫和沉默拉低了他的得分。遇到這種情況時，考官總是想在事後對考生說些鼓勵的話，但考官守則不允許我們這麼做。

16:00 考試中心

4:00 p.m. The interviews are over for the day. The supervisor carefully checks all the examination materials and then we wait for the minibus that will take us to the airport.

一天的口語考試結束了。等負責人員仔細檢查過所有考試材料後，我們等待小巴士接我們去機場。

17:40 機場

5:40 p.m. At the airport, we learn that the flight to Beijing is delayed by an hour. Not being able to get home because of transport problems is a constant worry for examiners. After a long weekend, and being out of bed early on Saturday and Sunday, we are keen to get home and unwind a little before Monday morning rolls around.

在機場等待時，我們得知去北京的航班遲到一個小時。因交通問題耽擱到家的時間是考官們長久以來的心頭之患。經過一個漫長的週末，在歷經週六和周日的早起之後，我們都渴望趕在週一的早晨來臨之前回家放鬆放鬆。

19:20 飛機上

Track 050

7:20 p.m. We take off and have an incident-free flight back to Beijing. Some passengers are sleeping; others are reading books, magazines or iPads. The plane is full and the efficient Air China staff serve hot bun sandwiches and drinks.

我們從機場起飛後平安飛抵北京。途中有一些乘客睡覺，一些人讀書、看雜誌或玩平板電腦。這班航班滿員，高效的國航工作人員為我們提供了熱的圓麵包三明治和飲料。

20:45 首都機場

Track 051

8:45 p.m. Walking towards the taxi rank at Beijing airport, I see a candidate that I tested the week before at BLCU. He waves at me and I wave back... I can't remember now what score he got, but I think he was one of the better ones that day.

在走向計程車候車處的路上，我遇見一週前在北京語言大學考試的一位考生。他向我揮手，我也向他揮手……雖然我已不記得他的得分，但我覺得他是那天表現比較好的一位。

21:04 計程車上

Track 052

9:04 p.m. The taxi pulls out into the evening traffic.「你們是從什麼地方來的？」asks the taxi driver.「從瀋陽。」「瀋陽天氣怎麼樣？」「比北京冷啊！」

我乘坐的計程車駛入夜晚的車流中。「你們是從什麼地方來的？」計程車司機問。「從瀋陽。」「瀋陽天氣怎麼樣？」「比北京冷啊！」

21:49 家裡

Track 053

9:49 p.m. The taxi pulls up outside the 7-11 near my building. I pop into the shop to buy some bread and fruit juice for the morning and then pull my suitcase — those wheels are sticking, gonna have to replace this suitcase soon — to my door. Home, sweet home!

計程車在我家附近的 7-11 超市前停下。我下車後鑽進店裡買了些麵包和果汁，留到第二天早上吃，然後拉著我的手提箱向家門走去。箱子的輪子有點卡，該換個新箱子了。終於到家了。家，溫暖的家！

特別收錄 ② 在學校學不到的口語妙招
Learning Habits Round-up

　　前面我們已經斷斷續續介紹了一些有效的準備考試方法。在本節中，我們會對一些重點推薦的方法進行總結和詳細介紹，希望你能踏踏實實地應用和練習。相信過不了多久，你一定能感受到自己的進步和提升！

　　下面這七種方法可以全面提高你的口語能力，幫助你準備考試：

1. 擴大詞彙量：瀏覽單字書

2. 擴大詞彙量：使用思維導圖

3. 提高語言流暢度：練習自我陳述

4. 改善語言的流暢和連貫性：勤記筆記

5. 學習文法：大量閱讀

6. 改善發音：練習的技巧

7. 使用 www.ieltsyes.net 網站上的資源

妙招 1 擴大詞彙量：瀏覽單字書

　　拿起一本英語單字書和一支螢光筆，瀏覽全書。每當看到某個吸引你的單字或你覺得會有用的單字，直接用螢光筆標出。中途不要停下來問自己為什麼選擇這些詞而忽略了其他詞。一直這樣標下去，直到看完全書。相信你的直覺。

　　第一次瀏覽時，你可能只會標出書中 10% 到 15% 的單字。沒有關係，這些是你的核心詞彙。學習這些核心詞彙，並努力記住它們，儘量運用到句子中。如果你覺得多寫幾遍有助於記憶的話，那就寫一寫。

當你逐漸熟悉了這些新單字，發現很容易就能記住和運用它們時，你的自信就會增添了幾分。現在就到了第二遍瀏覽詞彙書的時候了。再一次標出新單字。如果你想將它們與第一批區分開，可以用不同顏色的螢光筆標。這一次瀏覽時，你就能挑出一些平時比較少用的擴展詞彙。開始學習這些詞彙，但同時也不要忘記複習核心詞彙。照這個步驟學習下去。當你第三遍瀏覽的時候，再標出新的單字。反覆這個過程，直至你把所有你認為有用的單字都掌握住。你可以忽略那些沒用的單字。比如，如果你不是學生物的學生，你就不用學「細胞膜」這個單字，可以忽略它。

當你瀏覽到第五或第六遍時，你會驚訝地發現很多單字已經刻在你的腦海裡了。請記住，詞彙是我們交流的基礎。你學習詞彙不僅僅是為了通過雅思考試。沒有詞彙，我們就不可能表達自己的想法。

妙招 2 擴大詞彙量：使用思維導圖

利用主題學單字是很好的記憶方法，因為大腦喜歡進行聯繫，而且有聯繫的詞記憶起來也更容易。根據這一原則來有效記憶詞彙的方法就是利用思維導圖。使用這一技巧，你就能通過複習已掌握的詞彙，找到它們之間的聯繫，學到你以前不會的詞彙和表達法。

下頁就來試試看如何畫思維導圖吧！首先在一張紙的中間寫下一個主題，然後進行腦力激盪，把所有你能想到的和該主題有關的詞彙都寫下來。話題可以是實物，比如「一間公寓」，你可能會想到裡面不同的房間和物品；也可以是一個抽象想法，如「假期」，可能包括旅行、住宿、天氣和活動等。最重要的是不僅要寫下名詞、動詞和形容詞，而且要考慮到冠詞、介系詞和常用片語等。

下面是一個關於「健康」這一話題的思維導圖。這樣的圖不會對你有太大的幫助，因為只列出了一些名詞和形容詞。

然後請看下面這個思維導圖。兩張圖都是同一個話題，但下面的圖明顯就做得更好，因為它列出了一些有用的動詞和説法。

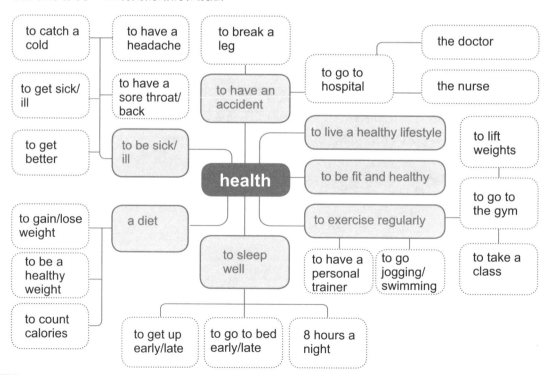

在畫思維導圖時，你可能會注意到有一些重要詞彙和表達的英語是你不會的。沒關係！先把中文寫下來就好，然後繼續畫圖。等到畫完了，再去查字典找出對應的英語表達。現在就動手開始畫吧！

一旦畫出一個思維導圖，你就可以進一步檢查你是否知道如何從過去、現在和未來的角度去談論這一話題。如果你對某個特定的主題想不出豐富的詞彙，那就過幾天再畫一次。畫思維導圖有兩種方法，一種是用很多顏色的筆在紙上畫；另一種是用專門的思維導圖軟體在電腦上畫。

總之，運用思維導圖不僅可以幫助你複習你已經掌握了的詞彙，還可以幫你學習新的詞彙。

妙招 3 提高語言流暢度：練習自我陳述

自我陳述也是一種有效的語言訓練技巧，也就是用英文講話給自己聽啦！這樣練習的好處是可以複習詞彙，並訓練用英語口頭表達的能力。訓練這種技巧有兩種方法，一種辦法是觀察和描述你周圍的事物。

舉個例子，當你在廚房中時，看看你能說些什麼……

首先列出你能想到的詞彙：kitchen, crumbs, tissue, junk mail, gas meter, shelf, cutlery, electric kettle, blender 等。

那麼我們如何使用這些詞彙呢？可以描述你看到了什麼：

Track 054

"I am standing in the kitchen and there is a long wooden bar running north/south and on the bar there is a diary and some paper tissues and also a pot with pens in it and a few crumbs and also a bunch of papers which appears to include bills and a letter and some junk mail. Behind the bar is the main part of the kitchen with shelves running along the back wall and on the shelves there are glasses and some photos and a big packet of tea and also I can see a gas meter. Under the shelves is the kitchen counter which runs around the whole area and on it there is an electric kettle and also a blender and a rice-cooker and a jar of coffee and some chopsticks and cutlery. If I turn the other way and look at the wall, I can see a painting of some people hanging on the wall on one side of the door leading into a bedroom, and on the other side of that door is a big wooden plate that looks like it comes from Xinjiang maybe or maybe from somewhere in Eastern Europe..."

訓練自我陳述的另外一種方法就是思考你的現狀和優先要做的事情，就好像在列一個事務清單一樣，並大聲説給自己聽。看下面這個例子：

"So, the situation is that today is the 10th of October 2012 and it's a lovely day but a little bit chilly and I have a lot of work to do this week and next week. I really must get my philosophy assignment done as soon as possible and then there is the math paper that has to be handed in next week. Also, I need to finish my personal statement and make sure all of my university applications are sent this week or else I will start to panic. I also need to remember to go to yoga class on Friday and to check on the Internet to see if there are any cheap flights for December. And I have to contact Katherine and see how things are going with her and whether I can stay with her when I go through Paris."

這種方法的好處在於你每天都能練習。經常進行這樣的自我訓練，你肯定能鞏固並提升自己的語言能力。

妙招 4 改善語言的流暢和連貫性：勤記筆記

練習記筆記可以增大你的詞彙量，改善你的語言流暢和連貫性。每天、每週、每年都可以使用這個手冊，用特定的話題來進行腦力激盪訓練和詞彙記憶。每當你遇到一個讓你感興趣的新話題，你都可以翻開手冊中新的一頁，寫下與其有關的中文或英語單字。

對於寫下的中文，查到對應的英語詞彙後再添加到話題頁上。下一步就是運用手頭的錄音設備。當你練習談論各種各樣的主題時，你就可以把自己的話錄下來，從中找出關鍵字匯，寫在紙上。再次練習時強迫自己説得更快一點，不要出現猶豫或卡住的情況，要囊括所有的詞彙。另外，還要訓練記筆記。如果你能在一分鐘內快速記下關鍵字，那麼你不僅能習得助你在第二部分拿高分的詞彙，還可以構建起發言的思路。你就可以一個接一個地運用那些詞彙來完成你的陳述。所以你必須練習速記，寫下可以助你完成兩分鐘表達的詞彙。給自己計一下時，只用 50 秒來寫詞彙。用這本書中的話題來練習，並習慣運用思維導圖。

妙招 5 學習文法：大量閱讀

多讀英文書，養成閱讀的習慣有很多好處，可以助你：

• 擴大詞彙量

• 激發想像力

• 擴充文法知識

• 熟悉語言的節奏和韻律

• 獲得樂趣

• 增長知識

• 通過瞭解他人經歷來開闊視野，豐富閱歷

• 學習看清事物間的聯繫，因此也可以訓練管理才能

• 通過熟悉書中出現的單字來減少拼寫錯誤

妙招 6 改善發音：練習的技巧

1 找出你有哪些發音讓別人很難聽懂。

2 再看看這些發音是母音還是子音。

3 聽聽母語是英語的人如何發這個音。

4 錄下你自己的發音。錄的時候，不要只是單獨發這個音，而是要放到一個句子裡面讀。

5 嘗試找出你的發音與母語人士發音的區別。

6 弄懂這個音的發音方法，也就是說發這個音時，嘴形應該怎樣，應該使用哪個部位發音。如果你身邊有母語是英語的人，在他們發這個音時仔細觀察並模仿。

7 在不同的語境中練習發這個音，可以將其放在句首，也可以放句子中間。錄下自己的發音，然後聽錄音。

8 讓母語是英語的人來聽聽你的發音並給出評價，或者將你的錄音上傳至 www.ieltsyes.net，讓我們來給你打分數。

妙招 7 登錄 www.ieltsyes.net：利用網站資源

www.ieltsyes.net 網站由本書作者創建，會定期更新學習資料，有空請上去看看吧！

NOTE

原來如此 系列 **E114**

不是權威不出書！
雅思考官教你征服**雅思口語**

最瞭解雅思+最瞭解考生＝最適合你的雅思口語惡補書！

作　　者	丹尼爾·科特拉爾、陳思清
顧　　問	曾文旭
總 編 輯	王毓芳
編輯統籌	耿文國、黃璽宇
英文主編	張辰安
美術編輯	吳靜宜、王桂芳
封面設計	阿作
法律顧問	北辰著作權事務所　蕭雄淋律師、嚴裕欽律師

印　　製	金濆印刷事業有限公司
初　　版	2015年02月
出　　版	捷徑文化出版事業有限公司
電　　話	（02）6636-8398
傳　　真	（02）6636-8397
地　　址	106 台北市大安區忠孝東路四段218-7號7樓

定　　價	新台幣320元／港幣107元
產品內容	1書+1光碟

總 經 銷	采舍國際有限公司
地　　址	235 新北市中和區中山路二段366巷10號3樓
電　　話	（02）8245-8786
傳　　真	（02）8245-8718

港澳地區總經銷	和平圖書有限公司
地　　址	香港柴灣嘉業街12號百樂門大廈17樓
電　　話	（852）2804-6687
傳　　真	（852）2804-6409

※套書《不是權威不出書─雅思考官、權威教你征服口語、單字》之其中一冊

本書原由外語教學與研究出版社有限責任公司以書名《雅思考官教你征服雅思口語》首次出版。此中文繁體字版由外語教學與研究出版社有限責任公司授權捷徑文化出版事業有限公司在台灣、香港和澳門地區獨家出版發行。僅供上述地區銷售。

捷徑 Book站

現在就上臉書（FACEBOOK）「捷徑BOOK站」並按讚加入粉絲團，就可享每月不定期新書資訊和粉絲專享小禮物喔！

http://www.facebook.com/royalroadbooks
讀者來函：royalroadbooks@gmail.com

國家圖書館出版品預行編目資料

不是權威不出書！雅思考官教你征服雅思口語
/ 丹尼爾·科特拉爾, 陳思清著.
-- 初版. -- 臺北市：捷徑文化, 2015.02
　面；　公分（原來如此：E114）

ISBN 978-986-5698-38-6(平裝)

1. 國際英語語文測試系統　2. 讀本

805.189　　　　　　　　　103026084

考官親自出馬與你分享，
教你練出最靈活、最讓考官喜愛的高分英文口語！
真的不是權威不出書！